HACEY MILLER

HACEY MILLER

A NOVEL

BY JAMES SHERBURNE

HOUGHTON MIFFLIN COMPANY BOSTON

To my mother
and
To Miss Emily Ann Smith
of Berea College

I will lift up mine eyes unto the hills,
From whence cometh my help.

CONTENTS

CONTENTS

HACEY MILLER

I

SPRING IN THE BLUEGRASS

IN my life I've never given much attention to religion, but if
I'd had a bent that way, I believe Cassius Marcellus Clay
would have made a Calvinist out of me.

Not that there was anything churchy about Clay. Quite
the opposite; he thought people ought to get out of their
messes the same way they got into them — by themselves,
unassisted by either divine or infernal intervention.

C. M. Clay just about destroyed any possibility of Free
Will for me. Talk about Predestination — there was a kind
of society I was expected to join, and a kind of girl I was
expected to marry, and the kind of work I was expected to
do, and I didn't get within a country mile of any of them,
thanks to Major General Cassius Marcellus Clay. The worst
of it is, when I say "thanks," I don't even know if I'm being
ironical or not. And *that's* a ridiculous thing for a seventy-
one-year-old man to admit!

It is the year 1903, and Cash Clay died two weeks ago —
so I know nothing more is going to happen to him. That
leaves me with one more job to do before I can say that nothing more is going to happen to me.

I must write this book.

*   *   *

My name is Hacey Fort Miller. I was born in 1832, but it wasn't until 1845 that anything very interesting happened to me, so that's when I want to begin this story.

I was an impatient two weeks away from my thirteenth birthday. My sister Rosalie was a year-and-something older, and my brother Boone was a year younger. We lived with my father, Sheldon Boone Miller, and my mother, Patience Fort Miller, in a house grandiosely called "Hazelwood." There wasn't a hazel wood within a twenty-mile radius, as far as I ever knew, but it was a nice house overlooking the north bank of the Kentucky River — the Fayette County side — about twelve miles from Lexington.

You'll notice a couple of names keep cropping up in my family, Boone and Fort. The Boone name comes, not surprisingly, from Daniel Boone — or, more exactly, from his brother, Squire Boone, who was some kind of shirttail relative of my father's. (Father always referred to the fabled frontiersman as "Cousin Dan'l.") The Fort name harks back to Virginia. My grandfather was a Fort, and also a Carter. His full name was Anson Carter Fort. His sister, my great-aunt Henrietta, also kept the Fort in her name, even after she married my great-uncle John Satterlee.

In our family we don't use up names very fast.

We weren't really farmers, even though Hazelwood was surrounded by some forty acres of Miller-owned farmland. My father owned a feed and dry-goods store in Lexington, and most of our income came from that. We had a family of tenants on the land — the Tates — who raised hemp, corn and a little tobacco, and kept most of the profits.

And, of course, we had our slaves, five of them, which was foolish for a house as small as ours. There was 'Shach, and his wife Aunt Hessie, and his brother Jubal, and his two children, Pierre and Opal. Jubal would drive Father into Lexington every day, and then help out in the store, and sometimes 'Shach would go in with them when it looked like a busy day shaping up — so we weren't quite as overstaffed as we sounded. But there certainly were plenty of Negroes around.

Especially if you count Star.

Star was a free Negro who lived in a shack right down on the river. Since it was on our land, he paid my father a few dollars a year rent, which he made by mending fences in the spring and other odd jobs. But he didn't work much. Mostly he fished and trapped varmints in the woods, and often I accompanied him.

I guess Star was my best friend — but of course I never thought of him in those terms, he being a Negro. But I spent more time in his company than that of any other person outside my own family. He taught me the best bait for catching bullheads, and how to skin a coon, and where to find wild grapes, and how to pop the head off a snake, and knowledge of that sort, which, unlike geography and geometry, has great relevance during the springtime of a man's life.

Star was a big man, well over six feet, and truly black, black with almost purplish highlights. His teeth were magnificently white, although his eye was yellowed. On his forehead was a great scar in the shape of a five-pointed star. The healed skin was livid, much lighter than that which surrounded it. The scar gave him a frightening aspect until you became used to it — and even sometimes afterwards, if you caught him wearing the cold and harsh expression that seemed so oddly at variance with his normal lackadaisical appearance.

On this particular day, however, there was no suggestion of still waters running deep — unless we consider the Kentucky River. It was about seven in the morning on a beautiful sunny Sunday — the thirteenth of April, it must have been. The mist — the wonderful pearly-cool luminous mist of the Bluegrass morning — was rising from the motionless water. Star and I were stretched out on the bank near his cabin; I was fishing with a line, a bent pin and a chunk of fatback; Star was whittling on what both of us knew (and neither of us had mentioned) was going to be his birthday present to me: a small flat box of cherrywood, about two by three inches in size, with curious figures carved in bas-relief on the top. There was a flash of scarlet in the nearby trees as a cardinal took flight; the first church bells of the day carried on the still air from Richmond six miles away.

"Your daddy happen to say anything about Mr. Clay's gal Emily going on trial Monday?" Star asked.

"Not that I recollect," I answered. "How come? Is the trial really going to get started after all?"

"So they saying." He whittled in silence for a moment. "Sure do look like it going to be some big trial all right. Wished I could see it."

"You know that Emily right well, don't you, Star? Do you think she really poisoned Mr. Clay's little boy?"

"Mr. Hacey," Star said, smiling with all his face up to but not including his eyes, "that's the kind of question you don't ask one black person about another black person. At least, not unless you hoping to get lied to."

I felt a quick tingle of resentment. Negroes shouldn't presume to tell white folks that they lied to them whenever they chose — although everybody knew it was true. But the irritation gave way to my curiosity.

"All right, I'm sorry I asked that question, Star. But look, answer me this. Just supposing Emily poisoned him, *why*

4

would she have done it? What could she have against a four-year-old?"

Star sighed. "Mr. Hacey, you do ask me the worrisomest questions. How I know why somebody who maybe didn't even poison somebody come to poison that somebody?"

"Aw, come on, Star. You must have some ideas."

"Yeah, I reckon I have some ideas." He looked up from his whittling, and his expression became stern. "You know about Mr. Cash Clay? You know how he all the time talking and speechifying about freeing the slaves? You know how he fighting duels and killing other white men 'cause he love black men so much? Of course you know that — everybody in Kentucky know that. Then how you think you feel if you are a nigger in his own house — you and your mama and your uncle and your little child — and you hear him all time talking about freeing *other* black people, while he keeps you on being a slave?"

"But Star, I heard the only reason Mr. Clay hadn't freed Emily and her family was 'cause he *couldn't*. He didn't really own them because they were in trust, or something."

"I don't know nothing about trusts, Mr. Hacey — but I know about slaves. You think anybody likes being a slave? You think anybody likes any of the *children* of anybody who keeps them being a slave?"

"But golly, Star — you mean that Emily might have poisoned the baby just because Mr. Clay wasn't able to free her and her family? It doesn't seem fair!"

The big Negro went back to his whittling, a half-smile on his face. "I ain't studying about 'fair,' Mr. Hacey, I'm studying about 'free.'"

Before I could express my disagreement with that statement, I heard the voice of my mother raised in maternal out-

5

rage. "Hacey Miller, you get into this house and get yourself cleaned up for breakfast. *Now!* And if you smell of fish and river mud, you'll take a bath before church."

So I hurried into the house to start the regular Miller Sabbath routine. I didn't get a chance to talk to Star about the Clay poisoning case anymore that day, but I thought about it a lot. And the more I thought about it, the more important it seemed to me that I should witness the beginning of the trial.

*   *   *

That Sunday after church, the Ledyards came over for Sunday dinner. I always dreaded the arrival of the Ledyard family. It meant that I had to stay dressed up after church, eat dinner at the second table in the kitchen and act as a kind of host to the Ledyard children, even though I really didn't have anybody to talk to. Bryan Ledyard was an argumentative nine-year-old, and his sister Robin was only seven. There was no basis for intelligent conversation there. Their stepbrother Galt Ledyard was pretty interesting, but he had graduated to the first table as soon as he started at Transylvania College in Lexington, the previous fall. So he wasn't there to give his courteous but slightly patronizing answers to my questions about duels and horse races and other such topics.

The Ledyards were kin to us. The head of their house was my great-aunt Henrietta — Henrietta Gordon Fort Satterlee. A formidable woman, five feet one inch tall and 175 pounds, with a bosom that looked like she had a bedroll wrapped around her chest, and a jaw like a Cherokee's stone ax. She was sixty-five that April Sunday, widowed for twenty-five years, and she was to die before the year was out. But you never would have guessed it then.

Her daughter Maud was my first cousin, once removed. She was a pretty brown-haired woman who always seemed

6

to me to be putting on airs and carrying on about "The Old Dominion" and people being "F.F.V.'s" and all that kind of Virginia talk. She was always nice enough to me, though, and so was her husband, "Cousin" Whitney Ledyard, a rather shy and soft-spoken gentleman hailing originally from Maryland, and one of the best breeders of racehorses in the Bluegrass.

Cousin Whitney had been married twice. I never heard anybody talk about his first wife, but I have the feeling that she was scandalous. Her only legacy to the Ledyards and Millers of 1845 was a son, Galt. His second marriage brought Cousin Whitney five children — of whom, by the cruel arithmetic of the times, two survived infancy, Bryan and Robin.

Those were the Ledyards as they came to call on us that Sunday afternoon.

There were five of us youngsters around the worn oak table in the kitchen — Bryan and Robin, my sister Rosalie and my brother Boone, and I. Old Aunt Hessie was serving us a Sunday spread of Old Ham and biscuits and Brunswick stew, wheezing and grumbling a little more than the effort demanded.

"Children won't eat no greens, going to grow up puny, no-count and crooked as a snake." Bryan Ledyard, the object of her complaint, hadn't touched a fork to green during the whole meal. "Eat them, child. They ain't going to poison you."

"How do you know? Look at Mr. Clay's baby. I bet that's the way he got poisoned," said my sister Rosalie in her smart-aleck way.

"Now you hush up about that. You don't know nothing about it," said Aunt Hessie sharply.

Bryan regarded his greens with new interest. "My father

7

says it's too bad it wasn't Cash got poisoned his own self, instead of just his baby. He says Kentucky would be better off." He poked through the greens looking for arsenic.

"That's a terrible thing to say," said Rosalie primly.

"Well, he's got it coming. He's just a murderer himself. Everybody knows that."

"Now, wait a minute, Bryan," I said. "I've never heard tell about anybody getting murdered by Mr. Clay."

"What about that Sam Brown at Russell's Cave, then?"

"Why, you can't call that murder. Brown didn't die. Anyway, they proved it was self-defense."

"Self-defense," jeered Bryan.

"Yes, self-defense. What would you want him to do, just stand there and get killed?"

The fight at Russell's Cave had happened two years before, and, with the trial that followed it, had been the biggest news of the year in Kentucky. I hadn't understood the political ins and outs of it, but I knew all the main facts. Robert Wickliffe, Jr., was running for Congress on the Democratic ticket, and most of the big slave-owning people were supporting him, so naturally Cash Clay supported Wickliffe's opponent, Garret Davis, the Whig candidate. As the campaign progressed, Clay learned that Wickliffe was reading a letter aloud at meetings which cast aspersions on Davis. Then Clay discovered that the alleged author of this letter repudiated it as a forgery. Clay communicated this fact to Wickliffe and asked that he stop reading the letter. Wickliffe refused, so Clay started following him around from meeting to meeting, and every time Wickliffe read the letter, Clay would interrupt to read the repudiation. This galled Wickliffe to the point of importing a gunman named Sam Brown from New Orleans, and instructing him to quiet Cash Clay the next time he interrupted a meeting.

8

The next meeting happened to be at Russell's Cave, on the Kentucky River. Wickliffe read the letter and Clay interrupted him again, but this time Brown and five or six companions surrounded Clay and struck him a number of times. Clay was dazed; the crowd fell back; Brown drew a pistol and fired a ball, which struck Clay above his heart and was deflected by the metal-studded sheath of his bowie knife. Before Brown could fire again, Clay was on him with his knife. He carved an ear, dug out an eye, and, in one savage slash, cut through the skull and exposed Brown's brain to the assembled Democrats. Then he pitched the unconscious body off the bluff to the banks of the river below.

Clay was brought to trial for mayhem before a hanging jury of slave-owners in Lexington. His distant cousin Henry Clay defended him. I think every fair-minded person in the state must have thrilled when he heard or read the words with which "Cousin Harry" concluded his plea. Pointing dramatically to Cash, he cried to the jury, "Would you have had him meanly and cowardly fly? Or would you have had him do just what he did do — there stand in defense or there fall? And, if he had not, he would not have been worthy of the name he bears!"

I guess that even if you are proslavery, when a man who has run for President of the United States three times lays his own name on the line like that, you haven't any choice but to go along with him. Anyway, the jury brought in a "Not Guilty" verdict, and Cassius M. Clay left the courthouse a free man in a city and a state whose feeling was, "We weren't mean enough to put you out of the way this time — but we'll get you next time!"

These facts ran through my mind as I argued with my cousin Bryan Ledyard in the kitchen of Hazelwood. As best I can remember it, I was not pro-Clay at that time. How could I have been? I had never heard a single person defend Clay's views on slavery. From my experience, the "peculiar institution" of slavery was as natural and inevitable as tenant farmers and poor whites — or for that matter, as sunrise and sunset. Rather, it seems to me that a kind of "anti-anti-Clay" feeling was just beginning to harden within me. I wasn't *for* him as much as I was against the people who were against him. Like my cousin Bryan, and all the tidewater-talking would-be blue bloods who had taught him to think the way he did.

"Listen, Bryan," I said, "Cash Clay is no murderer, and only a stupid brat like you would ever say he was!"

"Now Mr. Hacey —" said Aunt Hessie in a cautionary tone.

But it was too late. The words "stupid brat" had triggered Bryan's volatile temper. He scooped up the butcher knife from the platter of Old Ham, came out of his chair and around the table in a flash, screamed "Dirty abolitionist skunk!" at the top of his lungs and lunged at me. I went off the side of my chair, throwing my plate at his head as I did. I managed to kick him in the stomach, too. He went down in a welter of stew, ham and vegetables, and Aunt Hessie disarmed him instantly.

This hooraw naturally got all the youngsters up from the table. My little brother Boone was standing beside me as though the two of us were going to take on a regiment — he was always silent and loyal, even then — my sister Rosalie was jabbering like a trained crow, Bryan was crying with rage among the turnip greens and Robin Ledyard was staring at me with wide eyes as though I had just been brought over in a cage from Timbuktu.

Aunt Hessie managed to restore some order. I apologized to Bryan, with my fingers crossed behind my back, and we all sat down again to eat rice pudding with rum sauce. As I searched for plump and winy raisins, I thought again of the forthcoming Clay poison trial, and of how, somehow or other, I had to be there when it opened.

*   *   *

I don't remember what I did the rest of that day — but I'm sure I must have spent some of the time strengthening my resolution to play hooky on Monday. It always took me some time to prepare myself to commit crimes against law and order such as truancy. I was incorrigibly law-abiding. The enormity of any anticipated transgression awed me, and I was always ninety percent sure of being caught red-handed. Nonetheless, I have, I am glad to say, occasionally been able to carry out some minor outrages anyway.

Monday dawned a crisp and sparkling day. Rosalie, Boone and I walked single file along our shortcut path that led to the little two-room schoolhouse in the village of Foxtown, two miles from home. Around us rolling green fields alternated with dense stands of tulip, walnut, ash and beech trees, tall and green-glittering in the frosty air. But I was less concerned with the beauties of the morning than with working out a tactical problem — how to accomplish my truancy without being informed on by my sister. I knew Boone was no threat — he would keep my secret if he were tied to the mouth of a cannon — but Rosalie would normally like nothing better than to squeal like a shoat to both teacher and parents.

I decided to try a combination of flattery and bribery.

"Rosalie, remember that silver locket that Robin was wearing Sunday?"

"Yes," said Rosalie curiously.

"I couldn't help but think it would have looked prettier on you."

This unlikely remark was enough to stir my sister's curiosity. "What's the matter with you, Hacey? Don't you feel well?"

"I feel fine — just like you'll feel when you're wearing the beautiful silver locket I'm going to buy you out of my birthday money."

"Oh, go on — why would you spend your birthday money on me?"

"Because you're my sweet loving sister, and because you'd look pretty, and because you'd keep a secret so your brother wouldn't get into trouble."

Calculation gleamed in Rosalie's eyes. She wasn't slow to see opportunity, or to grasp it.

"What secret is that?"

"That I'm going into Lexington today."

"Alone?"

"That's right," I replied, with more bravado than I felt.

"How?"

"I'll hitch a ride on the back of a wagon. Nobody'll even see me."

"You going to that poison trial, Hacey?" asked Boone. "You going to see Mr. Clay and that Emily girl?"

"You've got it, Boone."

"Son of a gun!" breathed Boone in admiration. He looked at me as though I were a cross between Sam Houston and Jean Laffite.

"And you'd really expect me to tell a lie for you? Hacey Miller, you really must be conceited if you think I'd do that! Why, I wouldn't tell a lie for a beau — much less a brother!"

"Look, Rosalie — it's an awful little lie for an awful pretty locket. You just tell Miss Dowdie that I had to go into Lexington today, and let her think I went in with Papa. That way she won't think anything's wrong, so she won't send back a note about it. Then, after school, you just tell Mama that I went off with some of the boys and you don't know where I went. I'll be back by suppertime, and nobody'll ever say Boo about it."

Rosalie wanted to argue awhile, and she used both ridicule and outraged morality against me, but finally — as is so often the case in this life — virtue was defeated by raw avarice, and she agreed to my plan. A single handshake bound Boone, and I was free to take up a position behind a hackberry bush beside the Lexington pike where I could breathe in the intoxicating scent of spring as I waited for my wagon ride.

II

A Day in Court

I DIDN'T HAVE LONG to wait. Five minutes after I took up my position behind the hackberry bush a wagon loaded with feed and grain came creaking down the road, heading toward Lexington. There was a tarpaulin spread out haphazardly over some of the bags of feed, which offered ideal conceal-ment, not only from the driver but also from neighbors who might take notice and report back to my parents.

As the wagon passed by, I scooted out from behind the bush, belly flopped onto the floorboards and scuttled under the tarpaulin into darkness. But it was inhabited darkness. My shoulder, elbow and knee all hit something simultane-ously, and my nose and mouth were buried in what felt and smelled like human hair.

For a second I knew sheer animal panic. Whatever horror lurked beneath the tarpaulin had caught me now — "All hope abandon, ye who enter here!" — and it was the fault of nobody but wretched, miserable me. Then my mind auto-matically began to sort out the information my senses had gathered, and I realized I was clutching another human be-ing, of about my own size.

"Who are you?" whispered a high-pitched but menacing

14

voice. "And don't make no noise or I'll slit your gizzard!"

"Hacey Miller. Who are you?"

"Falconer Padgett. What the double-danged tarnation you think you're doing getting into my wagon?"

"*Your* wagon! It's just as much *my* wagon as it is *your* wagon! You got your elbow in my stomach!"

"Well, I was here first!" he whispered fiercely. "I might of killed you dead, and it would of served you right. Double-danged idjit!" But I was glad to notice he shifted his elbow from my solar plexus. We both moved quietly under the tarpaulin until we were lying side by side, and could resume our conversation in whispers.

"Where you reckon you're going?" asked my fellow traveler.

"Lexington."

"Me too. What did you say your name was? Hayseed?"

All possible jokes on a man's name are old and tired by the time he's twelve, but I answered patiently, "Hacey — H-A-C-E-Y — it's a family name. Falconer isn't the greatest name in the world either!"

"Well, don't get het up about it. Anyways, I'd liefer be called Falk than Falconer myself, so we ain't got no argument."

During the next two hours I learned a lot about Falk Padgett, even though I had yet to see his face. He and his family were hill people. They lived a few miles east of Paintsville, over near the Big Sandy. Falk was thirteen, and the oldest of seven children. His mother was always "poorly" and his father was a brute. Finally Falk decided he'd had enough of his father's sober sneers and drunken beatings, and lit out for the Bluegrass, which he apparently conceived of as the land of milk and honey.

I asked Falk what he expected to do when he got to Lexington, and he answered that he hoped to get a job and learn a trade. "Figured I'd try my luck at the blacksmiths' and the livery stables. I always done right good around horses."

I told Falk the names of all the smiths and stables I knew in Lexington, and then on impulse suggested that he might find a job at my father's store. "I know Papa's always saying what he needs is a likely boy to hustle around and learn the stock," I whispered. "And he's generous, so he'd probably pay you pretty good. The store's on South Broadway near Water Street, and if Papa's not there ask for Elam Yates — he's the clerk."

"Thank you kindly. Might I say you told me about the job?" Falk asked formally.

"Oh, sure, tell him we met under a tarpaulin in a feed wagon on the Lexington pike!" I hissed sarcastically. "I'm supposed to be in school right now. Nobody's supposed to know I'm going to town!"

"What's so big that's going on in town today?"

I told him about the Clay poisoning trial. "Mr. Clay's our neighbor. He's got a big old house called White Hall, about three miles from where I live. I've seen him and that slave girl both — hundreds of times! So naturally I got an interest in the trial, haven't I?"

Falk allowed as how he guessed I did, and then we lapsed into silence. After a couple of minutes, Falk whispered, "I never knowed anybody who had a slave."

"Shucks, everybody in the Bluegrass has slaves. If you don't have slaves around here, you're just nobody — just white trash."

"I wonder what it would feel like."

"What — having slaves?"

"Yeah — and being one."

"Well, having them just feels normal. But being one — I

guess you'd have to be a nigger to know how that feels."

"You reckon they're that different from us white folks?"

"Well, sure. My mama says slavery's the natural condition for niggers. Back in Africa they're always holding one another slaves."

"Then it appears to me that *owning* slaves is natural to them too. Ain't that right? So how is that different from us?"

"Well, you never heard of a white man *being* a slave, did you? That's the difference, you darn fool — *being* a slave, not owning slaves! Now hush up before the driver hears us!"

We rode together in silence in the hot and stuffy darkness under the tarpaulin, each occupied with his own thoughts. I wasn't too satisfied with my answers to the mountain boy's questions about slavery, so I tried to sort out the whole subject in my mind, but it was too much for me.

By and by the increasing sound of voices and horses' hooves told us we were drawing close to the center of Lexington. I popped my head out from under the canvas, blinking in the sudden light, and saw that we were on Main Street, a few blocks from my father's store. I ducked back under cover. "It's time we get out here," I whispered. "Let's just slide out now while the wagon's still moving."

Falk and I wriggled as silently as grass snakes over the wagon's tailboard and dropped to the ground below — and as we stood together in the road watching the wagon pull away from us, the driver looked over his shoulder and genially shouted, "Goodbye, boys!"

*   *   *

So Falk and I found ourselves in downtown Lexington — even if our entrance into the city hadn't been accomplished with the masterful stealth we had hoped for. Our reaction to the wagon driver's farewell was to stare at one another open-mouthed. That was my first view of Falk in daylight, and it wasn't impressive. He was above middle height, scrawny, shaggy-headed and densely freckled. His most prominent features were his ears, his Adam's apple, his hands and his feet. And his smile, a sudden, wild irreverent splitting of his whole face — a smile that slapped you on the back at the same time it mocked you, that always seemed to be saying, "Why the hell not?" — the purely ornery smile of the mountain man.

I guessed I looked as unprepossessing to him as he looked to me, because he burst out laughing and shouted, "Shucks — I thought as how I was under that old tarpaulin with a *man* — not some little old bug-eyed tadpole like you!"

"I'm as much a man as you are, you danged ridge-runner," I retorted, raising my fists and settling back into what I imagined to be a professional pugilistic position. "And it wasn't no picnic spending two hours under a tarpaulin with *you*, I can tell you!" I moved my left fist in a circular motion while I rocked back and forth on my toes.

Falk raised his hand pacifically. "Ain't no need of getting all antsy, boy. I'm not about to start fighting you in the streets of Lexington, especially when I might end up asking your old man for a job. Just point my nose toward your pap's store, and I'll be a-going."

I felt ashamed of my pugnacious stance. "I'm sorry, Falk," I said, reaching for his hand. "Good luck to you. You just keep walking the way we're going, down that way about four blocks, and you'll come to Broadway. Then turn left and go another block and you'll see it on your right. It says 'Miller's' on the sign outside the door."

"Thank you kindly — and I hope we meet again," said Falk.

"Well, you just get that job and we'll be sure to!"

Falk turned and took off with a vigorous stride down Main Street. I followed after him, but more cautiously, with many a furtive glance to left and right.

Lexington had a carnival air about it that day. You could feel that people were expecting something to happen — something which, if not exactly joyous, still was exciting and promised no unpleasantness to themselves. I was to sense this mood in the city often during the next fifteen years, and generally upon occasions when Cash Clay was in town and embattled.

I made my way down the sidewalk past the Phoenix Hotel and across Limestone Street. The courthouse was a block ahead, and I could see an unusually large crowd assembled outside it. I quickened my pace, and in a matter of moments was worming my way into the outer perimeter of the jostling group. My small stature gave me a suppleness of movement and kept me (I thought) safely below adult eye level, and I had threaded my way between most of the bodies and almost reached the great courthouse door, when a hand descended on my shoulder and gripped it — a small hand, but with fingers like wire cables. "What you doing here, Hacey Miller? Why aren't you in school?" asked a querulous voice that I immediately and with sickening certainty recognized as belonging to my father's chief clerk, Elam Yates.

"Well, I had to — I mean, I felt like I had to — well, that is, here was this trial, and Mr. Clay's our neighbor, and — what was the question again?"

"So you played hooky and come all the way into Lexington to see the opening of the trial, did you? Your pa'd skin you alive if he knew you was in town today, you know that?"

"I reckon he would, Elam," I answered humbly.

Then Elam's stern expression relaxed, and his face re-

19

sumed its usual monkeylike appearance. "Then I guess we better not tell him," he said with a grin.

Before I had time to digest my surprise at this stroke of good luck, it was topped by another. "If you'd like to get inside and get a seat where you can see and hear what's happening, stay with me. I got a message for Cash Clay, so they got to let me in."

With that, Elam slipped in front of me and began to weave his way through the crowd as easily as I had, even though he moved with a lurching gait — his right leg being two inches shorter than his left, due to a childhood accident.

At the door he showed an envelope to the guard and gestured toward me to include me in his carte blanche. We were readily admitted and made our way down the crowded corridor to the courtroom, where we were passed by another guard.

The large room was almost filled, but my eyes went to one imposing figure without hesitation. Cassius M. Clay sat in the front row of spectators' seats, and he was watching the door as if waiting for us to arrive. His eyes brightened with recognition as he saw Elam enter, and then his expression became momentarily puzzled as he noticed me following.

"Get us two seats there in the back, Hacey. I'll join you directly."

I did as Elam told me, sitting in one seat and laying my coat over the second. Meanwhile Elam limped down to Clay's seat. He handed him the envelope, Clay opened it quickly and read it, then the two exchanged a few words. Clay squeezed Elam's arm, and the clerk began to make his hobbling way toward our places.

At this time Clay was thirty-four years old, and in the full flower of his physical and mental capacities. He was six foot three and weighed 230 pounds or more, with a body proportioned and muscled like a wrestler's. His face was full, and his heavy chin was clean-shaven. A great shock of black hair fell loosely across his forehead, and his brown eyes flashed under heavy brows. He was one of the *noblest* looking men I've ever seen. No one who ever set eyes on him forgot him.

He sat straight in his seat, alone, looking neither to the right nor left (apparently Elam was the only person he had been watching for), waiting for the proceedings to begin as if he had nothing else to do all day. I marveled at his calmness in the midst of a crowd that was obviously hostile to him. He acted as such a magnet to my eyes that it was some minutes before I became aware that there were two other people I knew well in the courtroom. Four or five rows in front of us was a group of Transylvania College "bloods" — young dandies of wealthy, proslavery families, who affected high, shiny riding boots, which they slapped often with riding crops. Their leader was a handsome young man named John Hunt Morgan, and sitting at his side was my half second cousin, Galt Ledyard.

Galt leaned toward Morgan and said something to him, and Morgan threw back his head in a dramatic manner and laughed loudly. There was a callous quality about his laughter that managed to communicate scorn in the very hearing of it — and for a second Clay's eyes turned toward the Transylvania group curiously.

Then a moment later, I saw the other person in that courtroom whom I knew well. Against the back wall, in the far corner of the room, seven or eight free Negroes were sitting — one of them was Star. He was dressed in his Sunday best, a good but worn broadcloth suit, a white dress shirt and a black string tie. He was sitting quietly in his seat, his yellowed eyes hooded, unmindful of his neighbors, waiting as impassively as Clay himself.

My speculations about why three such unlikely persons as Elam Yates, Galt Ledyard and Star should all be present in this courtroom were cut short by the bailiff, who announced that the court was in session.

The judge that day was a fat man with a walrus mustache and an irascible tongue. He got the proceedings under way in short order, and in a few moments the prisoner was brought to the bar.

The slave and alleged poisoner, Emily, was a jaundice-colored mulatto of thirty or so, thin, with protruding bones. A hush fell over the courtroom as she acknowledged her identity. Her face was expressionless, but her eyes darted around the room, as though she were searching for someone.

Out of the corner of my eye I saw Star sit up straight and lean forward in his seat. Emily's eyes found him, and it was obvious that it was Star for whom she had been searching. Her eyes widened and her lips parted expectantly. It was almost as if you could hear her unspoken question: "Yes? Tell me!"

And then Star raised his hands up even with his shoulders, where they could be seen from the prisoner's box. He was holding a piece of yarn, and it was looped around his fingers in interlocking X's — a cat's cradle. He held his hands there, motionless — and I felt a sudden chilling tingle in my stomach. Someone, I thought, must have just walked across my grave.

The clerk began to read the indictment, while Emily stared at Star. She didn't appear to be listening to the charges against her. I heard the clerk's high flat voice reading ". . . did then and there put, mix and mingle a deadly poison called arsenic, to wit, five grains thereof, in a certain quantity of milk, to wit, half a pint, and did then and there, by reason of persuasion, threats and force, induce the said Cassius Clay, an infant of tender age . . ."

And then Star suddenly pulled his hands apart, and the intricate maze of intersecting angles disappeared and only a single thread remained. The clerk's voice faltered, ". . . ah — an infant of tender age, to — ah — I'm sorry, Your Honor, I seem to have lost my place."

"Well, find it again, and be quick about it!"

"Yes, sir."

Star's hands had disappeared from view, and I saw that Emily was standing taller than before, and there was the ghost of a smile on her lips. Then the clerk's voice began reading the indictment again. ". . . an infant of tender age, to drink and swallow down a great quantity of the poison aforesaid, with the evil intent that his death might therefrom ensue."

"You've heard the charge against you, Emily. How do you plead?"

The young lawyer whom the court had appointed to represent the defendant answered for her. "We plead not guilty, Your Honor."

"Let it be so noted. We'll now proceed to the selection of the jury."

A panel of veniremen was summoned into the court and took seats in the jury box. The lawyers began to question them, one by one. So many of them had to be excused when they admitted a bias against Cassius M. Clay that it was soon apparent it would be hours before a jury could be selected.

Elam whispered, "Looks like Cash is fixin' to leave. Ain't nothing more going to happen in court today. Let's go see if anything happens outside."

Nothing could have suited me better, for the monotonously repeated questions of the lawyers had begun to bore me, and I was ready to burst with curiosity about Elam's relationship to Clay, and the contents of the envelope he had handed him.

As we rose from our places, Clay made his way past the empty seats that had been occupied by the Transylvania bloods. I noticed that Star's seat was also empty.

We followed Clay into the corridor and caught up with him near the door. The big man smiled as he recognized us. "You brought me good news, Yates — the only good news I've had for weeks, it seems."

"I kind of thought so, Mr. Clay," said Elam in a proud tone. "Oh, this here boy is Hacey Miller. His father owns the store."

Clay nodded gravely, and put his great hand out to me. "I recognized you, Hacey, although I didn't know your name. You live out near White Hall, I believe."

"Yes, sir. Just across the river a couple of miles. I want to tell you I'm sorry about your little boy, Mr. Clay."

"Thank you."

". . . and I hope they hang that Emily!"

"Well, since it took a Lexington grand jury a year and a half to bring in an indictment against her, I don't believe she's in much immediate danger," he answered drily. Then, dismissing the subject, he turned to Elam. "About that other matter — I'm informed that the materials in question are now in Cincinnati, and can be expected in Lexington before the end of the month, depending on when transportation is available."

"Shouldn't be more'n a week," said Elam.

"That means we have to have a place to put them, and

the — er, craftsman to operate them. I think I've found the place. Have you had any luck with the craftsman?"

"There's a journeyman up in New York City I know pretty well. I wrote him and told him what's up, but I haven't heard back from him yet."

"Well, go ahead with it, Yates. We'll need him soon."

This exchange confused me utterly, as it was intended to. Clay began to walk slowly down the courthouse steps, Elam limping beside him, and I brought up the rear. We began to walk down the path that crosses the courthouse lawn and leads to the slave-auction block on Cheapside.

In the shade of an old elm tree, standing and leaning in postures of elaborate unconcern, were grouped the Transylvania bloods. There were four of them — Hunt Morgan, Galt, and two others I didn't recognize, a pudgy one whose skin looked too tight and a thin one with a face like a sheep. As we came up even with them, the pudgy one said loudly, "You know, John, I believe they ought to hang that nigger wench."

"Why's that, Charles?" asked Morgan, smiling.

"Why, to punish her for killing the whelp when she could have got the old dog instead!"

The four young men laughed loudly and artificially; Morgan's laugh had the same scornful sound it had had in the courtroom. Clay stopped. He turned his face to the group and studied them for a moment. Then he said quietly, "I believe that offensive remark was intended for my hearing."

The pudgy youth took a swaggering step toward us. "If you think it's offensive, you're free to do something about it, if you're man enough."

Clay dismissed the speaker with his eyes and looked at Morgan. "I don't know your friend, Mr. Morgan — but I do know you. So will you please explain to him that I don't fight duels. I got tired of allowing my enemies to import professional murderers whose job it was to use an obsolete code of honor to provoke me into making a target of myself."

Morgan smiled broadly. "Sir, as you request, I shall report to my friend that you lack the stomach to demand satisfaction."

"And perhaps you will be good enough also to tell him that I am always armed, and always willing to defend myself against attack."

"I will."

"And that if and when he attacks me I shall open up his body and let out his corrupt little soul the way a surgeon lances a boil and squeezes out the pus!" The controlled fury in Clay's voice was so intense that the pudgy young man blanched, but Morgan's smile remained unchanged. Galt Ledyard and Sheepface drew closer to their leader, as though to share in his confident attitude.

"I will see that he gets your message, sir," Morgan said. He bowed to Clay, Clay bowed to him and we proceeded down the walk. My heart was pounding like a drum in my ears, but Clay appeared completely unconcerned.

As we crossed Cheapside and skirted the slave-auction block, I heard the clock in the courthouse tower tolling three. Suddenly I remembered that I had twelve miles to cover before suppertime.

Much as I wanted to talk to Elam about the events of the day, and much as I wanted to know more about that calm and violent giant, Cassius Clay, I knew I must cut and run.

"Excuse me, but I've got to go now," I blurted. "Goodbye, Elam. Don't say anything to Papa. Goodbye, Mr. Clay — I'm really pleased to have met you!"

"My pleasure also. Goodbye, Hacey."

Ten minutes later I was stretched out in the back of a wagon headed for Richmond. This time the driver knew I was riding with him, so there was no foolishness about hiding under a tarpaulin. Which proves that some people can learn some things, sometimes, if they put their minds to it.

*   *   *

I returned home without incident, and was able to appear at the dinner table at the appointed time, looking well-scrubbed and virtuous. My brother Boone embarrassed me with his awe-inspired gaze, and Rosalie let me know by her complacent smile that she felt herself to be in the catbird seat, and was prepared to bring doom down upon my head if I didn't honor my promise to provide her with a silver locket.

In the course of the meal my father made an interesting announcement to my mother. "I think you'll be able to count on getting more work out of 'Shach around here from now on," he said.

"How's that?"

"I shouldn't be needing to take him in to the store with me so often. I hired me a boy to clean up and run errands and help with the inventory."

"A Lexington boy?" asked my mother.

"No, a boy from the mountains. An orphan. Name of Falconer Padgett. Poor lad, his father was killed feuding, and his mother died of consumption. His brothers and sisters all turned their backs on him, so he's had to make his way in the world all by himself. Since he doesn't have any place to stay, I put a cot into the storeroom, and he's going to sleep there. So he'll be a kind of watchman for us, too."

"Probably steal you blind, I shouldn't doubt," sniffed my mother.

That night in bed, it seemed as though I would never get

to sleep. It was as if all the things I had to think about were
arranged in a circle, and I was trying to get inside. I'd push
up against one thing for a while, and then see it was no use,
and move over to the next one. Falconer Padgett . . . what
it feels like to be a slave . . . Emily . . . Star and the
yarn . . . Elam Yates and the envelope . . . Cash Clay
. . . the "materials in question" in Cincinnati . . . Galt
and John Hunt Morgan . . . and Pudgy . . . and Sheepface . . .

I must have gone around the circle three times before I
went to sleep.

III

THE POLITICS OF SLAVERY

THE NEXT DAY, I heard that as soon as a jury had been chosen, the defense had asked for and been granted a continuance of one month. Whatever the technical reason, it established a pattern which was to continue in the Clay poisoning trial all through the summer and fall. The whole town understood the motive behind this legal delaying action: it was simply to prevent Clay from achieving any kind of conclusion for as long as possible — certainly until after the next election.

As that sunny April drew to a close, and I came within dreaming distance of my thirteenth birthday, the acrid smell of slavery politics oppressed the Bluegrass air. Even I was uneasily aware of it, although my main interest those days was discovering the way of a man with a maid, through the cooperation of Laurel Tate, the fourteen-year-old daughter of Fenn and Annie Tate, our tenants.

On the day before my birthday, Laurel and I were in our "secret place," a little open spot along the river, completely shielded by bushes and tall grass. We had been hugging and kissing one another for ten minutes, but the only other thing that had happened was that my left arm had gone to sleep. I was afraid of moving it for fear of breaking the mystical contact between us. I was sure this was the day our relationship could be advanced to a more intimate level. Even though I had only one hand to work with, I vowed to use it with a will. I used it.

"Oh, Hacey," sighed Laurel. Instead of thrusting my hand away, as she always had before, she pulled my head down for another kiss. The blood sang in my ears.

Just then my mother's voice carried down from the porch. "Hacey Miller, you get in here right away. Somebody's come to see you."

"Tarnation," I protested, looking at my hand resting squarely on Laurel's firm young bosom like an inert white spider. It looked so crude and obvious there. But to take it away suddenly might call even more attention to it. I sort of slithered it off.

"Hacey Miller, I'm calling you," shrilled my mother.

I struggled to my knees. My left arm wasn't much help. "Goodbye Laurel. See you soon," I whispered.

She sat up and smoothed her dress with surprising savoir-faire. "Make it *real* soon, Hacey," she said.

I left her there and hurried up to the house, silently cursing my unknown visitor. But my outrage disappeared when I found the identity of the caller and the reason for his call: it was Josh Brain, and he had brought me a birthday present.

Josh Brain was a lawyer and a bachelor. In his first capacity he represented my father's legal interests, and in his second he was a frequent guest at our dinner table, where he enjoyed vicariously the family life he had been denied. Perhaps it was his corpulence that had kept him from marrying — although no more than five feet four or so, he must have weighed close to 250 pounds. He was a trencherman, and our family never got over surprise at how much food that fat little man could put away.

He had developed a special fondness for me when he noted my avid enthusiasm for books. A bibliophile himself, he had a special sympathy for any other book lover, and always made it a point to give me books on my birthday and Christmas. That day he was holding a package of familiar shape in his small pink hands, and I could hardly wait to strip off the wrapping and see what treasures he had brought.

"Hacey," my mother said, "say, 'How do you do' to Mr. Brain. He's come to bring you a birthday present."

"How do you do, sir," I said.

"Howdy do to you, Hacey," replied the lawyer, his eyes glittering merrily in his puffy face. "I thought I'd get you something real unexpected this year — something you wouldn't guess if you studied about it for a coon's age. What do you think of that?"

At the thought that his present might not be books after all, my face must have fallen comically, for he burst out laughing and thrust the package into my hands. "See for yourself," he chuckled.

In a matter of seconds I husked the wrapping off and saw two beautiful leather-bound volumes, one blue, and the other brown. *"The Deerslayer,* by James Fenimore Cooper . . ." I read, ". . . and *Martin Chuzzlewit,"* by Charles Dickens!"

"That Cooper book is another one about Natty Bumppo, and it takes place before *The Last of the Mohicans.* It's a corker," said Brain, who always seemed to have read my books before he gave them to me. "The other one's brand new. It's by that Englishman who wrote *Oliver Twist.* It's about America — and he sure don't think much of us!"

31

"Oh, thank you, Mr. Brain," I gasped, transported with joy. "I can hardly wait to read them!"

"Well, I'm afraid you're going to have to wait, young man," said my mother. "You get yourself washed up. We're going to have dinner directly."

At the table Josh Brain did away with a rack of lamb, platters of creamed turnips, fried potatoes, greens with bacon, corn pudding and a sweet potato pie — or at least the lion's share of it. It was his usual impressive performance. Old 'Shach was waiting on us, and Josh kept him moving at an unaccustomed pace. The old Negro's eyes widened with incredulity each time the rotund lawyer filled his plate again, and meanwhile Brain's voice kept up an incessant chatter. It was during the dessert that I pricked up my ears and stopped kicking my sister's ankles under the table.

In answer to a question of my father's about the Clay poisoning trial, Brain answered, "Well, however it comes out, Cash isn't just sitting around waiting for a verdict. The word is, he's figuring to put out a newspaper."

"What? In Lexington?"

"It appears that way. First thing, Cash rented a building on North Mill Street, right across from Cheapside. Nobody knew what for, until about a week later three wagons come in from Cincinnati, all loaded down with machinery. Cash had them unloaded after dark, but a couple of fellers report that the contents included — mark this, Sheldon — a flatbed printing press, four or five job cases of type, two fourpounder cannons and a quantity of weapons of the sticking and shooting persuasion."

"Good God!" gasped my father.

"And," continued Brain, "at about that same time a cadaverous-looking workman appeared in one of our seamier saloons. He confided to his fellow drinkers that he was a

32

journeyman printer who hailed from New York, and that he was looking for Cassius Clay."

"Clay must be insane," said my father.

"Or at least he moves with a singleness of purpose that is unusual among those who profess sanity," amended the lawyer.

So Cash Clay was going to start a newspaper in Lexington! One of the several mysteries that had boggled my mind was suddenly solved: the "materials in question" and the "craftsman to operate them" — in Clay's cryptic phrases — were now explained. I don't know why, but I felt an exhilarating charge of excitement run through my whole body.

"I suppose he figures it's the only way he can foist his mad-dog abolitionist views on the public," said my father indignantly. "The Lexington *Observer* has refused to publish anything he's written for the last three months."

"They may regret that decision before too long," said Brain. "When they were publishing his cards in the *Observer*, at least they could have the last word. If he publishes a paper of his own, God alone knows how far he can go."

Observing that Josh Brain had finished his second piece of pie and seemed to be temporarily sated, my mother said, "Well, it really distresses me to hear about that terrible man — if you gentlemen will excuse me, the children and I will leave you to your Madeira."

This was the cue for Rosalie, Boone and me to rise from the table and excuse ourselves. Pa and Josh would stay at the table for two or three hours, drinking wine and cracking Louisiana pecans, while the rest of the family made itself scarce. But today I felt that, for the first time in my life, I wanted to stay with the men — and I felt that as a birthday boy I had the right to ask permission.

33

"Please, Mama, just this once — if it's all right with Papa and Mr. Brain — could I stay with the gentlemen?"

Mama's eyebrows shot up to the top of her forehead. "Why, Hacey Miller, I declare! What's gotten into you? Your papa and Mr. Brain don't want to be bothered with you when they're having a serious talk!"

"Your pardon, ma'am," the lawyer interjected, "but I'm curious. Why do you want to stay and listen to two dull old fogies palaver, friend Hacey?"

"Because you're going to be talking about politics, and Cash Clay and abolitionism and all that — and I'm old enough so I ought to know about those things, and I want to start learning about them."

"Well!" said my father in a surprised tone. Then he looked at Josh Brain and said with a smile, "I suppose we should be flattered that he chooses us for his mentors, eh, Josh?"

"It's a testimonial I will cherish. I vote Hacey be allowed to join the council of the warriors, for this evening at least. That is, if it doesn't do irreparable harm to the house rules," Brain said.

"Heavens, if you all can stand it, I'm sure the house can," my mother said tartly, and she swept from the dining room with Boone and Rosalie in tow.

Father passed the decanter of Madeira to Josh Brain, who filled his glass and passed it back. Father filled his glass; both men held their glasses up to the light and gazed admiringly into the ruby depths, and both men sighed together in complete satisfaction. Then Father said, "That damned Cash Clay."

"Oh, you know it's more than just Cash Clay, Sheldon. It's slavery. Slavery's the rock we'll break on."

"Well, damn it, I'm against slavery. You're against slavery. I imagine even old Wickliffe would be against it, if he could figure a way to get his money out of those hundred slaves of his."

"Of course most people are against slavery *in theory*. They're also against sin *in theory*. Clay happens to be against it in fact — and that is an equine of an altogether different hue." Brain paused to crack a pecan, extract the meat and munch it meditatively. "But still nobody would mind too much if he'd just keep quiet about it," he resumed. "But expecting Cash Clay to keep his mouth shut is like expecting the Mississippi River to flow north. And mark my words, Sheldon — before he's through he will have killed the Whig Party as dead as a doornail."

My father looked quizzically at his friend. "For a Whig, you don't show much confidence in the health of your party."

"Man alive, look what he did last year! If Henry Clay could have carried New York state he would have beaten Polk for the presidency. And why didn't he carry New York state? Because Cousin Cash went up there to campaign for him and scared the daylights out of half the Whig Party! Why, Henry's hardly spoken to Cash since then — and what's more, he says he's retired from politics for good! If Cash were a Democrat he couldn't have done any more harm!"

My father raised his glass in a silent toast. "You can hardly expect a Democrat like me to be upset about that, Josh."

"I think you should be, though, Sheldon, and I'll tell you why," said Josh seriously." Right now the Whig Party is law-abiding and constitutional and safely middle-of-the-road. The firebrands like Cash Clay only represent a minority opinion — a small minority, even up North. But if Cash keeps scaring conservative Whigs over into the Democratic Party, sooner or later that minority opinion is going to be a majority opinion — and then you'll have a real, true anti-slavery party to deal with."

"I can't believe that abolitionism will ever gain more than a handful of supporters," argued my father.

"Wait a minute. We're not just talking about abolitionism — we're also talking about emancipation. There's a whale of a big difference. Abolitionists believe in freeing slaves illegally, against the laws of the states and the national government. Emancipationists believe in freeing them gradually, and by law, and paying their owners a fair price in return. I agree with you that there will never be very many abolitionists in the country — since these are people who are willing to break the law — but there *will* be plenty of emancipationists. Why, Sheldon, we *create* emancipationists by the bushel basket! Remember two years ago, when that girl who was only one sixty-fourth Negro was sold at auction on Cheapside? Remember how the auctioneer ripped open her blouse and showed her titties to the crowd? I bet that made more emancipationists in one afternoon than William Lloyd Garrison's made in his whole life! I tell you, slavery's the rock that will sink the Whig Party — and you Democrats better worry about whether it will sink the Union as well!"

"Josh, you manage to destroy the Union every time you come to dinner. It seems to me we have a situation in which our 'peculiar institution' works effectively in certain areas and doesn't work in others. Logically we can assume it will continue where it works and disappear where it doesn't. And remember that the cost of slaves has been rising steadily, year after year. This is bound to restrict slavery to those areas where it makes good economic sense . . ."

". . . and as the costs rise, fewer and fewer slaves can be operated at a profit, so finally the whole institution just dries up and blows away," Brain interrupted. "I've heard the argument before. The only thing wrong with it is that it just isn't true."

"Oh, come now, Josh. Calhoun says —"

"I don't give a damn what Calhoun says. Look what happened when we passed the Non-Importation Act in 1833."

"You mean the Nigger Law?" asked Father, giving it the name by which Democrats called it.

"If you like. I don't care what it's called. The point is, us Whigs worked for five years to pass a law that made it illegal to bring niggers into the state to sell. That was supposed to make slavery gradually dry up and blow away, too. And what happened? Why, there's more niggers in Kentucky now than there were then!"

"Then why don't you side with the Democrats who are trying to repeal the law? You say yourself it doesn't work?"

"Why, Godalmighty damn, Miller, if slaves are increasing *with* the law, what do you think would happen *without* it? Man, there would be a black flood that would swamp the state! Don't you know that bastard Robards —" here the fat little lawyer checked himself, glanced at me apologetically and amended his words — "that scoundrel Robards and the other slave-traders like him would bring in blacks for stud? They'd have stud farms here in the Bluegrass to supply every plantation in the Deep South!" He paused to empty his glass and refill it, spilling wine on the tablecloth in his agitation.

Father sat quietly, meditating for a few seconds. Then he said, "Assuming you're right, Josh, which I don't — you're always too ready to drive the Four Horsemen of the Apocalypse through my dining room — what do you think is the answer?"

"I wish I knew," said Brain. "One thing I'm sure of — repealing the Non-Importation Act will only increase the pressure that's beginning to pull us apart already."

"So will Cash Clay's newspaper."

"As I am sure he intends." Brain sighed loudly and raised his glass. "God protect us from virtuous men."

"Here, here," seconded Father. "Although I must say you're usually pretty safe from contact with them in the Whig Party."

"Sheldon, is that kind? Why, we have a positive gaggle of virtue in the party. Virtuous people falling over one another in their zeal to build a greater and more Christian commonwealth."

"Have you all decided which one of that virtuous gaggle you're going to run for State Senator this summer?"

Brain pursed his lips, hesitating before he answered. "I don't know why I shouldn't tell you — it will be announced in a day or two anyhow. We're putting up Bob Todd."

Bob Todd was Robert S. Todd, a respected Lexington businessman who — although I didn't know it at the time — had been for the past two-and-a-half years the father-in-law of an Illinois lawyer named Abraham Lincoln.

"A good man," said Father. "But I doubt if he can beat Colonel Moore."

"I've got a bottle of twenty-year-old Kentucky bourbon that says he can," said Brain.

"Done!" said Father.

As they shook hands, my mother's voice came from the doorway. "So this is the valuable instruction the boy is getting from his elders — how to gamble with bottles of whis-

key? Come, Hacey — I think you'll profit more from a hot
bath!"

I thanked Father and Mr. Brain and said good night, leaving the two of them looking a bit sheepish over their nuts and
wine.

IV

The True American IS BORN

FINALLY my birthday came. My father gave me a shotgun
— breech-loading, with a percussion lock that took copper
caps. It had a beautifully carved curly maple stock. Mother
gave me a new suit of clothes. Boone gave me a gutta-
percha slingshot he had whittled himself, and Rosalie gave
me three linen handkerchiefs — worth, I'm sorry to say, a
good deal less than the silver locket she had extorted from
me.

After school I brought five or six friends home with me
and we had a little birthday party, with ice cream and cake.
By the time they left it was after five o'clock, and I had just
enough time to get down to Star's shack for a quick visit
before dinner.

The big Negro, stripped to the waist, was stretched out on
his bed, his hands at his sides, his eyes wide open and staring
at the ceiling. His face was expressionless, his body completely immobile — he lay as if in a trance.

The door was open. I hesitated a moment on the threshold, then tapped on the wood. "Star," I said softly, "it's
Hacey. Mind if I come in?"

Slowly the eyes rolled toward me. For a moment or two

they seemed unfocused, as though he were looking at something far beyond the walls of the room — something beyond the limits of the Bluegrass — even beyond the borders of the "dark and bloody ground" of Kentucky.

Or maybe it was my imagination, for suddenly Star's teeth flashed dazzlingly, and the ugly scar on his forehead became simply a familiar landmark on the map of friendship. "Well, I do declare, if it ain't Mr. Hacey. Come in, boy, and set a spell. I hoped you'd come to see me today."

"I can't stay long, Star. We're going to eat in a few minutes."

"Well, you can stay long enough for what Star want to do." He sat up and swung his legs to the dirt floor, and the husks in his mattress chattered. "I reckon about today you due to have a birthday, ain't that right?"

"That's right. It's today. I just finished having a birthday party up at the house."

"And you got all kind of presents, I expect."

I told him happily about all my new acquisitions.

"Lord, Lord! Alongside all that, my little old present won't be worth a picayune!"

"Oh, no, Star!" said I, anxious to reassure him if I had hurt his feelings. "Anything you gave me would be just about my favorite present. Really!"

He walked across the room to a battered old chest of drawers in the corner, pulled one out and reached inside. When he withdrew his hand, he was holding the familiar small cherrywood box which he had been carving for the past two months.

He handed it to me, smiling. "Happy Birthday, Mr. Hacey," he said.

The design on the lid was finished now, and stood out clearly in relief. There were three human figures and a giant snake. The snake was curled around the feet of the center figure, and its head was raised in the air, fangs exposed. The person in the center seemed to have the features of a white man, while the other two persons appeared to be blacks. The one on the right was a woman of gentle expression, the one on the left a very fat man who was glaring at the snake and gesturing at him.

"Oh, it's beautiful, Star! I'll keep it for my most important things!"

"You like it?"

"I love it! But what does the design on top mean?"

"Don't fret about that, boy. It's just some old nigger nonsense."

"But who are these people supposed to be? And what's that snake doing? Is he going to bite the fellow in the middle?"

"They all just made-up folks out of old nigger stories, Mr. Hacey. That lady, she called Maitresse Ezille, and the fat man, he called Papa Legba. The snake named Damballa, the bloody one."

"Who's the one in the middle?"

"He ain't got no name."

"He looks like me!"

Star laughed loudly. "Looks like you? Why, I don't think he look a bit like you. He too good-looking to be you!"

"Well, anyway, is the snake going to bite whoever it is?"

"That depend. Papa Legba and Maitresse Ezille can stop old Damballa when they want to. They got him stopped now. But any time they feel like it, they decide to let him strike, and bang — that man, he dead!"

I studied the design for a few moments in a silence. The execution of the figures was superb. As I looked at it I could almost feel the constricting pressure of the serpent around my legs.

It was hard to take my eyes off the box, but I knew I had to get back for dinner. "Well, whatever it means, it's the greatest piece of woodcarving I've ever seen, Star, and I thank you."

"You welcome, Mr. Hacey. May it bring you luck."

As I was preparing to leave, I remembered I hadn't seen Star since the day I went to the courthouse in Lexington. "Say, I didn't know you were planning to go to town to see the trial when it opened. Why didn't you tell me?"

"Me? Go to Lexington to see some trial? I never went to no trial."

"Why, sure you did, Star. I saw you there. Right in the back row."

"I reckon you mistaken, Mr. Hacey." He smiled with his mouth. "You know how all us niggers look alike. And anyway, you couldn't have seen nobody, because that would mean you was playing hooky in Lexington instead of going to school, and you'd never do that."

We looked at each other in silence. After a moment I said, "I guess you're right. How could I have seen anybody? Thanks for the box, Star."

"You're most welcome."

On the way up to the house I was glad I hadn't mentioned the yarn I'd seen stretched between those strong black fingers that day in Lexington.

* * *

April blossomed into May. The school year ended, and suddenly there was the banquet of a Bluegrass summer spread out before me. Hunting and trapping with Star, learning to use my own shotgun, riding out to see friends at

43

neighboring farms, swimming and boating on the river, picnics, barbecues and burgoos, horse races — there couldn't be a happier life for a boy. It was two weeks before I gave a thought to Cassius M. Clay, his poisoned son and his newspaper.

One Monday in the middle of May, I was planning on riding into Lexington and buying a new pair of boots. Pierre, 'Shach and Hessie's son, had saddled my little brown mare, Sacajawea, and he stood holding a stirrup for me by the front porch. Birds were fussing in the trees, the sun was shining, I had money in my pocket and not a care in the world. I vaulted into the saddle, kicked Sackie into a canter, and sped down our private lane toward the Lexington pike with the wind in my hair and my heart.

I slowed down to a walk on the pike, and began to plan my day. Then I remembered that it was Monday. Was it the second Monday in the month? Yes it was — Monday, May 12.

That meant it was Court Day again. The justices of the peace would be sitting in the courthouse, and outside, Cheapside would be clamorous with the cries of hucksters and odorous with the smell of fresh-cooked food. And on the rickety platform in the southwest corner of the yard the autioneer would be selling Negroes.

My spirits rose even higher, if possible. What an exciting day was in store for me! First I'd stable my horse. Then I'd buy my boots, high, brown and shiny. Then I'd go past the store and see Elam and find out whether he was going to the poison trial again. Then maybe we'd go to the courthouse, or, if he wasn't going, maybe I'd get my friend Falk Padgett to sneak off with me, and we'd go down on Cheapside and see what was happening. We'd make our meal off the foods sold by the vendors, and maybe we'd find something to buy — a knife or a compass, perhaps. And then we'd go by the Melodeon Theater and see if there was a matinee — often there was on Court Day. And if there was, I'd treat Falk to a ticket and show him what the high culture of the Bluegrass was like.

I left Sacajawea at Pruitt's Livery Stable and walked up Broadway to the store. Papa must have been in his office in the back, because I didn't see him, but Elam Yates was waiting on a customer and Falk was wrestling a forty-pound keg of nails behind the counter. I went over to him, and said, "Howdy, Falk. How are you?"

He looked up, and his face split in two with that ornery mountain grin. "Tolerable, Hayseed. How's yourself?"

"Look, if I'm a hayseed, I'd hate to think what you are, coming out of some little hidey-hole out by the Big Sandy that they haven't even figured a name for yet!"

"I reckon I went and did it again, didn't I? I declare, there's something about that name of yourn that just downright makes me forget my manners!" His expression was uncontrite.

"Well, try to remember them," I growled. "How have you been getting on? Do you like your work?"

"Your pa's been real good to me, Hacey, and so has Elam. I got me a bed in the back, and I get me a free hot meal every day at the tavern that I don't even have to pay for, and Elam's even teaching me how to read, whenever we get the spare time."

"You didn't tell Papa you knew me, did you?"

"Sure not. I said I wouldn't."

"He told us about you at dinner, the day he hired you," I remembered. "You sure did string the long bow with that story you told him!"

"I did?" asked the mountain boy innocently.

45

"You know you did! All that flapdoodle about your father being killed feuding and your mother dying of consumption and all your brothers and sisters turning their backs on you! Why, I'd be ashamed!"

"Well, I guess you and I don't rightly look at it the same way. The way I figured, your pa don't really pay no nevermind to where I come from or who my folks are or whatever. The only thing he really cares about is that he can help out a poor homeless boy, and that makes him feel good. And the more desperate off he thinks I was, the better it makes him feel to help. You follow me?"

"Well, I follow you, but —"

"Why, shucks, Hacey, I'm only sorry I didn't think to tell him I had epilepsy, the blind staggers and some kind of loathsome foreign disease besides."

Elam had finished with his customer, and was clumping across the floor. He smiled at me in welcome. "Howdy, Hacey! Nice to see you again."

"Hello, Elam. I had to come to town to buy a pair of boots, and I wondered if you might be going over to the courthouse for the trial this morning?"

"The Clay trial? No, it's been continued a month. That was the first order of business this morning. Ten o'clock the bailiff called the case, ten-o-two and the judge continued it. Christ on a handcar!" Elam was a railroad enthusiast, and his profanity often indicated as much.

"Oh, pshaw. I was sort of hoping to see Mr. Clay again," I said.

"Cash? You want to see Cash Clay?" A mischievous smile appeared on his monkey face, and his eyes searched the store quickly. "That ain't the safest thing to do these days, you know. A lot of folks are saying some pretty mean things about him, and it looks like there's worse to come.

Maybe you just better decide you'd like to see somebody else!"

"Well, I'm on Mr. Clay's side, no matter what they're saying."

"Your father ain't, you know," said Elam, lowering his voice.

"I know," I said, remembering his conversation with Josh Brain. "I can't help that. All I know is, I think he's a great man!"

Falk was looking at me with interest, a half-smile on his lips. Elam gave me a piercing glance. Then he turned to Falk and said, "You stay here and mind the store, son. Tell Mr. Miller that Hacey and I have gone out to get our lunch and do a couple of errands. We'll be back around two or so."

"Yes, sir," said Falk, and the little clerk and I left the store.

On the street outside, I expected my companion to turn to the south, in the direction of the little tavern where he and my father customarily took their luncheon. Instead he turned north, toward Main Street. He walked briskly along the crowded sidewalk, in spite of his impediment, and I had to trot to keep up.

"Where are we going, Elam?"

"Well, you're so danged interested in seeing Cash Clay again, I thought you might want to go see where he's fixing to put out his paper."

"We're going to his newspaper office?" I said incredulously. I couldn't believe my good fortune.

"That's right. *The True American*, he's going to call it. The building's just around the corner on Mill Street."

When we arrived at Six North Mill Street, there was a crowd of perhaps fifteen men standing around in front of the building, mainly idlers, by the look of them. They were watching and commenting derisively about a tall young man in his shirtsleeves, who was engaged in the peculiar task of bolting a six-foot sheet of iron to the inside of a door.

The *True American* building had two doors on the street. One opened directly into the first floor, and the other opened on a narrow flight of stairs leading to the second floor. It was on this second door the young man was working. Elam walked up to him and said, "Good Morning, Lewinsky. Clay inside?"

The man called Lewinsky pushed a lock of sweat-dampened hair from his eyes, looked out from under a lot more of the same, and recognized Elam.

"Oh, Yates — good morning. How are you? Yes, Mr. Clay's upstairs." He spoke with a heavy accent which I did not recognize.

"Then excuse us," said Elam, and squeezed past him, up the stairs. I followed. As he passed the sheet of iron, Elam tapped it. "Heavy sucker, ain't it? Reckon it'd turn back a cannonball?"

Lewinsky smiled bleakly. "Let us hope so," he replied.

As we ascended the narrow stairs, Elam explained to me that Lewinsky was a Polish émigré, reputedly from a titled family, who had fallen in love with the Bluegrass, bought a house in Lexington, married a local girl, and attached himself to Clay's cause with true Slavic zeal. Which I found no stranger than the fact that the man telling me this, a laconic little clerk with a monkey face, should have done the same thing himself.

We reached the top of the stairs, pushed open a pair of folding doors, and entered the newspaper office. It was a single room that ran the length of the building, about twenty by fifty feet. It contained a printing press, job cases of type, work tables, two desks, most of the other usual equipment of a newspaper office — and some things not so usual.

Cassius M. Clay and another man were conferring beside a four-pounder cannon mounted on a low sloping platform so that its wickedly flaring muzzle angled downward. A carpenter was nailing together what looked like a rifle stand in one corner of the room, and two other men were unpacking a crate which contained at least a score of rifles and shotguns. Fifteen or so lances of the Mexican type leaned against the wall.

"No, no, Neal," Clay was saying. "The angle's wrong. I want it so it will sweep all the way down the stairs right at belly height. I want those rusty nails and Minié balls to hit them right in their belly buttons. The way you've got it now, it'll hit them at knee level at the top of the stairs, and go clear over the heads of the people at the bottom!"

"Then we'll have to raise the platform and increase the angle of descent," said the other man. "That means the platform will have to be built solider."

"Then make it solider," said Clay. He turned away from the cannon and noticed us. His heavy, handsome face broke into a smile. "Elam, glad you could come over," he said, reaching out his hand.

"Wanted to see how things were going — and young Hacey was deviling me to let him see the notorious Cash Clay again."

I blushed a fiery red. "He's funning, Mr. Clay. I didn't call you notorious. I don't even know what it means."

"When you find out, you'll discover they coined the word to describe me." He shook my hand too. "How do you like our establishment?"

I assured him I admired it very much, particularly the cannon. He responded eagerly, "I have two of them, both four-pounders. They were cast specially for me in Cincinnati. I had coin silver mixed with the brass — one hundred silver dollars went into each barrel."

"Seems a shame to shoot old rusty nails out of such genteel guns," Elam said dryly. "When do you expect the ball to begin?"

"We'll have the office in condition to repel boarders in another day or two. When Lewinsky finishes lining the downstairs door with sheet iron, he's going to do the same thing to the folding doors up here, and then to the shutters of the windows. I'll have the two cannons in position to sweep the stairs, and there'll be guns and pikes for forty men."

"Where'll you find forty men?" interjected Elam. Clay ignored the interruption.

"The escape route is up that ladder and through the trapdoor to the roof," he continued. "From there it's an easy jump to either of the adjacent buildings. And if worst comes to worst, and we're driven out of the building, there'll be a new crop of widows and orphans in the slavocracy — look here!" He showed us four small barrels standing inconspicuously in a corner. "There's enough black powder here to blow this building and everybody in it to Kingdom Come. As I go to the roof, I'll light a powder train. It will give me twenty seconds to get clear. I've timed myself going up the ladder and through the trap, and I'm assured twenty seconds is adequate."

My eyes must have been bugging out of my head, for Clay suddenly smiled at me and said, "I bet you'd hear the bang way out on the Kentucky River, Hacey!"

"That's all well and good," said Elam, "but have you got an editor yet?"

Clay frowned. "You know that Stevenson from the Frankfort *Commonwealth* had agreed to come? Well, since then I've heard nothing from him but excuses. It begins to appear he's thought better of his decision."

"Where does that leave you?"

"With ink on my fingers, I should imagine. Emancipationist editors don't sprout from trees in Kentucky. And just in case we don't find one, I've been working on an editorial for the first issue myself. Would you care to hear a bit of it?"

Elam answered in the affirmative, and I added my enthusiastic agreement. Clay went to one of the desks and leafed through a pile of papers, finally extracting one. "You know that Old Wickliffe has been bragging that if I put out an antislavery paper in Lexington, he'll suppress it? Well, this editorial is addressed to Wickliffe. I say, 'You are a living, but ungrateful, monument to the forbearing mercy of the people. Old man, beware! Old man, remember Russell's Cave — and if you still thirst for bloodshed and violence, the same blade that repelled the assault of an assassin . . .' "

"Golly!" I breathed.

" '. . . is once more ready, in self-defense, to drink the blood of the hirelings and sycophants of the father of assassins!' How does that sound?"

"You don't think it's a little too temperate?" asked Elam gravely.

"No, I didn't— do you?" asked Clay in a worried tone. "Perhaps I could strengthen it a bit. What would you think of 'blood-reeking old ghoul' in place of 'father of assassins' ? "

"No, no — on second thought, it's fine the way it is," said Elam quickly. Starting out in a minor key like that, it lets you build up to something dramatic later."

"That's a good point, Elam," said Clay judiciously.

Elam changed the subject. "Well, I reckon I better get Hacey here some lunch and get him back to his pap's store,

Mr. Clay. I'll be back this evening, if I can lend a hand."

"Appreciate it," answered Clay. Then he put his hand on my shoulder and said, "Hacey, feel free to tell anybody anything you want about what you've seen up here."

"Oh, I wouldn't do that, sir!"

"No, I want you to. Tell them about the cannons, and tell them that we put the newspaper office on the second floor because there's only one way in — up the front stairs. And tell them about the escape route and the black powder. Don't worry — I'll be writing about all this in *The True American* in a week or two."

"I don't understand."

"Son, I want them to know just one simple fact. That Cassius M. Clay is capable of — and willing to accomplish — the destruction of large numbers of slavocrats in the execution of his duty to God and the Republic."

"Substitute 'eager' in place of 'willing' and you've got it," amended Elam.

"Come over to this window — I want to show you something," said Clay. He unlatched the shutter over the front window and pulled it back. We were looking east, toward the courthouse. In front of us was Cheapside, with all sorts of livestock on sale — horses, mules, dogs and cats, pigs, goats, sheep, men, women and children. You could hear the voices of hucksters hawking their wares: "Here's your next saddle horse! Look at this beauty — just four years old, with a mouth as soft as butter! She'll move through all five gaits with nary a touch of the spur. She'll make you look like Light-Horse Harry Lee, the little darling!" "Get it here — the world-renowned Dr. Tibee's Intestinal Fumigator! Do you suffer the excruciating tortures of the unfortunates of Dante's famed inferno when you pass water or attempt the connubial act? Have you suspected — but feared to ask a physician — that you suffered from a disease whose name is more familiar abroad than here at home . . ." "Here's a likely yellow wench, skilled in the household arts, an excellent cook, dependable and trusty — the kind of female who can deny her master nothing! What am I bid for this bedworthy — my excuses, I meant to say this *most* worthy young creature? As you can see, she's handsomely endowed, gentlemen!"

"Look down there, Hacey," said Clay. "There are a lot of animals for sale in Cheapside, aren't there? Now look over there at the auction block. There's an animal there, too — just *one* animal. It's called slavery. It's as savage as a tiger, as filthy as a hyena, as meanly and slyly destructive as a wolverine! Hacey, that animal will turn on its master, eat its own young, sleep in its own excrement! There's nothing evil it won't do — and the hell it brings to the poor devils it enchains is no worse than the hell it will bring to those who forge the shackles! Do you understand what I'm saying?"

"Yes, Mr. Clay, I think so."

"Then listen, and remember. While this beast is alive and at large in the Southland, its stinking breath will suffocate every attempt to improve the lot of mankind, both black *and* white. No artisan class will grow in states where slavery exists — no industry will take root — no culture worthy of the name will ever flourish, unless, indeed, it be the culture of the slave himself!"

I remembered the songs that Star had hummed as we bent to the oars in his rowboat on the river, and compared them to the piano pieces my sister Rosalie would perform when the Ledyards came to visit. I nodded.

Clay turned away from the window and slowly walked back toward his desk. "Boy, the first time I met you, you were kind enough to express your sympathy to me on the death of my little son. Now let me tell you something about that." He paused and looked at the ceiling, and a half-smile crossed his face. "Do you know that my father was the greatest slave-owner in Kentucky? Why, when I was growing up at White Hall, I had more darkies around me than old Wickliffe does today. Even though I was the youngest of seven children, I still inherited a considerable number of slaves, as you can imagine. And you know what I did with them? I freed them all, as soon as I was legally able to do so. Every wooly-headed one of them, Hacey — every single Negro on my land — with four crucial exceptions!" He suddenly swung around to face me, and his eyes blazed with the same fury I had seen when he challenged John Hunt Morgan on the courthouse lawn. "There were four slaves I couldn't free, because I only held them in trust — they were actually owned by my wife's family, the Warfields. Four slaves — an old crone named Rachel, her worthless brother Solomon, her daughter Emily, and Emily's child, Margaret. Four slaves — that I didn't want and would have freed if I could. You wouldn't think that was many, for the son of the richest slave-owner in Kentucky, would you?"

"N-no, sir!"

"But it was enough to cost me my son! It was enough to put arsenic in his milk and leave him screaming and puking until merciful Death came for him and took him away!"

"This ain't doing anybody any good, Mr. Clay," Elam interjected.

"No, I want the boy to understand this, Elam. It's important. Hacey, Emily didn't kill my son, even though it was her fingers that dropped the poison in his glass. *Slavery* killed him, Hacey, *Slavery* — nothing else. That great filthy beast out there, outside the window, *that's* the killer.

54

And if we don't destroy it, then God help us all — it will get every one of us just like it got my boy!"

When Clay's great voice stopped, I became very conscious of the quiet in the newspaper office, and the cries of the hucksters in the square outside. I knew I would never hear that fascinating web of sound with joy again until the cries of the slave auctioneer had ceased to be a part of it.

Shortly thereafter Elam and I left, to get a bit of food and return to the store. As we were walking along the crowded sidewalk, Elam summed up my feelings in two sentences: "Mr. Clay may not have the most effervescent sense of humor in the world, but that's the only thing he don't have. Christ in a caboose!"

*   *   *

Clay didn't get his paper out as soon as he had hoped. It took him three weeks. But on the first Tuesday in June, father brought home a copy of *The True American*, Volume I, Number 1. He waved it at Mother. "Look at this devilish, scurrilous, incendiary piece of corruption, Patience!" he shouted.

"If it's Cassius Clay's newspaper, I'd rather not see it, thank you," she replied primly.

"Can I see it, Papa?" I asked.

"Here." He handed it to me. "Just be sure you burn it when you've read as much as you can stomach." He stamped out of the drawing room and up the stairs.

The True American seemed too puny to bear the weight of all those adjectives father had piled on it. It was a flimsy four-page sheet with classified advertisements and filler stories on the front page and editorial matter inside. I quickly opened it, wondering if the article Clay had read us would be in print. It was, altered slightly, but in no way less blood-

55

thirsty. As I read Clay's furious challenge to Wickliffe and the slavocracy again, the paper ceased to seem puny. It seemed as formidable as a cavalry saber.

Cassius M. Clay, baited like a bear in his attempt to gain justice from his fellow townsmen for the murder of his son, had unleashed an antislavery newspaper in the heart of a proslavery community. Even then I knew that nothing would ever be the same again.

V

Hoodoo

Every June I decide that June is the most beautiful month of the year in Kentucky — just as every October I decide October is the most beautiful, and similarly every April and every May. In the Bluegrass, every month comes up at the right time, contains the right amount and type of weather and never wears out its welcome. You just can't ask for more than that.

June of 1845 was up to the usual high standard. If it hadn't been for the increasing tension generated by the coming election, and heightened by the weekly forays of *The True American* into the camps of slavery, the placid and schoolfree days would have been halcyon indeed. It was the time for the pubescent male to consider God's marvelous plan for the reproduction of the species. I seemed to consider it an average of twelve hours a day.

Laurel Tate was the focus of this obsession. My last few encounters with her had gone so well that I was positive I was on the verge of complete success. But I had been equally positive on the eve of each previous encounter. Somehow I seemed to remain teetering on the brink of bliss, day after day. This inexplicable suspension of the laws of motion was

57

puzzling enough — and added to it was my puzzlement at my own ambivalent attitude toward my lack of success. Each evening when I shinnied up the elm tree outside my window and climbed into my bed of frustration, a voice inside me seemed to breathe a sigh of relief. "Another day gone, and you're still safe," it whispered.

One Sunday morning in church my randy thoughts did not turn even briefly to the Blessed Redeemer. In the afternoon I was able to escape the Ledyard children long enough to arrange a rendezvous with Laurel for eleven that night at our secret place. The day seemed to creep toward evening, and the evening, when it came, seemed as immobile as a statue, as impenetrable as a bog. I thought it would never end.

I was pretending to read *Martin Chuzzlewit,* Father was turning the pages of the Lexington *Observer and Reporter,* Mother and Rosalie were sewing, Boone had already gone to bed. "Looks like Cash Clay is finally going to get some action in the poison trial tomorrow," said Father.

"Oh?" Mother said politely, without raising her head.

"It says here that two witnesses are expected to testify. That would be those two house niggers of the Porters, over near White Hall. I understand Emily bragged to them that she had poisoned the Clay boy. Unfortunately for her, she misjudged their characters. They told Major Porter the whole story, and he told Clay."

"What a sordid business it all is," sighed Mother.

"Sordid enough, but I can't hold with those who'd like to see Emily acquitted because they hate Clay so much. Murder is murder, after all."

"Any engagements or marriages announced today?" asked Mother.

My mind was so full of sensual imagery I barely heard

this conversation. But I had occasion to remember it well before the night was through.

It was just eleven by the Foxtown church bells when my feet touched the ground outside my window. Clouds covered the moon, and the night was almost totally black. I made my way along the path through the trees down toward the river. An owl hooted, and something scurried through the grass at my feet. The wind blew across the water, damp and chilly with fog. For a second I wished I was back in my bed again, then I chased the unworthy thought from my mind.

I parted the tall grass that surrounded our secret place, and found that Laurel had arrived before me. I could see her dimly in the darkness; she was sitting on the ground, her legs tucked under her, her hands toying with one of her braids. She was wearing a white shirtwaist and a skirt of some dark-colored material. She had heard me approach, for her face, a pale soft blur, was turned toward me. "Hacey, is that you? Honey?"

My heart thudded and I couldn't get enough air in my lungs. "It's me, Laurel," I whispered as I knelt down beside her. I put my arms around her. "I'm glad you've come," she breathed. "I was getting scared." One of her hands brushed the back of my neck. "Don't be scared, Laurel. I'm here now." She raised her mouth to mine and we kissed. I didn't think anything in the world could be more exciting than that moment.

Presently we lay down together in the grass, which was even more exciting. This time my arm didn't go to sleep. I was conscious of every inch of my body and every inch of hers. One sentence kept ringing through my brain: "Tonight's the night! Tonight's the night! Gosh all hemlock, tonight's the night." Which was why I didn't hear them till they were almost on top of us.

Four people were walking single file along the path on the river's edge. They came within five feet of us, as we huddled together in sudden fright, fearing to breathe, with our arms trembling against one another's bodies. The moon broke through the clouds, and we could see their faces through the tall grass as they passed.

They were blacks. First in line was Star, leading the way. Next was a bent old woman, toothless, a hag. Then a fat middle-aged man. Then a child of about my age, a girl. Except for Star, I had no recollection of ever having seen any of them before, but suddenly, lying there in the chill damp darkness with Laurel's shivering breath on my cheek, I knew infallibly who they were.

Rachel, Solomon and Margaret — mother, uncle and daughter of Emily, who would face her accusers in the Lexington courthouse the next day.

As they passed by, their faces momentarily highlighted by the cold white light of the moon, Laurel whispered in my ear, "Niggers!" Shhhhhhh!" I hissed at her. Suddenly it was very important that Star not discover me a witness to whatever was happening tonight beside the river.

We lay as quiet as two field mice as the footsteps moved away from us along the riverbank. After a few moments they were swallowed up in the murmurous silence. "They must be headed for Star's shack," I whispered.

"Who were they?" asked Laurel.

"I reckon they're the family of that Emily girl that poisoned Mr. Clay's little boy."

"I declare, I just hate niggers." She shivered, and I realized with surprise that my arms were still around her and our bodies were still pressed together. "What you expect they're doing down here at this time of night?"

I began to free myself from our embrace. "I don't know,

but I'm fixing to find out." I gathered my knees under me and started to stand up.

Laurel gasped, and her arms tightened around my neck. "You ain't going to follow them, are you, Hacey?"

"I sure am," I replied with more confidence than I felt. "They're up to something, and I aim to find out what it is."

"Well, what about me? You expect me to come with you to spy on some niggers and maybe get my throat cut, or stay out here in the woods alone and get et by a bear or something?"

It didn't sound as if there was much to choose between the two alternatives, but I wanted to reassure her. "Come along with me. There's nothing to be scared of. Star would never do anything to hurt me."

"Hacey, honey, whyn't you just stretch out beside me and pick up where you left off? I bet you won't regret it!"

I hesitated a moment, as curiosity and lust engaged in their age-old battle. This time, curiosity won. "Shucks, Laurel, we can do that any time," I said incautiously.

"Oh, we can, can we?" She struggled to her feet, ignoring my proffered hand. "If I were you, Hacey, I wouldn't hold my breath!"

We began to pick our way cautiously along the riverbank, each silently considering his own emotions; Laurel smarting with the resentment of a "woman scorned," me frightened and exhilarated by our midnight adventure.

It was only a few hundred yards to Star's shack, but it must have taken us all of fifteen minutes to cover the distance. Every night sound — a surfacing bass in the river, birds in the trees, tree frogs and varmints and the sighing wind — raised gooseflesh on my skin. In no time at all Laurel forgot her anger and pressed close to me for protection.

There was a light in Star's window, shining with a golden

glow through the oiled paper that served in place of glass. As we approached it, I noticed a small triangular rip in the lower right-hand corner of the window. Gesturing to Laurel for absolute silence, I put my eye to the rip and looked in on one of the strangest scenes I've ever beheld.

Star was standing at one end of the room, his hands pressed flat on a small table in front of him. The table was covered with a white cloth, and Star was wearing a loose-fitting white robe over his clothes. Draped over his shoulders was the skin of the largest rattlesnake I've ever seen; when it was alive, it must have measured eight feet from fangs to rattle, and been as big around as a man's arm. On the table in front of him were a small earthenware bowl, a number of lighted black candles, a little wooden box and what appeared to be two lumps of meat.

The other three blacks were facing Star. The hag was standing, leaning forward eagerly. The fat man and the child were sitting on the bed. The man was tapping his fingertips on the skin of a small homemade drum, and for the first time, I became aware of the sound of drumming, so low as to be almost below the threshold of hearing.

Star was leading the others in a kind of chant or song. Star would say a line, and they would say it back to him.

"Damballa *loa*, Damballa *loa*," said Star.

"Damballa *loa*, Damballa *loa*," replied the others.

"We welcome you to this *houmfort*, Damballa."

"We welcome you to this *houmfort*, Damballa."

"We ask you to aid us against our enemies."

"We ask you to aid us against our enemies."

"And if you would devour our blood and bones, Damballa."

"And if you would devour our blood and bones, Damballa."

"We have a cock you can devour instead."
"We have a cock you can devour instead."

The old woman leaned over and picked up something from the floor. It was a black rooster. Its legs were trussed together, but its wings were flapping feebly. The woman crossed the floor and handed the fowl to Star. He quickly presented it to the four corners of the room.

"Damballa *loa*, devour and be satisfied."
"Damballa *loa*, devour and be satisfied."

I felt Laurel tugging on my arm. She mouthed the words, "What's happening?" soundlessly. I waved her away and kept my eye glued to the rip in the oiled paper.

Star then placed the rooster on the table, where it rested quietly. The sound of the finger drum increased in volume. For a moment nothing moved inside the room but the hands of the drummer. Then Star deliberately broke one of the rooster's legs — *snap!* — then the other. He paused a moment, then quickly broke both the bird's wings, pried open its bill, thrust two fingers and a thumb down its throat and tore out its jugular vein. Blackish blood spattered across the tablecloth as Star grabbed the earthenware bowl and held it to catch the flow. Rachel, Solomon and Margaret sighed in unison. The rhythm of the drum pulsed louder, and the black candles flared.

And suddenly the thought flashed in my mind: *Something has just entered the room.*

The rooster's blood had all drained into the bowl, and Star set the bird back on the table. He held the bowl in one hand, and with the other raised the malevolent head of the snakeskin draped around his neck.

"Drink the blood of the fat cock, Damballa," he chanted.

"Drink the blood of the fat cock, Damballa," answered the others.

"Drink that you may help us destroy our enemies . . ."
"Drink that you may help us destroy our enemies . . ."

Star placed the rattlesnake's snout in the bowl, and in the flickering candlelight it appeared to be drinking. After a few seconds he withdrew it, snout and fangs stained with black blood, and raised the bowl to his own lips. He drank deeply. Then he passed the bowl to the hag, who was trembling with eagerness as she waited her turn. Then to the drummer, who kept up the rhythm with one hand as he drank with the other. Then to the girl . . .

I turned away from the window. "Dang you, Hacey," whispered Laurel fiercely, "what are those niggers doing in there?"

"I'll tell you later. You don't want to look," I answered.

"It ain't fair. I should get a turn too! And anyway, I'm scared, just standing here!"

"Hush up now. You don't want them to hear us, do you?"

She shivered and pressed her body against my back. She was silent except for the quietly audible chattering of her teeth. I returned my eye to the triangular rip in the window.

Star had resumed his place behind the small table. The rooster had disappeared, as had the bowl. He had placed the two lumps of meat squarely in front of him, and I identified them with surprise as lamb tongues. In some subtle way, the rhythm of the drum had changed. The feeling of the *presence* was strong.

Star took two small pieces of paper from the wooden box. He made a slit in each tongue with a knife he took from the box, and pressed the papers into the slits. "These are now the tongues of our enemies," he chanted.

"Damballa *loa*, Damballa *loa* . . ." answered the others.

He produced a number of needles from the wooden box.

64

"These are the needles with which you pierce their tongues . . ."

"Damballa *loa,* Damballa *loa* . . ."

Quickly he thrust all the needles into the two tongues. "Make them feel the pain of the needles, and gladden our hearts!"

"Damballa *loa,* Damballa *loa* . . ."

Again he reached into the wooden box. He drew out a ball of yarn, and quickly began to weave it around the ends of the needles, crisscrossing the surface of the lambs' tongues many times. As he worked, he intoned, in a singsong chant:

> Now we tie their tongues, Damballa,
> So they don't speak the truth.
> Around the needles of pain, Damballa,
> So they forget the truth.
> They will not speak the white man's words
> They will not pull the black man down
> One say yes and one say no
> One say come and one say go
> One say hot and one say cold
> One say new and one say old . . .

"Damballa *loa,* Damballa *loa* . . ." keened Rachel, Solomon and Margaret. The rhythm of the drum began to speed up. Excitement inside the shack increased. I felt it, and moved closer to the window — and then disaster struck.

Laurel leaned heavily against my back. "Hacey, I tell you I'm scared . . ." she began, in a tremulous whisper. I was off balance, drawn too much toward the window by the accelerating chant inside. As I felt myself begin to fall toward the oiled paper, I instinctively threw up my arm. My elbow hit the taut surface of the window and ripped through, with a noise that sounded like a close clap of thunder.

Instantly all sound within the shack was silenced.

In this terrible and endless moment of discovery, my only thought was flight. We had to get away. God knew what would happen if Star — my erstwhile friend, Star — caught us and took us into that room!

"Run, Laurel, run!" I grabbed her hand and pulled her after me, running for all I was worth, through the darkness, down the river path. I heard her stumbling behind me, her breath panting and sobbing in her throat, and behind *her* I heard the swift opening and closing of a door, and then Star's deep voice calling, "Who's that? Stop, you hear?"

I don't know how close Star was behind us — or whether he chased us at all — but as I dragged Laurel across roots and stumps, through brush and creepers, tripping and falling and scrambling up again, I was sure he was only inches away. And if his hands had closed on my shoulders, I had no doubt what my fate would be, and Laurel's. I had seen what happened to the rooster.

Finally, somehow, we reached our secret place. From there a path ran up the bluff to the field in front of our house. Resting a few moments, and hearing no sound of pursuit, we took to the path at a slower pace. Once out of the woods and into the moonlit field, we looked at each other in wonder, as if we couldn't believe we had escaped.

"Hacey — that nigger Star — you reckon he'd a-killed us?"

"I don't know, Laurel. Probably not. Come on, I'll walk you home."

"What were they doin' in there?"

"I'll tell you some other time. It's awful late, Laurel. Come on." I took her hand, and we walked the quarter-mile to the Tates' house in silence. We said good night in whispers, in the dark shadow of the house. "Don't tell anybody about tonight. Promise?"

"I promise, honey. Who'd I want to tell a thing like that to? Good night, Hacey." She raised her lips to be kissed and I kissed them. But my mind wasn't on it.

The next morning the last person in the world I wanted to see was Star. But Star didn't feel the same way. As I walked toward the stable to see to Sacajawea, Star was sitting against the stable wall, whittling and whistling, apparently without a care in the world. I would have ducked back around the corner of the house, but I was too slow. His face lit up with his brilliant toothy smile.

"Morning, Mr. Hacey. How you feeling this fine bright morning?" He began to get to his feet, his expression affectionate, respectful — and something else.

As I heard his rich Southland Negro dialect, I suddenly realized that the voice I had heard invoking Damballa the night before had not contained a trace of accent. The realization so shook me that I stammered as I replied.

"J-just fine, Star. Sure is a nice morning, all right. I was just fixing to take Sackie for a ride."

"Why, that's just dandy. Old Star will just rub her down a little for you, and then throw a saddle on her." He opened the stable door and stood waiting to follow me inside.

"Oh, don't bother, Star . . ."

"It's no bother, Mr. Hacey. It'd pleasure me." His smile widened. "You come on now, hear?"

I stepped into the stable with considerable trepidation, resolved that if he should attempt to close the door behind us I would seize a pitchfork from the wall and fight my way out. But he left the door wide open, so the interior of the stable

67

HACEY MILLER

was bright with summer sunshine. He crossed to Sacajawea's stall, picked up a currycomb, and gentled her as he
began to groom her already glossy coat. She snorted with
pleasure.

"You know, Mr. Hacey, I been meaning to talk to you
about something for quite a spell, but it just ain't happened
to come up."

"Oh, what's that, Star?"

"Well, it's about that little old no-account box I whittled
for your birthday — the one with the funny pictures carved
on the top."

"What about it?" The temperature in the stable dropped
a degree or two.

"You ever hear of a wanga, Mr. Hacey?"

"A wanga? No, what's a wanga?" I asked uneasily.

"Well, some ignorant niggers got a superstition — I don't
take no stock in it, now, mind — but they think there's
things that are sacred to the spirits, and that if you have one
of them, it's going to bring you good luck all your life long.
And these good luck things, they call them wangas." His
great black hand moved steadily up and down Sacajawea's
flank. She shifted her weight, and her hooves clattered on
the floorboards of the stall.

"You mean, like a rabbit's foot?"

"Well, not *exactly* like a rabbit's foot. You see, a rabbit's
foot *may* do you a little good, and sure won't do you no
harm. But a wanga either going to do you a whole mess of
good, or one *whale* of a lot of harm. See, these ignorant
people, they think the spirit is right there inside the wanga,
and as long as the spirit like you, it going to do good luck
things for you." He stopped speaking. A horsefly buzzed in
the silence.

"What happens if the spirit stops liking you?"

68

"You don't need to study about that. Just make sure it don't stop."

"What would make it stop?"

Star turned his yellowed eyes to me. "People who believe this foolishness, they think the spirit stop liking you if you do bad things to black folks, or if you try to throw away the wanga. Otherwise, your good luck stay with you all your life."

I forced a laugh. "Well, even if my box is a wanga, I guess I got nothing to worry about, 'cause I sure don't figure to do any bad things to black folks, and I wouldn't sell it for a thousand dollars!"

"Why, I knowed that, Mister Hacey." Star lifted down a bridle off a peg on the wall and fitted it over Sacajawea's head. "I was just telling you about wangas for fun. I know you won't pay it no nevermind, no more than I do." He led Sackie out of her stall, threw a saddle blanket over her, and cinched my saddle tight. Outside in the sunlight he held my stirrup and smiled up at me. "Have a nice ride, Mr. Hacey, you hear?"

*   *   *

Father had been in town that day, and when he returned in the evening he told my mother the newest development in the Clay poisoning trial. As I listened to his voice, I had no feeling of surprise. It was as if I were hearing confirmation of what I already knew.

"Damndest thing happened at the Clay trial I ever heard of, Patience."

"Please, Sheldon — the children."

"All right — the *dangdest* thing happened. Those two niggers of Major Porter's who were going to testify, you know? Well, one of them contradicted the other one, flat out. Come out and denied that Emily ever said anything to her about poisoning the Clay baby. Blew the prosecution to hell in a handbasket."

"Sheldon!"

"Blew the prosecution to *smithereens,* Dog nab it! Anyway, after that, the prosecutor had to ask for a continuance. But it appears to me Clay hasn't got any more chance of getting a conviction than a snowball in . . ."

"Sheldon!"

". . . than a snowball in a hot oven. Sometimes, Patience, carrying on a conversation with you reminds me of trying to avoid the hazards in a steeplechase!" He lapsed grumpily into silence, turning the pages of his paper with vigor.

That night I looked for a long time at Star's carved wooden box. It took me quite a while to fall asleep.

VI

BURGOO

As JUNE GOT READY to turn the sunny corner into July, politics became more than ever the prime subject of conversation in the Bluegrass. The two races attracting the most attention were the contest for United States Congressman between Democrat Thomas F. Marshall and Whig Garret Davis, and for State Senator between Democrat Charles Moore and Whig Robert S. Todd. Tempers were hot and became hotter, and Cash Clay's *The True American* did nothing to cool them off. Clay supported Davis and Todd, as did the Whiggish Lexington *Observer*, but both Davis and the *Observer* denounced Clay as bitterly as the Democrats did, and even Todd, who was personally close to Clay — their wives had been close friends from childhood — received *The True American*'s support with an embarrassed silence.

Father and Josh Brain got into a fierce argument over Todd which almost broke up their friendship. Democrat Moore had charged that Clay's support of Todd made it clear that Todd was antislavery. Todd felt this was so damaging to his chances that he published a statement in the *Observer* in which he said, "I am a slaveholder. Were I an abolitionist or an emancipator in principle, I would not hold a slave." The effect of this, as Democrats like my father were quick to point out, was to make Todd appear a wishy-washy candidate, supporting slavery on the one hand and the Non-Importation Act — the notorious "Nigger Law" — on the other. Father presented this view forcefully at dinner one night, when Brain was our guest, and by the time Mother excused herself and us from the table the fat little lawyer was well on the way to losing his temper. For the next half hour we could hear their voices raised in burgeoning anger through the closed dining room doors. Suddenly the doors flew open and Brain stalked out, mumbling under his breath and livid with rage.

He crossed the hall and swung the front door open, then turned on the threshold and saw us gaping at him. "Poor innocent children, what chance have you, growing up with a blatherskite for a father!" he shouted, and stamped out. Moments later, Father emerged from the dining room, glowering. "Damned abolitionist skunk — he's as bad as Cash Clay! No more free meals for that wretch!" He went to his study and slammed *his* door.

Of course Josh and Father made up a few days later — they enjoyed arguing with each other too much to give it up for any reason short of divine intervention. But the fact that they became estranged at all indicated the depths of passion and rage that were being plumbed by the slavery controversy that summer.

Since I had met Cassius Clay and visited the *True American* office, I had become interested in Bluegrass politics. My father noticed me reading the speeches of the candidates and the editorials in the *Observer* and was pleased. He assumed that my sympathies would develop in the same way his had, and I never disabused him of that assumption.

When I wasn't reading the paper, I was generally hiking

through the woods or swimming in the river with my brother Boone. I had avoided Star since our last encounter in the stables, and had also failed to arrange any more nocturnal trysts with Laurel. She claimed she couldn't get out of the house at night because her mother was suspicious. I didn't believe that, but had stopped asking.

So Boone and I hunted and fished and swam, and through the long slow days we often talked about slavery and politics. I told him about Clay and his paper, about Morgan and the bloods, about the Non-Importation Act and the speeches of Marshall and Charles Moore denouncing it. We talked about the Negroes who were sold on Cheapside, and the coffles of black livestock that trudged through the streets of Lexington, foot shackled to dusty foot, on their way from Megowan's Slave Jail to some plantation "down the river."

Clay had fired my idealism and my imagination. The more I thought and talked about him, the more he appeared to me as a knight in shining armor battling an obscene and evil dragon. But Boone's cast of mind was different from mine. The keystone of his character was loyalty. To me as a brother, he felt he owed sympathy and solidarity against the outside world, but to our father, he owed fidelity to political beliefs. It was simply and literally impossible for Boone to conceive of slavery as an evil as long as Father supported it.

Against his silent stubbornness I pitted all the arguments I had heard and some new ones I had made up. And there, beside the river, Boone and I exercised and strengthened the muscles of our consciences.

*   *   *

The Ledyards always had a barbecue on the Fourth of July, and on that day I was willing to forgive the Ledyard children anything. It was a red-letter day in all our lives and

73

a memorable occasion for everyone fortunate enough to receive an invitation. Between two and three hundred guests attended — nobody ever knew the exact number. There were juleps for the gentlemen and wines for the ladies and lemonade and ice cream for the youngsters. There was the brass band of the Lexington Light Infantry to provide a program of martial airs. There was a horse race in the afternoon and dancing and whist in the evening, with the dance floor illuminated by hundreds of lanterns, under the stars. There were games for the children. There was Cousin Whitney Ledyard shooting off a real cannon, in memory of the "shot heard 'round the world." And there was burgoo.

Burgoo is like mint juleps — no Kentuckian will admit that anyone else can make it better than he does. But since burgoo is rarely made in less than twenty-gallon batches, the physical labor involved is so disheartening that most amateurs are willing to hire a burgoo cook and relinquish all responsibility except for a modicum of supervision. But not so Cousin Whitney. He started thirty-six hours ahead of time, and engineered the building of the fires. Then he oversaw the filling of the huge copper kettles, the cutting-up of the various meats — beef, pork, wild turkey, partridge and squirrel — and watched like a hawk as they were added to the pots in proper proportion. He checked every peeled potato, every scrubbed turnip, every plump tomato and pungent onion before it was added to the bubbling mixture. As it began to change its consistency from stew to burgoo — from solid-cum-liquid to semisolid and homogeneous — he added the flour, cream and butter to make it smoother and the spices to enhance its subtle combination of flavors. And finally, as his waiting guests salivated, he upended the small kegs of bourbon over it and stirred in the ultimate ingredient necessary for a Kentucky imprimatur.

It was a glorious dish. I could eat a quart of it at a sitting and still have room for fried chicken and Old Ham and corn pudding, and wash it all down with ice-cold lemonade. So could everybody else. And they did.

Our family arrived about one-thirty. The festivities were in full swing. The band was playing a march as the adults promenaded on the newly cut grass and the children rioted nearby. The Ledyard house slaves circulated through the crowd with trays of mint juleps in frosty pewter tumblers, and white and red wine in tall-stemmed and graceful glasses. Tables were set under the trees, and other retainers piled food upon them. It was almost time to start eating, if we wanted to be through in time to see the horse race.

Of course Bryan Ledyard had to be sitting next to me at the young'uns' table. At first, I ignored him after a perfunctory greeting — after all, it *was* his party, or anyway, his father's — and concentrated on a long-standing argument Boone and I had over whether George Rogers Clark could have beaten Andrew Jackson in a battle. But finally Bryan succeeded in breaking in.

"Lucky for your friend Cash Clay he isn't out here at our barbecue. I reckon he wouldn't ever get back home again," he said provocatively.

Mastering an urge to tell him to go fry his face, I replied, "How come not?"

He pointed a spoon dripping with burgoo toward a group of elegantly dressed young men and women promenading a few yards away. "Look over yonder. If my brother Galt didn't fix him, then John Hunt Morgan would for sure. I know 'cause he was out here visiting last week, and I heard him say Cash Clay ain't fit to live."

"Isn't," said my brother Boone. "You'll sound like a poor white if you keep saying 'ain't.'"

75

"You can worry about sissy stuff like that if you want to. I'd rather learn about fox hunting and cock fighting and being a gentleman."

In an effort to change the subject, I asked Bryan, "Who's the girl who's holding on to Galt's arm?"

"That's Galt's sweetheart — or maybe not quite his sweetheart, but he's mighty sweet on her. Her name's Beckie Bruce. Ain't she a pippin?"

It was my first sight of Rebecca Gratz Bruce, one of the loveliest girls of her, or, for that matter, any age. She was fifteen, and a student at Madame Mentelle's exclusive boarding school, where my sister Rosalie passionately wanted to go. She was as fresh and glowing as morning glories in May. My heart leaped at the sight of her.

Although she was holding Galt Ledyard's arm, her face was turned toward Morgan and he was smiling down at her. All the charm of his magnetic personality was concentrated in that smile. At the moment, it appeared to be the only thing in the world of which Beckie Bruce was aware.

"You say Galt's sweet on her? Then if I was him, I'd speed up my sparking, before Morgan gets her away from him," I said spitefully.

"Oh, you think you're so smart! That don't mean nothing. Beckie's just friendly by nature, and interested in what you say to her. She'd look that way even if she was talking to some real idjit — like you!"

Remembering the source of the burgoo, I didn't rise to the bait. Instead, I changed the subject. "I hear Galt's entered in the race. Think he'll win?"

"Why, sure," Bryan answered smugly. "He's up on Sheba, and she's the fastest horse in the state, just about."

"What's the prize?" asked Boone.

"Coin silver cup. My sister Robin's going to present it, and since Galt's going to win it, we'll keep the whole thing in the family."

"Who else is riding?" I asked, trying to keep my mounting irritation out of my voice.

"There's Perry Owsley from out on the Harrodsburg pike, and Dick Porter and some fellow from over in Versailles. That's all I can remember — excepting John Hunt Morgan there."

"Morgan's riding against Galt? Wonder which of them Beckie Bruce will be cheering for?" I said innocently.

"Oh, go swallow a brick," said Bryan. He turned away from us angrily, leaving Boone and me to pick up the threads of our interrupted strategic argument.

A half hour or so later we pushed ourselves away from the table and headed for the improvised race track in the pasture behind the big house. We skirted the slave cabins — freshly scrubbed inside, with new straw for the beds, and with saucer-eyed pickaninnies staring out at us in fear and wonder. By the time we arrived at the shady grove where the guests were gathering, it was almost time for the race to begin.

In the few minutes that remained before Cousin Whitney fired the starting gun, I idly swept my eyes across the assembled spectators, looking for familiar faces. I saw many people I knew, mostly friends of my father's. Then I realized a surprising thing, something that would never have occurred to me three months before — of those present whose politics I knew, every single one was a proslavery man and an ardent one at that. There was not one moderate Whig among them.

That point would hardly be worthy of comment in Vir-

77

ginia or Georgia, but Bluegrass society, though traditionally proslavery, always accepted and occasionally welcomed a little mild dissent. But apparently no more.

The race was a mile and a quarter, straight across the pasture to the stone fence and back again. The ground was unusually flat, but not so much so that a rider could take it for granted. About two hundred yards from the starting pole, a sudden narrow gully cut across the racecourse, presenting a definite hazard.

There were seven riders up at the post, but two commanded most of the attention. There was spirited betting going on among the spectators, and the names of Morgan and Ledyard were being mentioned the most, with Ledyard the favorite, as far as I could judge.

"Look at that horse of Galt's, Hacey," said Boone excitedly. "That's the kind of horse I'm going to have when I grow up!"

Ledyard's Sheba was as beautiful an animal as I had ever seen. She was big — at least sixteen and a half hands, and deep-chested — coal black, with three white stockings, an arching neck and a wicked eye. She didn't want to take her place in line at the starting pole, and Galt had his hands full with her.

Morgan had less horse, but more confidence, I thought. He was mounted on a small chestnut stallion with clean lines and a look of competence about him. Morgan rested comfortably in his saddle — almost lolled — a more-than-slightly patronizing smile on his lips, as Galt sweated and swore over Sheba.

Then suddenly all seven horses were shoulder to shoulder, and Cousin Whitney's pistol cracked. They were away, and the thud of their hooves on the turf was like muffled thunder. They bunched together as they covered the first two hundred yards to the gully, then they flew apart, as one missed his footing on the far side and fell, and another shied at the jump and collided with the horse behind him. Three horses were down; the other four were stretching out for the drive to the rock fence. Nobody in the crowd could tell who was still in the race and who was out, and everybody was yelling questions at his neighbor at the top of his lungs.

As Cousin Whitney and four of his stable hands ran to the gully to help the fallen riders and horses from the track (none of the riders was injured but one of the horses had broken a leg), the four remaining competitors separated far enough to be identified. The Versailles horse was in the lead, Morgan was number two, Galt and Sheba were third, and Dick Porter was last. They remained in that order until they pulled up at the rock fence, turned and started back. Then both Morgan and Galt began to move up. Morgan passed the Versailles entry, and then Galt, three lengths behind Morgan, also passed him. Then Galt made his play. Sheba's long legs stretched, her neck flattened out and she began inexorably to overtake Morgan's chestnut stallion. The three-length interval shortened to two, then one and a half.

Morgan glanced over his shoulder and saw Galt coming up on his left. They were almost to the gully. As the little chestnut gathered his strength for the jump, Morgan unhesitatingly pulled his head to the left, requiring him to take the jump at an angle and cross Sheba's path in midair, and also lengthening the distance of the jump by at least a foot.

Galt had three choices. He could continue on a collision course, trusting to Sheba's size and weight to keep her on her feet. He could turn her head to the left, hoping she would parallel Morgan's horse and recover from the jump in spite of the sudden change of direction. Or he could check her and give Morgan time to get clear.

79

He checked her.

The crowd acted like a single person. A sharp intake of breath marked its reaction to Morgan's maneuver, and a kind of sighing groan followed Galt's response. Morgan drove the last two hundred yards at the peak of fury, using his whip on every step, and even though Galt began to close the gap again, there just wasn't enough time for him to catch the chestnut stallion before it crossed the finish line.

The crowd's reaction was muted. Ledyard's supporters didn't say anything, and even Morgan's backers seemed a little subdued. It was as if we all had seen something we wished we hadn't, and it made us feel soiled.

Morgan leaped from the saddle and trotted over to Galt as he dismounted, throwing an arm around his shoulders affectionately. His smile lit up his handsome features, and Galt smiled weakly in return. Then Cousin Whitney came up to congratulate the winner, and little Robin Ledyard presented him with the silver cup.

I turned my eyes to the place in the crowd where I had seen the Bruces watching the race. Beckie was there, flushed with excitement, her bright eyes riveted on John Hunt Morgan. She didn't seem disappointed in the outcome.

*   *   *

We youngsters played games like stoop tag and blindman's buff until dusk, when we restoked our fires with ice cream and cake. After that we were expected to mind our manners, because it was time for the dancing and the whist to begin. An old darky shuffled around the outdoor dance floor, lighting innumerable paper lanterns with a taper. The Lexington Light Infantry Band began tuning up, and, since neither of us cottoned much to dancing, Boone and I ambled up to the big house to peek in on the card playing.

Mother and Father were at one of the tables in the drawing room. They must have just won a hand, because Father was beaming and Mother had a trace of a ladylike smile on her face. Father lifted his glass of claret and squinted through it toward the glittering chandelier. "Ever notice what a truly magnificent color wine is when the light shines through it? Like something from Rembrandt or Leonardo."

"Deal the cards," grunted one of their opponents.

We watched from the hall until an old house servant shooed us away with "You chillun go out and play now, hear?" Ostensibly obeying, we doubled back when we were out of his sight and went up the wide curving staircase to the second floor, where the billiard room was located, hoping to eavesdrop on some man-talk.

The door was ajar. Inside, the room was crowded and filled with tobacco smoke. Though there was an occasional click of ball striking ball, it was obvious that politics, not billiards, was the focus of interest.

Among the fifteen or so men around the big green table, I recognized quite a few. Standing next to Cousin Whitney was Tom Marshall, the Democratic candidate for United States Congressman. Bending over the table and sighting along a cue was a slight, white-haired old man with a long nose and pale blue eyes; I recognized him as the "Old Duke" — Robert Wickliffe, Sr. Grouped behind him respectfully were Morgan and his two cronies, whom I had mentally named "Sheepface" and "Pudgy." There were others I knew by sight, if not by name.

A man I didn't know was speaking. ". . . mistake was to let him get started in the first place. Suppressing the God-damned rag now will cause a stink worse than a hog wallow in July."

"I can imagine what the locofoco abolitionist papers up North would say," said another stranger. " 'Heroic antislav-

ery editor mobbed by lowdown slave-owning skunks.' "
There was a murmur of agreement from several of the
others.

"Please, gentlemen," said Wickliffe. In the silence that
followed, he made his shot. Two clicks signaled his success.
He studied the position of the balls for a moment, then
raised his cue. "The question isn't *if* the paper will be suppressed, it's *when* it will be suppressed. I gave the renegade
fair warning before he began publication, and I'm not in the
habit of going back on my word." He made his next shot,
and again it was followed by two clicks.

"You're saying we should decide whether we do it now or
wait till after the election," said Cousin Whitney.

"Since it's my election we're talking about, I'm perhaps a
bit more concerned with it than you gentlemen," said Marshall. "The way you see it, if we clamp down on Clay now,
I'll lose some votes out of sympathy for him, but I'll gain
some who might have been converted to his way of thinking
during the next month. Right, Mr. Wickliffe?"

"Substantially right, Mr. Marshall, although rather subjective," said the old man dryly.

"I'm afraid I happen to be rather subjective about my career, sir. And here's what I think. I don't think Clay's going
to switch over so God-all-many people during the next
month, and I'm worried about how many fence-sitters would
sympathize with him if we took it upon ourselves to suppress
the paper prematurely."

"Then you'd wait until after the election, sir?" asked John
Hunt Morgan.

"It seems the lesser of the two evils, John. God knows I'm
not happy about it. Every time a new issue of the wretched
sheet comes out, it affronts everything I hold dear. But I've

got my hands full with Garret Davis, and I can't afford to take chances."

"We won't wait long after the election, I hope," said Morgan.

"You should be able to control your impatience for the necessary time," replied old Wickliffe. He started to say something else, but just then I heard a step behind us, and the old house servant who had shooed us out before whispered, "What you boys doing out here? Didn't I tell you get out the house and play? I got a good mind to tell your ma and pa on you!"

We assured him we were actually on our way out, and left him grumbling to himself as we trotted off down the stairs. "Golly, they sure have it in for Mr. Clay, don't they, Hacey?" said Boone.

"Don't you worry, he'll be ready for them. You should see his cannons! Why, if they try to come up the stairs, there's not a one of them will even get to the top!" But I was worried nonetheless, and resolved to tell Clay or Elam about the conversation around the billiard table at my first opportunity.

Outside, it was full darkness. The band was playing a polka, and the dancers, illuminated by the golden light from the lanterns, hopped and spun to the gay rhythm. My sister Rosalie had a partner I didn't recognize; Beckie Bruce was dancing with Galt.

"That durned John Morgan," said a small and sullen voice at my elbow. I peered through the darkness and saw that Bryan Ledyard was standing a foot or two away, watching his half brother dance.

"Hello, Bryan," I said.

"He cheated, that's what he did. I'd be ashamed to be

such a cheater!" There was a tremor in his voice that showed he was close to sobbing. I was a bit sorry for him, for the first time in my life, and was about to give him the small comfort of agreeing with him, but Boone spoke first. And Boone didn't know how to lie.

"No, he didn't," he said levelly. "He bluffed Galt out. Galt should have called his bluff. If he had, he would have won."

"Or maybe gotten killed!"

"Or maybe gotten killed," agreed Boone. "That was what the bluff was."

"Are you saying my brother's a coward?" screamed Bryan.

"No, you're saying it. I'm saying he let himself be out-bluffed."

"You're a dirty polecat," shouted the infuriated boy, and swung his fist at Boone's face. Boone took the blow on the shoulder, then hit Bryan as hard as he could, full on the nose, which instantly began to bleed. Gibbering with rage and pain, Bryan grappled with Boone, and they both went to the ground, with Boone on top.

I was debating with myself about how long to let the fight go on when my father appeared and pulled the two combatants apart wrathfully. "Can't I leave you alone for five minutes without you behaving like a wild Indian?" he growled. "I declare, sometimes I feel like giving up on you, Boone! Now, you apologize to Bryan, and say it like you mean it!"

"I apologize, Bryan," said Boone, putting out his hand.

"I'll get you, Boone Miller," answered Bryan, ignoring the proffered hand.

"Now, come on, Bryan," Father intervened. "He says he's sorry. Shake hands now. It's almost time for the fireworks, and we'll all watch them together, like good friends."

So they shook hands, and then we went back into the house to staunch the flow of blood. A few minutes later the fireworks started. I remember they were very beautiful, but for sheer excitement I didn't think they could compare with some of the other things that had happened that day.

VII

The Election

Elections in those days lasted for three days, to give country people plenty of time to get into town and cast their votes. In 1845 the dates selected were August fourth, fifth and sixth. Toward the end of July, Josh Brain appeared for dinner one night and gave us his analysis of the situation.

"I'd say Marshall and Davis are neck and neck, and Bob Todd is a hair behind Charles Moore," he said, his mouth not entirely free of sweet potato pie. "But at this point the game is still on the table."

"A lot depends on Clay," said my father.

"Which Clay, Sheldon? Henry, or — the other one?" asked Mother.

"Both of them," interjected Brain, before Father could answer. "After his defeat last year Henry Clay retired from politics, or so he said. But the question is, can he stay retired? He's the most popular man in Kentucky, with a personal following of thousands of voters that would jump off a cliff if he told them to. And right now, they're all after him to tell them how to vote. If he doesn't tell them, the Democrats will probably win — if he does, it's five to four on the Whigs."

"I'd quarrel with your odds, Josh, but you're right in principle," said Father. "A Whig endorsement from Henry Clay would certainly make the race closer."

Brain snorted, "Closer, hell — pardon me, madam — it would put us a mile ahead!"

"You said a lot depended on both Clays," said Mother. "What about the other one?"

"Well, you know that two weeks ago Cash came down with typhoid. I understand he was tuckered out from working on his newspaper, and he caught a real bad case. It laid him out. He took to his bed, and they've got him packed in ice to break the fever, so I hear. I understand he's out of his head."

Mother looked puzzled. "Then I don't see how anything could depend on him now."

"The problem is, when he felt himself going under, he called in some of his friends and told them to keep the paper going till he got on his feet again. Last Tuesday they brought out an issue on their own. And if you think Cash Clay's editorials are harebrained, you should see those! Jehosophat!"

"They practically advocated slave insurrections," said Father.

"Well, I'd say they *predicted* insurrections, not *advocated* them," corrected the fat little lawyer. "But howsomever, the effect was the same. They've really got people stirred up. I don't know when I've ever seen so much high feeling in Lexington. A few months ago I wouldn't have believed it possible." He shook his head in wonderment and stirred a spoonful of sugar into his coffee.

"There's a lot of talk about forming a mob to attack the *True American* office," said Father grimly.

"I can certainly understand why," said Mother.

"But the Democratic Party doesn't want the paper sup-

87

pressed, at least not now. It's common knowledge that the chief muckety-mucks — Wickliffe and Company — have decided not to take any action until after the election."

"I wish I had your sources of information, Josh," said Father ironically.

"I'm sure you do, Sheldon," replied the lawyer. "So you see, Mrs. Miller, here is a chain of possibilities to consider. *If* Cash Clay remains ill with typhoid, as he is now, his friends will continue to publish the paper. *If* they continue to publish the paper, they will provoke an armed mob into attacking them. *If* the mob attacks them, it will inevitably destroy the presses and no doubt kill some of Clay's friends. And *if* that happens, there'll be some people who'll sympathize with Clay because he was the underdog — flat on his back with typhoid, unable to defend himself and so on — and maybe they'll sympathize enough to vote for the candidates he's endorsing, Davis and Todd. That's what the Democrats are afraid of, and I think they're right to be afraid."

Father laughed ruefully and rubbed his chin. "I never thought of it in just that way, but I have to admit you're right as rain. If that don't beat all — us Democrats crossing our fingers for Cash Clay, and hoping he gets back to his newspaper office and starts writing his editorials again real soon!"

Josh smiled quizzically at Father. "But only for the next two weeks, eh, Sheldon?"

Father was silent for a second, then he returned Josh's look solemnly. "Yes. Only for the next two weeks, I'm afraid."

* * *

During those next two weeks Father informed us daily on the course of the campaign, and in such detail that my mother often objected. "Goodness, Sheldon, what makes you think the children are interested in all that?"

"Well, Hacey is, anyway. We're going to make a good solid Democrat out of you, aren't we, boy?"

"I expect so, Papa," I replied guiltily.

He reported that Cassius M. Clay was on the mend and able to dictate his own editorials; that Henry Clay had shut himself up in his beautiful home, Ashland, and would see nobody; that Robert S. Todd had published a pamphlet in which he described the "Old Duke," Robert Wickliffe, as "a habitual and notorious falsifier, and unscrupulous and indiscriminate calumniator, reckless alike of fame, of honor, and of truth"; that Wickliffe had replied that Todd was "a slander merchant, dealing in the basest calumnies and foulest abuse . . . weak and vicious, a craven spirit"; that not less than three well-known political figures had either given or received challenges.

"It's beginning to look like the only person who's going to win in this election is the undertaker," said Father.

Finally Monday, August fourth, arrived, and the voting began. It started slowly, because most of the country people didn't arrive in town until Monday evening or sometime Tuesday, and planned to vote on Tuesday or Wednesday. The first day's counting followed Josh Brain's prediction almost exactly: Davis and Marshall were within thirty votes of one another, and Robert S. Todd was trailing Charles Moore by almost a hundred votes. It looked bad for Todd because the Whig Party was stronger in the city than in the countryside, and for Todd to win, he should build an early lead that couldn't be offset by late-voting rural Democrats.

The second day, Whig hopes sank a little lower. At sundown Todd was trailing by almost two hundred votes. Davis was doing slightly better, trailing Tom Marshall by a hundred or so.

Wednesday dawned sunny and hot. The last — and largest — part of the electorate began to head for the polls, Whigs dispirited, Democrats jubilant. Simultaneously an open barouche appeared in the streets of Lexington, making the rounds of all the polling places in the city. Two men sat in it, conversing quietly and occasionally acknowledging friends and acquaintances on the street. One of them was Robert S. Todd. The other was Henry Clay.

The news that Henry Clay had come out of his secluded retirement to support Todd flashed around town in minutes. Crowds gathered around the polls, farmers and city folks, people who had voted and people still to vote, worried Democrats and jubilant Whigs. Clay spoke at each polling place, endorsing Todd and requesting his friends to vote for him. Although he was obviously an ailing old man, more frail than anyone remembered him, his hearty laugh was infectious, and his deep throbbing voice had lost none of its persuasiveness.

It was enough. During the rest of Wednesday, stunned Democrats watched their majorities melt away, and by the time the polls closed, Todd and Davis had been safely and solidly elected.

The chagrin and indignation of the losers knew no bounds. For two days they had felt the fruits of victory in their hands, only to have them snatched away on the third. They blamed two people for their misfortunes — both of them named Clay.

They paid their debt to Henry Clay first. Although not a

man of great wealth, Clay owned three or four small busi-
nesses in and around Lexington. One of the more profitable
was a factory that processed hemp into ropes and bags.
Hemp is very inflammable material, as was proved on the
night after the election, when the factory burned to the
ground.

Then they turned their attention to Cassius Marcellus
Clay.

* * *

The following Tuesday my father brought home a copy of
The True American, and read parts of it aloud to us. The
tone of the writing was provocative, to say the least. Cassius
Clay seemed to feel that he had won a partial victory with
Todd's election, and was now resolved to press on at increased speed toward the eradication of the South's "peculiar
institution."

"Listen to this, Patience — 'But remember, you who dwell
in marble palaces, that there are strong arms and fiery hearts
and iron pikes in the streets, and panes of glass only between
them and the silver plate on the board and the smooth-
skinned woman on the ottoman!' "

"I declare, Sheldon, I don't know why they let him write
things like that," said Mother indignantly. "Doesn't anybody in Lexington have the gumption to put a stop to it?"

Father looked at her soberly. "If you mean individually,
I'd say no. But if you mean collectively, in a big safe mob
where everybody thinks he can stay in the back and let his
neighbors go up the stairs first — I'd say yes, plenty of
people have that much gumption."

Mother glanced up at him curiously. "What's gotten into
you? You almost sound like you sympathize with the man!"

Father sighed. "No, I don't sympathize with him. I dislike everything he stands for. I think he's brought all his troubles on himself, and I'll be glad to see the day when his irresponsible newspaper ceases publication. But —"

"But what?"

"But sometimes I almost wish I could *believe* the way he does."

"Sheldon!"

"It's all very well to know that slavery is a complex problem — that it is peculiarly suited to certain areas of the Southern economy — that most darkies are better off being cared for by affectionate masters than they would be fending for themselves (although I own I've never been too sure of that myself!) — that if it were not logically and ethically effective, it would wither away — that the Bible tells us that the destiny of the sons of Ham is to be servants to servants — that the whole problem was brought on by unscrupulous Yankee slave-traders — that Athens was a republic which sanctioned slavery, which was why its patricians had the leisure to create a Golden Age — that the U.S. Constitution intended that the slavery issue be handled by the individual states concerned, and not by Northern meddlers — that abolitionists believe in Free Love and frequently form immoral relationships with the opposite sex —"

"Sheldon — the children!"

"Let's see — have I missed anything? No, I guess not." He slumped down in his favorite chair and tossed *The True American* onto the floor in front of him. "I know all of the answers, Patience — I should, we keep saying them to one another often enough. And yet, with all the answers on our side — how do we explain the fact that it's *we* — not Cash Clay — who are preparing to break the law? If our cause is as just as we all say it is, would we need to be working ourselves up into a mob to prevent one critic from telling us he disagrees with us?"

"But Sheldon — you've told me a hundred times yourself! He's trying to destroy the Southern way of life!"

"So he is — but *legally*, my dear. He's trying to change public opinion so that new laws can be passed to bring a gradual end to slavery — as he has every right to do. Meanwhile the word has gone out for a public meeting at the courthouse day after tomorrow to consider what action should be taken to suppress *The True American*."

"Well, finally!" said Mother with satisfaction.

"Yes, finally, now that the election is out of the way, and terrorism can't cost us any votes from the squeamish." He stared at the toes of his boots, stretched out in front of him. "Well, I won't be there. I won't ally myself with a lynch mob, whatever the cause."

He lapsed into moody silence. My mother apparently felt no good would be served by arguing with him, and she remained silent too. And as the silence lengthened, I thought to myself, as I had on the eve of the Clay poisoning trial, five months before, "Somehow I've got to be there."

* * *

Thursday afternoon found me, in company with Falk Padgett, on the fringe of a dense crowd on the courthouse lawn in Lexington. It had taken a certain amount of dissimulation — not to say prevarication — to get me there. (My mother believed that I was helping to break a horse to the saddle on a neighboring farm.) When I arrived in Lexington I stabled Sacajawea and then made my way through the already crowded streets to the back door of my father's store. Next to the door was a small window that gave me a view of the back room, where Falk slept. I waited a few minutes, and then Falk came into the room. I tapped on the window, and he recognized me and opened the door.

"Well, Land of Goshen, if it ain't Hasty Pudding Miller!" he grinned.

"You keep that up and someday I'm going to tell you what 'Falk' sounds like," I replied. "Is my father here?"

"Not yet. He stayed in town last night, at the Phoenix Hotel, but I don't reckon he's got hisself out of bed yet."

"There's a meeting today at the courthouse, and I wondered if you could skip out of here and go over there with me."

"You figure there's going to be anything to see?"

"I figure there might be, if Cash Clay comes to the meeting!"

"Shucks! Everybody knows Cash Clay's had a ree-lapse, and is flat on his back in bed again," said Falk scornfully.

"Well, do you want to come with me or don't you?"

"Oh, I reckon. You wait here, and I'll tell Elam to think up some lie about sending me on an errand to tell your pap. Don't that make you ashamed?" he asked wickedly, and disappeared.

By the time we were on the courthouse lawn, it was about two in the afternoon. We'd been milling around the yard with everybody else for almost three hours, and nothing had happened except a lot of windbags had tried to show off how dangerous and desperate they were, with suggestions about marching off to Cash Clay's house, pulling him out of bed, stringing him up on a tree and so on.

Falk hawked and spat, narrowly missing the polished boot of one of the daring would-be lynchers. "I guess I've about had enough of this," he said.

I was about to agree, when there was a commotion over near the street. People began saying: "They're coming!

94

Meeting's about to begin!" and then the crowd parted to
allow a small group of men to come up the path to the courthouse door. Some of them I recognized — I had last seen
them in Cousin Whitney's billiard room on the Fourth of
July. Cousin Whitney himself was there (causing me to
duck back into the crowd suddenly) and Tom Marshall, the
recent unsuccessful candidate, and John Hunt Morgan.
There was another man who had not been in the billiard
room, but whom I recognized instantly: James B. Clay,
Henry Clay's son, who had repudiated his father's moderate
politics and had joined the fire-eating wing of the Democratic Party.

During the next ten minutes, that group was followed into
the courthouse by other arrivals, singly or in clusters, until
probably thirty citizens were assembled in the large first-
floor courtroom. Falk and I had wriggled our way into posi-
tions just outside the courtroom window, which was open,
due to the heat of the day. We had box seats indeed.

The meeting was just coming to order — James B. Clay
had accepted the chair and was calling on Tom Marshall —
when my attention was diverted by a new disturbance outside. This time the crowd sounded different — ugly. There
were hisses, boos, catcalls, fists shaken in the air. Then, as
the loafers pulled back to open a path to the courthouse door,
my skin began to prickle, and I heard Falk whisper beside
me, "Jesus Christ — it's Cash Clay!"

Slowly and carefully, with a sort of stumbling gait, Cassius
Clay made his way down the path, supported on one side by
the tall Pole, Lewinsky, whom I remembered bolting iron
sheets on the doors of the *True American* office, and on the
other by the man called Neal, whom I had last seen planning
the angle of fire for a four-pounder cannon. Between their
vigorous and concerned faces, Clay's pale face was a study in

95

debilitating weakness and an indomitable hatred of weakness — of the imminent need to collapse and the absolute refusal to collapse. He was parchment-white, and his fine black broadcloth suit hung on him in unsightly bags and folds. He seemed oblivious to the cries and jeers of the crowd around him; it was as though his full awareness was needed for the task of getting into the courthouse, and he had none left for nonessentials.

He had an arm around the shoulders of each of his supporters. His coat was unbuttoned, the lapels were pulled wide apart, exposing a good deal of the shirt underneath — and the bowie knife in its sheath, strapped under his left arm.

"Lord A'mighty," said a man near me in the crowd, half sarcastically, half in admiration, "the son of a bitch can't even walk, but he's packing his fighting knife!"

The three men continued their slow progress along the path and then up the steps to the courthouse door. They paused there a moment, as if to allow the bent figure in the middle to draw more strength from some hidden source, and then went inside the building. Falk and I pressed up against the open window, and a few moments later the courtroom door opened, and Clay and his two friends joined the meeting.

Tom Marshall, who was speaking, was obviously taken aback at Clay's arrival. He stopped in midsentence, then shouted, "What's the meaning of this? You weren't invited to this meeting, Clay!"

Clay answered, his deep voice so low I had to strain to catch the words, "An hour or so ago I was fortunate enough to find out there was a little get-together scheduled for today to discuss my future. I was sure the reason I hadn't been invited was due to some oversight — some sort of error, no doubt. So I have rectified that." He swayed forward, and only his friends' support kept him from falling. "Don't let me interrupt you — I'll just sit here and watch the proceedings."

He sank upon a bench, but even sitting upright was too much for him, and a minute or two later he asked his friends to move from beside him, and stretched out full length on the bench, his hands folded on his breast, looking like nothing so much as a corpse laid out in a parlor.

Meanwhile the meeting resumed. James B. Clay called on two men I didn't know, then on Cousin Whitney, then on Tom Marshall. They all said substantially the same thing — that *The True American* was a threat to domestic tranquillity, an inciter of violence and rebellion, an affront to the simple Christianity of Kentuckians, a seducer of the young and a callous slur on Anglo-Saxon womanhood — in support of the last point an editorial of Clay's was quoted advising the ladies of the slave-owning South that they would be happier, handsomer and healthier if they started doing their own housework.

"Mark him there!" shouted Marshall, pointing a finger at Clay. "The assassin! He has assassinated the peace and order of Kentucky. And why? Because he aims at nothing less than revolution — nothing less than a reversal of the status of master and slave! It matters not to him that the Creator has placed the brand upon the African's brow, the badge of physical and mental inferiority and past servitude that dooms him while amongst us to remain a slave and be protected by our benevolence, or be an outcast and face the righteous wrath of a superior people. The assassin of order cares not a rap for such obvious truth. In the madness of his vanity . . ."

"Apostate!" cried Clay, in a voice that hardly carried to

the windows. "Apostate Whig! Admit it — you were the enemy of slavery until the slavocracy bribed you and bought you off. You sold your moral birthright for a mess of pottage, apostate!"

This was true, as everyone in the room knew. Marshall had run for office on the Whig ticket only a few years before, and had been quite articulate in his opposition to slavery. Clay's accusation stopped Marshall in his tracks, but James B. Clay took up the indictment.

"All right, Tom, let's get on with the business at hand. We're here to talk about a certain abolitionist newspaper —"

"Emancipationist," cried Clay weakly.

"— which has proved to be a threat to law and order in this community. Now, do I hear a motion that the editor of that paper be informed that he is required to cease publication immediately or face the certainty of suppression at the hands of his fellow citizens?"

"Why don't we put it a little more diplomatically?" said Cousin Whitney, in his insinuating soft Maryland drawl. "Why don't we say he owes it to his own safety, and the safety of his friends, to accept our suggestion?"

"I demand a hearing," said Clay hoarsely.

"Would you put that in the form of a motion, Ledyard?" asked James B. Clay.

"Stop this and listen, damn you. You can't suppress my paper. God and all his Heavenly Hosts couldn't suppress my paper." He struggled up on his elbows, and his voice grew stronger. "I demand you stop this kangaroo court and listen to me . . ."

"I move that the editor of a paper known as *The True American* be informed that his newspaper has had and is having a detrimental effect on the peace and tranquillity of this community . . ."

98

"Do you even know what you're doing?" cried Clay. "Do you even know my position on slavery? I'm not an abolitionist . . ."

". . . and that if he does not cease publication immediately, his fellow citizens cannot be responsible for his safety."

"Second," said John Hunt Morgan.

". . . I believe in *gradual* emancipation. You fools, I'm not trying to attack your pocketbooks, I'm not trying to rob your widows and orphans of their inheritances . . ."

"It has been moved and seconded," intoned James B. Clay. "All in favor vote Aye." Everybody voted Aye. "Opposed, Nay." Nobody voted Nay. "Motion is carried," announced James B. Clay.

"Listen to me — listen to me!" Cassius Clay's voice was a barely audible croak. "Can't you see, you're sowing dragon's teeth here! For every man you kill who loves freedom, a thousand will be born! For every drop of their blood the ground sucks up, a thousand drops will spurt out like a fountain tomorrow!"

"Hear a motion to adjourn?" asked the chairman.

"Move to adjourn," said somebody I didn't recognize.

"I'll be waiting — and you know I won't be alone!" Clay whispered. "If you try it, there better be plenty of you!"

"Second," said Cousin Whitney.

"Moved and seconded — favor, vote Aye." Everybody voted Aye. "Opposed, Nay." Nobody voted Nay. "Moved and carried. Meeting adjourned." All thirty members of the meeting rose briskly from their seats and prepared to leave the courtroom. Only one of them showed any awareness of the sick man stretched out on the bench — John Hunt Morgan. As he passed out of the door, he paused, turned his head and took a long look at Cassius Clay. Clay raised his

99

leonine head and looked back at Morgan. For a moment neither of them moved — then Morgan gave him a flippant
wave of his hand and disappeared.

The crowd on the courthouse lawn greeted the thirty
emerging delegates with cheers. Five minutes later, with
Lewinsky supporting him from one side and Neal from the
other, Cassius M. Clay received the full expression of their
disagreement, but I don't think he heard any of it. His head
was hanging, his feet were dragging and all his weight
seemed to be carried on his friends' backs. With considerable difficulty they wrestled his impressive bulk into a waiting carriage. The coachman cracked his whip, the magnificent matched grays leaped forward, and, trailed by the
groans and jeers of his fellow townsmen, Cassius M. Clay
went back to his bed.

"You reckon that was worth waiting three hours to see?"
I heard Falk ask sardonically.

"You dang bet it was! I'd wait longer than that just to see
Cash Clay scratch his ass!" I answered angrily.

Falk laughed. "How come — you think he'd do it with his
bowie knife?"

"Listen, Falk Padgett, if you're trying to get my dander
up, you're doing just fine. Why, don't you have sense
enough to see that all those other poltroons rolled up together don't have as much grit as Cash Clay has all by himself?"

"What the heck are poltroons?" asked Falk irrelevantly.

"Yellowbellies, for gosh sakes!"

"Then whyn't you say so?"

"Cause I keep forgetting I'm talking to an illiterate ridge
runner is why! Gosh all hemlock, haven't you ever read any
books about how gentlemen talk?"

"No — all I know is how gentlemen act, like those gentlemen in the meeting here. And come to think of it, I guess I *do* know what poltroons are, after all."

We walked together up Main Street, through the excited crowd. "What you think is going to happen now, Falk?" I asked.

"Appears to me the hounds got the coon treed. Next thing is gather round with a long stick and knock him down." We walked on in silence. When we reached Broadway, where we would separate, Falk turned to me seriously. "Hacey, I josh a lot — too much, maybe — but I reckon you know whose side I'm on in this here Cash Clay business. Me and Elam, we get to talking down at the store, and some of the time it's about slavery. I figure I'm agin it, and I figure you're agin it, and I figure Cash Clay's agin it. I just wanted to tell you that so's you'd know next time I'm funning you a little."

Then he walked away, quickly, as if ashamed.

An hour or so later, as I was claiming Sackie at the livery stable, a man came in with the latest news of the day: Cassius Clay, assisted by his two friends, had no sooner arrived at his Lexington home, Thorn Hill, and gotten into bed, when three delegates of the afternoon's meeting had waited upon him with a written ultimatum, based on the motion they had passed previously. Clay had dictated a characteristic answer: "Your advice with regard to my personal safety is worthy of the source whence it emanated, and meets with the same contempt from me which the purposes of your mission excite. Go tell your secret conclave of cowardly assassins that C. M. Clay knows his rights and how to defend them."

As I rode home along the Richmond pike, I thought to myself that Falk's metaphor was poorly chosen. Clay was no coon to hang tamely on a branch waiting to be knocked down with a stick. He was a badger who had gone to ground. The dogs might dig him out all right, but I wouldn't want to be one of them.

VIII

THE NIGHT OF THE BLACK INDIANS

ALL DAY FRIDAY the excitement continued, with Clay's friends keeping a vigil in the *True American* office, and an angry crowd in the street outside. There was also a cluster of idlers on North Limestone outside Thorn Hill, shouting obscenities, insulting ladies and passing bottles of liquor from hand to hand. Lewinsky and Neal had armed themselves from Clay's arsenal and stayed beside the invalid's bed all through the day and evening.

Saturday, a handbill appeared calling a mass meeting on the courthouse lawn the following Monday, for the purpose of suppressing *The True American*. The slavocracy apparently was not lacking for volunteer couriers. The flyer appeared as far away as Cynthiana and Harrodsburg within a few hours of its release in Lexington. By sundown the entire Bluegrass knew that Monday was the day to dig out the badger.

Sunday was a strange day. There was only one piece of news that day: we heard after church that Cash Clay had had his camp bed carried down to the *True American* office, and was established in the second-floor editorial room, supervising the reloading of all the cannons and rifles.

Aside from that, it was as if we had all taken time out from history. All the cards were on the table; no one could improve his hand, and yet the game had been suspended for twenty-four hours. It seemed unreal.

The Ledyards stopped by, as usual. The afternoon visit passed without incident until they were preparing to leave. Then, after seating his family in their phaeton, Cousin Whitney swung himself to the driver's seat, and, taking the reins in one hand and the whip in the other, saluted my father. "As one Indian to another, Sheldon — 'How!' " he drawled, smiling.

Father answered sharply, "I'm not one of your Indians, and I'm not about to become one. You know me better than that, Whitney."

"I swear, if this was Boston, you'd be eating baked beans and fretting about your immortal soul while the rest of us were throwing the tea overboard," said Cousin Whitney in a tone of gentle reproof. "Time has run out, Sheldon."

"Good day, Whitney," said Father firmly.

"Your absence will be noted."

"Good day, Whitney."

And the Ledyards drove away, leaving us to spend the rest of Sunday disquieted and irritable. Father wouldn't answer any of Mother's questions and finally escaped to his study; Mother then transferred her frustrations to us children; we excaped her only to turn on one another. And so it went until we were in bed, and I lay unsleeping, torn between dread of the morrow and a fierce impatience for its coming.

*   *   *

The next morning I was on the Lexington pike before dawn, and by 9:00 A.M. I was tapping on the back window of my father's store to summon Falk.

When he came to the back door, he waved me away.

"You'll have to wait a mite, I can't get away right now. Your pap's here, and he's as mean as a rattlesnake with piles," he whispered. "But he'll be going out directly."

Ten minutes later, Falk slipped out the door and we headed for the courthouse lawn. The streets were unbelievably crowded; men overflowed the sidewalks and blocked the passage of horsemen and vehicles. A pall of dust hung in the air, and you had to shout to be heard by your nearest neighbor. "Didn't Elam mind letting you leave work today?" I yelled.

"Elam ain't there. He's at the *True American* office with Clay. That's what made your pap so goldarned mad."

"Who's minding the store?"

"Nobody. I locked it up. Don't reckon no customers will be coming round today, with all this hooraw going on."

"How come my father knows where Elam is?"

"Elam told him. Said it was a day for a man to stand up for what he believed in, and he wasn't going to try to hide the way he felt no more. Said he was sorry if it hurt your pap's feelings, but that's the way it is."

"Did Papa fire him?"

"No — he was so busy cussing about Cash Clay and Tom Marshall I reckon he forgot to."

There were more people on the courthouse lawn that morning than I ever saw in one place before; the *Observer* later estimated the number at 1200. It was a fairly orderly crowd, but it was also a purposeful one. I didn't see any drinking going on. From the comments I heard, it was clear these people expected to close down *The True American* that Monday, whatever the cost.

After forty-five minutes or so, a man climbed up the steps onto the slave-auction platform and raised his arms to quiet the crowd. I didn't recognize him at first, but Falk, with the sharp eyes of a mountaineer, said, "It's that windbag Marshall feller — and I do believe he's fixing to make *another* speech!"

He was — and he made it for an hour. It was the same stuff we had heard at the meeting the previous Thursday — that Clay was assassinating the peace of Kentucky, and such — but Marshall spoke well, and the crowd began to get excited. Shouts interrupted him: "Let's cowhide the bastard!" "Lynch him!" "What are we waiting for? We've talked enough!" Marshall let them continue until it seemed he was in danger of losing control of the crowd, then he ended his speech and produced a list of resolutions, to be voted on by the assembly. They prohibited any abolitionist newspaper from being published in Kentucky, either presently or at any later date; promised that if *The True American* were surrendered peacefully, the presses would be carefully dismantled and shipped out of the city, and no harm would come to the building or its occupants; charged that if any resistance were offered, the blood would be on C. M. Clay's hands; and authorized the appointment of a "Committee of Sixty" of the group to take possession of the office of the newspaper and begin dismantling the equipment.

The resolutions were adopted by acclamation, and Marshall then read a list of the men he proposed for the Committee of Sixty. There were familiar names on the list — Cousin Whitney, James B. Clay, John Hunt Morgan — as well as unfamiliar ones, but at the end of the reading I breathed a sigh of relief, for my father's name was not on the list.

Again by acclamation the list was approved, and the Committee of Sixty assembled along Cheapside as the rest of us watched. Directly across the street was the *True American* office, iron-plated door locked, iron-shuttered window closed.

"All right, now — the rest of you folks stay right here on the courthouse lawn and wait," shouted Marshall. "We're going across the street and through that door, one way or another. You back us up. We'll let you know if we need you."

The crowd fell silent as the Committee started across the narrow street. A battering ram had materialized from somewhere — a foot wide by a foot thick, and about fifteen feet long — carried by five burly roughnecks in homespun. The Committee closed in behind them. Some of the men produced pistols from under their coats. John Hunt Morgan held his pointing to the sky, like a duelist about to begin his pacing. I drew a long breath and held it.

Then, incredibly, the iron-lined front door opened and a man stepped out into the sunlight. It was the Lexington town marshal, Loyall Davies, and he held a key ring in his hand. He closed the door behind him, locked it with one of the keys, then turned to face the Committee with his arms folded.

"Davies, what in tophet are you doing here?" asked Tom Marshall.

"My duty, sir," replied Davies.

"Are those the keys to this building?"

"They are."

"Then speaking for this duly constituted citizens' committee, I demand that you surrender them to us."

Davis smiled and unfolded his arms. "Let it be noted that I formally protest this action, but am forced to comply," he said, and handed the keys to Marshall.

Marshall stepped by him and unlocked the door, and then, stepping to one side, threw it open. Nothing happened. He poked his head around the doorframe and looked up the stairs. Still nothing happened. After a moment's hesitation, he found the courage to plunge ahead. "All right, men, we're going up. Follow me." He started up the stairs, followed by the five roughnecks and the rest of the Committee.

"That takes a certain amount of grit for a poltroon," said Falk.

"What happened, Falk? How come they just walked in that way? What happened to the cannons and the rusty nails? What about the barrels of gunpowder? What about —"

"What about waiting till we get some answers before you break your jaw asking questions?"

Later, when we got the answers from Elam Yates, we found out what had happened. Early that morning a group of leading proslavery figures, including Robert Wickliffe himself, had persuaded Judge Trotter of the police court to issue an injunction against *The True American,* covering the building it was printed in and the equipment used to print it. Cassius Clay was given no opportunity to hear the charges against him or answer them in court. The town marshal procured a writ of seizure and took it to Six North Mill Street. There he found Clay in bed with a pistol in his hand, and seven other men, including Elam, armed with loaded rifles. The cannons were in position to sweep the stairs.

"When he presented that damned writ, the rest of us were for tying him up and setting him on top of the gunpowder as a hostage," Elam explained. "But Clay has that legal bug up his bum. He'll go to hell and ask the devil for a light, but only if the law's on his side. The law! Christ on a cow-catcher — in this town the law is Wickliffe, and everybody knows it. But just because that damned rascal had a piece of paper signed by a judge, Cash Clay give up! He handed over his keys, laid his pistol down on the table and turned his face to the wall — and that was that for *The True American!*"

As Falk and I watched from across the street, a melancholy little band came down the stairs. Clay was at the head, leaning heavily on Lewinsky. Aside from the lines of pain around his eyes, his pale face was blank. Behind them came the others, either staring stonily ahead or glaring about defiantly. The last down the stairs was Elam, hobbling on his short leg. When they all reached the sidewalk, Clay and Lewinsky began to walk north on Mill Street toward Short Street, where Clay kept his carriage. The others followed, as the silent crowd pulled back and opened a way for them. In a few moments they were gone.

During the afternoon the Committee dismantled the press and carried out all the office equipment. Everything was crated up, loaded in wagons and carted off to the Lexington & Ohio railroad station to be shipped out of the state, C.O.D. to Mr. Cassius M. Clay in Cincinnati.

It seemed anticlimactic to us, and during the afternoon we discovered it seemed that way to many other people too — people who had keyed themselves up for a desperate scene of derring-do, with cannons roaring, pistol balls whistling down the stairs and Clay's bowie knife running red. Although the bulk of the 1200 people who had been at the meeting seemed happy enough to go quietly back to their homes, there was a substantial minority that wasn't ready to call it quits yet.

As Falk and I walked down Main Street we passed a number of groups of such diehards. They seemed to be of two types. Most of them were either the town idlers or poor whites from the countryside — men from the bottom of the Bluegrass social ladder — but there was a smattering of

"Quality" among them, often the same men who had been at the first meeting in the courthouse, or had been listed among the Committee of Sixty, such men as Morgan and his friends, and Tom Marshall and James B. Clay. From snatches of argument and exhortations I heard as I passed, I gathered that "Now's the time to teach 'em a lesson" — "Now, while the iron is hot" — "Tonight, before everybody goes home" — "We owe it to ourselves and our society" — "Never be another chance as good."

Something was in the wind. I felt a prickling along my backbone — not the good, healthy kind of fear that comes before a fight and prepares your mind and body for it, but the sticky kind that makes you feel damp all over. This was danger, I knew, but from whom, and under what circumstances, I had no idea.

"Trouble," said Falk briefly.

"I'm going to stay in town tonight," I decided suddenly. "Can I sleep in the back room with you?"

"Your pap'll raise Ned if he finds out."

"He won't find out. He'll either stay at the Phoenix or go on home. Either way, he won't be around the store tonight."

"If he finds out you stayed in town, I'd as lief you didn't mention where you stayed. Your pap's so mad at Elam, it wouldn't seem rightly fair for him to have to be mad at me too."

We went in the back door of the store, checked to make sure nobody was there, then lit the lamp in the back room, and we were as snug as two bugs in a rug, waiting for the sun to go down and for whatever was going to happen.

Falk nipped out to the tavern and brought back some bread and cheese and side meat and cider, and we had ourselves a quiet feast. Outside the sun went down. The days were getting noticeably shorter. There was a winter waiting for us, just around the corner of Indian summer, with its deceptive warmth laid like a blanket over a bed of coldness from which the sun had already departed.

"Falk, what do you think is going to happen now?" I was sitting on the floor, hugging my knees, and he was leaning back in an old kitchen chair propped against the wall, his feet braced on the highest set of rungs, so his knees were even with his ears, looking for all the world like the folded wings of some skinny angel or demon.

"I reckon some people are going to get stomped," he answered. "Back on the Big Sandy you could sort of smell stomping weather. Partly it smelled mean, and partly it smelled kind of hot and sluggish, and partly it smelled drunk. All run together, like it smells now."

We sat together in silence for a moment. Then I asked, "Who's going to get stomped, Falk? Cash Clay?"

"I figure Cash Clay still has too many teeth. Anyways, why would they need to stomp him? They already took his newspaper away, all legal-like. No, if I was Cash Clay, I'd sleep comfortable tonight."

"Then who, Falk?"

Before he could answer, we heard the beginning of it outside — far away to start with, over west of us, down in the gully by the Frankfort pike, where the shanty city called Iristown was — the sound of men baying like dogs, and keening above it, the cry of a human being screaming in pure terror. The hair stood straight up on my neck.

"The niggers, Hacey — who else would you reckon but the niggers?"

And it was the niggers, of course, who were the target. This was an opportunity for the slave power to show them just how futile, how foolish, was any dream of emancipation — how helplessly they lay in the palm of the hand of the white society around them — how suicidally dangerous were any thoughts of independence, let alone resistance.

Falk blew out the lamp and we stepped into the areaway outside the back of the store. The sounds of pursuers and pursued were closer now, as we hurried along the side of the building and out onto Broadway. "It's coming down toward Main Street," said Falk, and we turned left and headed for Main Street too.

At the corner we got our first look at the mob. They were half a block away, coming toward us at a loping run. A number of torches flared among them, serving both to illuminate them and silhouette the desperate figures running ahead of them, zigzagging from one side of the road to the other, looking for a place to hide.

We were standing in front of a waist-high fence, and the gate was closed beside us. Inside the yard were the dim shapes of bushes, offering concealment from which we could watch the mob as it passed. We ducked through the gate, closing it behind us, and knelt down behind a lilac bush.

The baying of the crowd swelled into a wordless roar, and then the first of the blacks came into sight, running in a loose, disjointed manner, his head turned and his eyes distended as he watched his pursuers pounding after him. He crossed our field of vision and was followed almost instantly by two more Negroes, one gray-polled, one a boy scarcely out of his teens. Then the first of the hunting pack came into sight — and for a moment I couldn't believe my eyes.

"Why, they're blacks too!" I whispered.

"Black Indians, you mean," replied Falk.

Then I saw that what I had taken for black faces were actually black masks covering white faces, and surmounting them were Indian headdresses! Black Indians! In the flickering glare of the torches they looked like fiends from hell.

The street was full of them, screaming, capering, parodying Indian war dances. They had captured two Negroes. One disappeared from sight immediately; he either fell or was knocked to the ground. The other was held by two men, while a third deliberately bent his fingers backward and broke them, first one, then another, then another —

"God!" I breathed.

"Hush up!" rasped Falk, as the gate in the fence opened, and a small black figure came through it. It was a Negro boy, about my own age. He was dressed in an oversized pair of overalls and nothing else. He ducked so that he was concealed behind the fence, and began to close the gate behind him. He had somehow eluded the mob and seemed on the verge of escape.

And then the gate flew open again, and a burly masked figure with a headband of feathers burst through it and seized the boy by the shoulders. "Here's a little nigger that needs a lesson!" he shouted. "Ain't that right, little nigger? You want something you can remember all your life long?" He grabbed each of the boy's bony little arms, two or three inches below the shoulder; then he began twisting them so the elbows were forced inward and the upper ends of the bones began to strain the muscles that bound them to their sockets. The boy screamed as the muscles started to tear, the "Black Indian" giggled; Falk and I leaped to our feet, all fear of discovery forgotten. Suddenly a piece of blackness seemed to separate from the other darkness around it, and there was a black man standing behind the "Indian," with a thick black arm around his neck. Immediately releasing the screaming boy, the "Indian" clutched the constricting arm with both hands and tried to wrench it loose. As he struggled and clawed and kicked, his headdress and mask came askew and fell off, and his fat, white, terror-filled face was revealed. He was the man I had mentally named "Pudgy" when, in company with John Hunt Morgan on the courthouse lawn, he had tried to provoke Cassius Clay into a duel.

Pudgy was in a different kind of duel that night, and as we watched aghast, he got his comeuppance. A second black arm snaked around below the first, there was an open jack-knife in its hand. And as Pudgy hung in the air, back arched, feet completely off the ground, the jackknife cut his throat from ear to ear.

Blood exploded into the air for a second, then the massive black arm withdrew its support, and Pudgy dropped to the gound like a bag of corn. There was nothing between us and the murderer, and we looked straight into his face. I didn't need to see the livid scar on his forehead to know who he was; I had already known when I recognized the jackknife; I had seen it often enough, moving across a curiously carved cherrywood box.

"Star," I whispered.

The Negro took a step toward us, stepping over Pudgy's body without a glance. Beside me I felt Falk hunch forward tensely. My eyes were riveted to that blood-dripping knife. I knew for sure I had reached the end of my days.

Then Star spoke. It was the voice I had heard in his shack on the hoodoo night, rich and pulsing, without a trace of darky accent. "Hacey Miller, remember Damballa. If you want to live, remember Damballa."

And I swear, as I stood in that garden beside a lilac bush, separated from a capering, howling mob by ten feet and a picket fence, and from a dead man and his killer by less than that, I felt something massive and scaly and cold press against my legs, move around to encircle them and gradually tighten its grip. The intermittent flicker of the torches showed there was nothing there.

"I remember, Star. I'll always remember. And I'll never tell."

He stood for a second staring at me, and I had the feeling he was weighing the odds on some vital bet. Then he put his free hand around the shoulders of the black boy in the overalls — still sobbing quietly, as he had been since Pudgy let him go — and, pushing the boy ahead of him, walked past us into the deepening darkness of the garden. "Remember the *loa*, Hacey Miller — and the *loa* will protect you," he said softly. And the two figures disappeared as completely as if they had never existed. The pressure on my legs stopped.

Only the lumpy body on the grass remained.

For a long moment Falk and I stared at it. Then Falk let out a long, shuddering sigh. "I declare, Hacey, you do have some downright interesting friends," he said. "I wish they'd clean up after themselves."

"Falk, promise me you'll never say anything about this. Cross your heart and hope to die!"

"Oh, I promise. I didn't really cotton to that feller much anyhow, what I seen of him with the little nigger, so I'd just as lief forget it. Only — you and me better get out of here fast, or we ain't going to be *able* to forget it!"

That was so obviously the better part of valor that it needed no debate. Falk and I turned from the street, and the corpse, and felt our way through the garden, the darkness increasing with every step away from the torches on the street. Falk stumbled once, and I tripped over a little wire wicket and fell flat on my face, and then we were at the back of the garden, with a high wooden fence in front of us. I boosted Falk up, then he pulled me after him, and we were over and out.

We kept to the alleys and back areaways on our way home to the store. We didn't see much of the "Black Indians," and their high-spirited doings, except one more incident: we saw on old darky tarred and feathered.

People laugh when they talk about someone being tarred and feathered, as though it's a comical sport that affords pleasure to the participants without doing any real harm to the victim — sort of like snipe hunting. It isn't like that at all. It's as cruel and vicious a thing as men can do to men. To my dying day I will never forget the screams of that poor old man as the molten tar scalded his flesh, or his wild, babbling pleas for help as the tar hardened and each movement of his body pulled the skin away from the parboiled flesh underneath it. And how the mob laughed as he stumbled down the street with a pillowful of feathers adhering to the tar, like some clumsy earthbound bird in the last extremity of pain.

Minutes later we were in the back of the store with the lamp lit and the door locked behind us. We didn't feel like talking and we couldn't sleep, so Falk and I lay awake till dawn began to brighten the sky, listening to the sounds of the mob outside. There was light coming in the window before the cries and shouts dwindled away and I was able to fall asleep.

*   *   *

The Lexington *Observer* never admitted that there was such an occurrence as the "Night of the Black Indians," but there happened to be three or four correspondents for Northern newspapers in town at the time to cover the climax of the story of Cassius Clay and *The True American,* and they got the word out to the rest of the country. For all who had eyes to see, the shame of the slavery power in the Bluegrass was revealed.

Following in the wake of the Night, I was disciplined by my father to the extent of being confined to the house for two weeks, but managed to keep Falk's complicity a secret. Father fired Elam Yates, but had to rehire him two weeks later, because nobody else knew the stock. Star disappeared from his cabin. No arrest was made for the murder of Pudgy. Cassius Clay slowly regained his health, and remained in seclusion. A noticeable coolness developed between my father and Cousin Whitney Ledyard. School started again.

And finally, on October 13 — Court Day in Fayette County, Kentucky — Emily, alleged murderess of the infant Cassius Clay, Jr., was found innocent and discharged. Almost immediately, she and her mother, her uncle and her daughter were sold down the river by their actual owners, Cassius Clay's in-laws, the Warfields.

IX

GROWING UP A LITTLE

THE FALL OF 1845, Great-aunt Henrietta died. Even though she was not officially a Ledyard herself — her name was Henrietta Gordon Fort Satterlee — she was the fountainhead of Ledyardism. She looked at the world through Tidewater-tinted pince-nez. Three years before, when the Lexington *Observer* published the news that Robert Todd's daughter Mary Ann had wedded an Illinois lawyer named Lincoln, Great-aunt Henrietta sniffed and commented, "Well! I would have thought the Todds could have done a mite better than *that!*"

After Aunt Henrietta's remains were entrusted to the no doubt grateful earth, we Millers drove back to Hazelwood, each bound in his own reflections on mortality. The solemn mood continued through dinner, and afterward, when we moved to the drawing room, Father opened a discussion on the future course of our lives.

"A day like today makes us all slow down and take a good long look at where we are headed," he began. "Sometimes it comes as a blessing in disguise, because it lets us see how we may have started to go wrong. We each have only one life to live, and all the credit that attaches to it, or all the blame, is ours alone."

"And our souls will be sifted before God's Judgment Seat," added Mother coolly, without raising her eyes from her sewing.

I began to feel uncomfortable, and a stealthy glance at Boone showed he was too. Serious invocation of the Deity was rare enough in our household to make us wonder what we were guilty of.

But not so my sister. Father smiled at her and said, "Fortunately Rosalie presents us with no problems. Next week she begins at Madame Mentelle's School in Lexington, whence she will no doubt emerge in four years with all the maidenly virtues necessary to inspire a young man's intellectual regard while inflaming his amorous desires . . ."

"Sheldon!"

"My dear, why do you think the good Lord told Noah to bring *two* of every sort of living flesh onto the Ark? The Divine Plan of the Universe doesn't seem to regard the existence of two sexes as an impediment."

"I have heard," replied Mother complacently, "that the Devil quotes scripture for his own purposes."

"The Devil would have a hard time getting a word in edgewise around here! Quote scripture? Hell, if he could squeeze in 'Jesus wept,' he'd earn a reputation as a champion windbag!" He snorted and walked in a circle around the room, and we waited for him to regain his composure. After a few moments, he picked up the thread of his discourse and continued, "As I said, Rosalie presents us with no problems. It's Hacey and Boone we have to think about. Particularly Hacey, after his overnight escapade in Lexington."

"Shucks, Papa, I've already been punished for that."

"I'm not going to reopen old wounds. I merely mention it to point up my contention that it's high time we looked at the road before us. Have you given any thought to your future, son? To what you want to be in life?"

"Well, sir, I think I'd like to go to college, either at Transylvania or at Centre College over in Danville . . ." I began, and then left the sentence hanging because I couldn't think of anything else to say.

"And study what? What do you want to prepare yourself for?"

"Gosh, I don't know. I suppose I could run the store, like you . . ."

"Hacey, have you ever thought of being a lawyer?"

His question surprised me, because I *had* occasionally toyed with the idea of entering the law — when I wasn't thinking about going to West Point or becoming captain of a clipper ship on the China run. "Yes, sir, every once in a while I've thought about it — usually after I've seen Mr. Brain, I guess."

"I've noticed how you've started reading the political news in the *Observer*, and I wondered if you might not have a talent for politics. You seem to get on well with everybody, and that's a start."

"Well, I suppose I wouldn't mind being a senator or congressman or something."

"If you ever want to enter politics, the law is your steppingstone. Nine out of ten politicians in this state were lawyers to start with, and when they're out of office, they take up the practice again." He paused, then said reflectively, "I've never really understood why that is, but I suppose it's because both professions concern themselves almost exclusively with the baser aspects of mankind." Mother looked up from her sewing and shot him an admonitory glance, and he cleared his throat defensively. "Well, howsoever, if you hanker to enter politics, you've got to read law first. Now you mentioned Josh Brain a minute ago."

"Yes, sir."

"You know he's taken quite a shine to you, son, bringing you books for your birthday and all. Well, when I mentioned to him that you just possibly might be heading for the Bar, he allowed as how he'd be proud to have you read law with him, in his office in Lexington."

I was suddenly convinced that I wanted nothing more from life than to be a Lexington lawyer and politician. "That's the best news I ever heard, Papa," I cried.

"The way I figure we'll do it is this. You'll stay here and go to school at Foxtown for the rest of this year. Then next year we'll get you a room over in Lexington and you can enroll at Transylvania. We'll send Jubal over to take care of you, and when he's not working for you he can come over to the store and work for me. And when you're not studying your college work, you can spend your time at Josh Brain's office reading law. How does that sound?"

"Gosh all hemlock, you mean I can have my own room, and everything?"

"I don't know about the 'everything,' but you can certainly have your own room. After all, a young college gentleman has to have a place to spread his wings," said Father.

"Just make sure he doesn't singe them," warned Mother.

After that Father talked about Boone's future, but Boone couldn't think of anything he wanted to do but farm Hazelwood and raise racehorses. After a while I stopped listening and concentrated on thinking about Father's plan.

I was going into politics, like Cash Clay. Honorable Hacey F. Miller — Senator H. Fort Miller — Chief Justice H. F. Miller — President Hacey Fort Miller — I tried them

on my mental ear like a prospective bride tries out the per-
mutations of her married name.

But how in the world could I possibly survive the year
ahead, stretching out like a desert between me and my destiny?

*   *   *

Actually the year sped by. Every copy of the Lexington
Observer brought excitement into the house, as the possibility of war — whether with Mexico or England or both —
grew more and more likely. President Polk was pressing for
the annexation of Texas in the south and of Oregon in the
west. If the options were, as the expansionists shouted,
"Fifty-four forty or fight," then "fight" seemed the more
likely.

As Josh Brain pointed out every time he came to dinner,
the United States had charted a course squarely between
Scylla and Charybdis. Great Britain and Mexico were natural allies; British interests were opposed to American annexation of Texas, and Mexico could gain small comfort from
the prospect of her California territory being flanked by
Yankees on the north as well as the east. "They just plain
can't afford *not* to get together," the fat little lawyer insisted.

But when the war came, it was only with Mexico; somehow the Polk administration had managed to divide its opponents and settle the Oregon question with England blood-
lessly. When the call for volunteers went out, the famous old
Lexington Light Infantry was among the first militia units to
respond. Its muster roll was filled to capacity, and one of the
new enlistees was Cassius Marcellus Clay. Although he enlisted as a private, he was immediately elected captain.

There are two questions that everybody who ever knew
Cash Clay has asked himself at one time or another: Why
did he enlist in the Mexican War to begin with, and why did

his fellow soldiers, many of whom had been part of the mob outside the *True American* office nine months before, elect him their commanding officer?

I can't answer either question with absolute confidence, but I think the second is easier to answer than the first. Clay was an aristocrat whose father had commanded the "Old Infantry" in the War of 1812, and had brought a measure of glory to the Bluegrass. He was also a fighter, as fearless and resourceful as any man in the state. Since he supported the Mexican War, it appeared that he had altered his emancipationist views and found common cause with the slavocracy. All this being true, there was no one better qualified to command the company.

The question of why Clay supported the war is more difficult. It seems against reason. He had said for the record time and time again that expansion into Mexican territory was simply a device of the South to increase the number of slave states in the Union. He had campaigned vigorously against the Democratic Party both locally and nationally; he abhorred President Polk and ridiculed the idea of "Manifest Destiny." What in the world, one asks oneself, would cause him to volunteer for an "Imperial" war?

Clay used to laugh whenever anyone asked him the question, and answer only that he had joined the Old Infantry to gain prestige to help him politically. His friends never believed that.

The best answer I can come up with is that the drums and flags and new blue uniforms and pretty girls blowing kisses snagged him as solidly as if he had been an eighteen-year-old farm boy with manure on his shoes.

But whatever the reasons were, Cassius M. Clay was captain of the company, and Falk and Boone and I watched from the crowd as he led his men down Main Street toward the railroad station, to begin their journey to New Orleans and Mexico.

Watching that splendidly turned-out company of men marching proudly down the street, heads high, backs straight, ranks in faultless alignment — watching their captain striding before them with a drawn saber in his hand, a stern and inward-looking expression on his face, the very embodiment of the God of War — watching all this on a spanking brisk May afternoon was almost enough to make me want to shift my goal from Transylvania to West Point. Almost, but not quite.

The band played "Yankee Doodle Dandy," and the crowd sang a new set of words that had swept the country:

> We're the boys for Mexico
> Sing Yankee Doodle Dandy
> Gold and silver images
> Are plentiful and handy!
>
> And when we've laid aside our arms
> With nothing more to vex us
> We'll vote ourselves extensive farms
> Each one as big as Texas!

Somehow the human race convinces itself, every time, that marching off to war is a joyous occasion. The faces in the crowd that lined the street were flushed with pride and excitement, and they waved and cheered wildly as their fathers and brothers and sons paraded past.

"I wish I was old enough to go," said Boone wistfully.

"Want to shoot yourself a Mexican?" asked Falk. "Reckon you better grow up fast, then, 'fore they all get used up."

Boone cast a cold look at Falk. "You see anything wrong in wanting to fight for your country?" he asked.

"Sure not. I'm just as mad as you are that them dirty Mexicans are planning on capturing Washington city and putting the Pope in the White House. Anybody's got a right to defend himself against rascals like that!" Innocently he began to whistle "Yankee Doodle." Boone started to say something else, but I interrupted to point out an acquaintance in the ranks, and the moment of growing tension passed. Still, it bothered me that Falk and Boone never seemed to get on together. They were oil and water — Boone with his straightforward mind, his intense loyalties and his basic humorlessness, and Falk with his mischievous wit and irreverent view of men and institutions. When the three of us were together, more and more I had to act as a buffer. I wished each of them could appreciate the other as I did. I was too young to know that life rarely allows this to happen with those we love.

A week or so later, we heard that the Old Infantry had seen its first action of the war — in Louisville, Kentucky. As I heard the story recounted in the livery stable — with much guffawing and knee-slapping — a handful of young recruits had left camp, without permission, for a night on the levee. As the evening got drunker, they decided the war could go on without them, and persuaded some of the fair tenants of a celebrated house of ill fame to allow them to remain hidden on the premises until the Lexington Light Infantry departed downriver.

Somehow Cassius Clay learned their whereabouts, and reacted in a characteristic manner. He turned out the balance of the company under arms, marched them into the red-light district, surrounded the house in question and ordered the miscreants to surrender.

125

"Come and get us, you damned nigger-agitator," replied one of the acolytes of Venus, as he swayed in a window, naked from the waist down. He clutched a lady in one hand and a pistol in the other, and discharged the latter in Clay's general direction.

At that, Clay stormed the house.

Furniture and glassware crashed, women screamed, civilian patrons cursed, the madam howled, half-clothed soldiers dashed up and down stairs and hid under beds and in closets — and in a few minutes the objective was secured. Clay took his prisoners and marched the Lexington Light Infantry back to quarters, after the successful completion of its first mission since the Battle of the Thames in 1813.

That bit of burlesque came back to haunt Clay in later years. After the war his enemies prevailed upon the owner of the bordello to sue Clay for violating the civil rights of the house staff, and, incredibly enough, the court found for the plaintiff. However, the United States Government reimbursed Clay for the damages, even though it could do nothing to silence the snickers of his fellow citizens.

Three weeks later there was another parade, as another Lexington unit left for the war. This time it was K Company for the First Kentucky Cavalry, and in its ranks were many of the bloods of the city, including John Hunt Morgan and some of his friends from Transylvania.

I had reason to wish they had left a week earlier.

It was June, and I had finished another — and my last — year at the little two-room schoolhouse in the settlement of Foxtown. It was the United States' first wartime summer in over thirty years, the papers were full of General Taylor's victories at Palo Alto and Resaca, and I thought long thoughts on mortality. Since thinking on one's mortality often seems to stimulate those generative impulses which are man's only answer to that mortality, I began to spend a considerable part of my time being accidentally near Laurel Tate's house.

My relationship with Laurel had never recovered from the hoodoo night. It was as if she held me personally responsible for the terror she had felt during that awful chase through the darkness, and the feeling of repugnance she had for Negroes seemed to include me as well. All during the fall and winter months, she had found excuses for not coming out at night to court, until I had given up asking her.

Lately, however, I fancied I could detect a change in her manner. She had developed a provocative way of looking at me sideways, under arched brows, and she tossed her head like Sacajawea on a frosty morning. Her figure had developed impressively over the winter months.

I "accidentally" encountered her one morning as she was feeding the family poultry. "Well, if it ain't that dashing gentleman, Hacey Miller," she said, with one hand on a firmly rounded hip. "We're surely flattered to see him again, ain't we, Goosey?" she asked a nearby fowl.

"Hello, Laurel," I said in my most casual manner. "It's a nice day, isn't it? How you been? I see you're feeding the poultry."

"Well, if that don't beat all! I never suspicioned a big strong man like you would know anything about woman's work."

"There's all sorts of things about women I know about," I said significantly.

"Oh, is there? How'd you learn them? Out of books? Or from looking in niggers' windows?"

"Don't you wish you knew?" I replied with a leer.

"No," she said crushingly, and cast a handful of corn to the flock.

I tried a new tack. "You know, I've been thinking about you a lot, Laurel."

"You have? Well, I declare."

"Yes, I really have. About how nice it was to — to talk to you, and everything. You know, those nice walks we used to have, at night? And how well we got along together? Remember?"

"Lots of water run over the dam since then, Hacey."

"I know, Laurel, but — what if I was to come by tonight and whistle under your window, like I used to? I mean, we wouldn't have to *do* anything. We could just talk and get to be friends again, like last summer."

She took a deep breath and arched her back. "Maybe I've got plenty of friends now, new friends. Maybe I don't need no more friends. Did you ever think of that?"

"Look, Laurel, everybody needs all the friends they can get," I said desperately. "Now you just keep awake tonight, and I'll come by and give you a whistle, and we can have a nice walk like before. All I want to do is talk to you, really," I lied.

"Tonight?" asked Laurel, with a little frown of concentration.

"Yes, tonight, about eleven."

"Well, there's nothing to stop you from walking anywhere you want to, and if you want to whistle under somebody's window, I don't reckon you're breaking no law. I ain't promising you'll do yourself any good, though." And turning away, she resumed her chores.

But I didn't get a chance to whistle under her window that night. Josh Brain came to dinner, and he and Father sat late at table. After dinner they decided to begin my instruction in the law, and I was invited to join them for what would have been under other circumstances a stimulating discussion of Anglo-Saxon jurisprudence. However, it was wasted on me that night. My eyes kept turning to the face of the clock on the sideboard as the hands inched toward eleven. Normally Brain took his leave by ten o'clock at the latest, for he lived over an hour's ride from Hazelwood. But tonight he was on his hobbyhorse, and quite oblivious of time. Finally Father suggested that he spend the night with us, so as not to interrupt the discussion. My inward groans were inaudible, and the conversation continued until well past one o'clock.

The next evening found me chafing at the bit. The family retired early, and by eleven I was under Laurel's window, whistling imitation birdcalls. There was no response. "Laurel," I whispered, "I'm sorry I couldn't come last night. A man came over to talk about me studying law. I couldn't have got out of the house till after one in the morning. Laurel? You hear me, Laurel?" No response. "Laurel? I know you can hear me. Gosh darn it, there's no reason to get mad. I said I was sorry."

After five minutes of whispered explanations and apologies, I gave it up. Either she was sleeping like a log, or she had moved her bed to another room, I thought. The moon was almost full, trees and meadow were brushed with silver, and there was that nighttime feeling of *presence* in the air — of a multitude of unseen and almost unheard creatures close about me, carrying on their invisible lives with never-ending vitality. I just couldn't go straight back home and go to bed, with all the unexpended energy within me and around me. I decided to cut across the fields to the pike and then walk down it to our cutoff, making my return home a sort of semicircle instead of the straight line by which I had come.

The pike stretched out empty in the moonlight, a track of silence running through the murmurous trees and fields on either side. I walked slowly along it, enjoying its loneliness in a self-pitying way. "You're never going to get a girl, Hacey Miller," I said to myself. "All your life long you'll hear other people talking about it and you'll never get to do it yourself, you'll never know what it feels like, and that miserable little peewee thing you're carrying around between your legs might just as well be an extra thumb for all the good it's ever going to do you." Then I branched off into a speculation on what it would be like to have an extra thumb there, and what you could do with it if you had it. This was such a rewarding line of thought that it almost made me miss seeing the buggy that was pulled off the road, about twenty feet up a grassy path that led into the trees.

Instinctively I stepped off the road and out of the moonlight, into the shadowy woods. I could see the buggy clearly, with the horse in the shafts, placidly grazing, and the man on the seat, who was sprawled out in a way suggesting boredom. He was whistling a waltz between his teeth. Something about him seemed familiar. Curious, I slipped quietly between the trees until I was only ten feet from the buggy, where I had an unobstructed view of it and the little clearing around it.

A gentle breeze caused the branches overhead to sway, so the silvery moonlight shifted and swam like reflections on water. But it was enough to allow me to identify the man in the seat of the buggy. It was Sheepface — Morgan's crony, whom I had last seen in the company of Pudgy. At the memory of my last sight of Pudgy — a memory I had stubbornly refused to recall — a shudder of horror and disgust ran through me.

Then I saw something else, something on the ground, a few feet from the buggy. For a second my eye was baffled by its shape and movement, and the play of light and shadow upon it. Then Sheepface spoke.

"Lordy, Galt," he drawled, "don't ream her out. Leave something for me, boy — I want to get mine off too."

From the chiaroscuro on the grass emerged two figures, joined in thrusting urgency. Laurel Tate lay on her back, white thighs raised in the air, legs wrapped around her partner's waist, face almost unrecognizable in its lascivious abandon. Panting over her was Galt Ledyard, a look of desperation on his face, as though he were struggling with a task beyond his powers.

I stood there in the shadows and watched, unable to move. The lovers grunted and gasped, the horse nickered softly as he grazed, and Sheepface shifted his position on the buggy seat. A little voice in my brain spoke with dreadful irony: "At least now you know how it's done, Hacey."

A minute passed, two minutes, and suddenly my paralysis was gone and I knew I had to get away before Sheepface took his turn. I regained the road quickly, and dogtrotted along to the cutoff, and then down it to our house, without a moment's pause.

All during the sleepless hours that followed, the knowledge kept returning to me that now there were three things that didn't bear thinking about: a cherrywood box with curious carved figures, a fat young man with an opened throat, and a gasping girl with her legs silver in the moonlight.

How many things can a person not think about in this life, I wondered.

Five days later, the First Kentucky Cavalry rode off to war, and in the ranks, riding beside his friend John Hunt

Morgan, was the man I knew as Sheepface. Galt Ledyard was not with them. It was understood that his family felt he was too young.

If Laurel was in the crowd that saw them off, she watched them with new life already quickening in her womb.

Before the summer was over, she married the tenant farmer of a tobacco farm near Nicholasville. Their baby was some four months "premature."

X

The Handwriting on the Wall

I MOVED INTO LEXINGTON in late August. My rooms were
on North Upper Street, three blocks from the college. I had
a large parlor, a bedroom for myself and a little cubicle for
Jubal, and the privilege of the kitchen. It was comfortable
as well as convenient.

The prospect of living my own life free of direct supervision excited me mightily. I indulged in erotic fantasies and
staged great festivals of debauchery in my mind. But that
palled quickly enough, and within a week or two I was settled in a routine which was to last through most of my three
years at Transylvania.

Five days a week, I attended lectures in the mornings.
Two afternoons a week, Wednesday and Thursday, I reported to Josh Brain's law office at 1:00 P.M. Court Day
afternoons I spent in the county courthouse, watching whatever legal actions Brain felt would be most educational. The
rest of the time was my own, for studying mathematics, rhet-
oric, philosophy, Greek, Latin and the law. Weekends Jubal
and I returned to Hazelwood. Since I was a year or two
younger than most of my classmates, and since I was by no

means a mental marvel, this schedule allowed me little time for idle amusement.

Jubal also settled easily into our routine. His duties were simple — preparing breakfast and supper, shopping two or three times a week, keeping my small wardrobe presentable and our rooms in order — but he managed to make them occupy most of his days, so that whenever my father needed him at the store he had to send over for him. Jubal wasn't especially lazy, but, like an old soldier, he saw no point in volunteering for any task.

The day we moved in, Jubal was hanging up my clothes as I unpacked a small chest full of my personal possessions. Right on top was the little cherrywood box. I picked it up and started to put it on top of my bureau, then I noticed Jubal. He stood motionless, and his eyes were fixed on the box.

"Oh, Jube, did you ever see this? Look here." I handed it to him, and he took it reluctantly. "Star carved it for me for a present. You know what it is?"

"No, sir, Mr. Hacey, I sure don't," answered Jubal vehemently.

"It's what they call a wanga. It's kind of a good luck charm. Star said it would bring me good luck all my life." I didn't feel it was necessary to go into the conditions.

"I don't know nothing about nothing like that — I ain't never learned, and I ain't about to now." He handed back the box. "You want I should sponge off your good black suit?"

"Oh, I guess so." I set the box on top of the bureau and studied the carved design for a moment. "Jube, did you or 'Shach or Hessie ever hear anything from Star after he disappeared last year?"

"No, sir."

"Not even where he might have been going, or anything?"

"No, sir, Mr. Hacey. He be anywhere in the whole creation for all I know." He lowered his voice and added, "Or
for all I care, either."

I looked at him in surprise. "Why, Jube, I thought you
liked Star!"

"Sometimes folks act nice to somebody 'cause it ain't
healthy not to. I don't know where that nigger is, or what he
done, and I ain't studying to find out. And if I was you, Mr.
Hacey, I wouldn't either. I better get at sponging that suit
now."

And that was all I could get out of him, then or later.

Although Jubal and I lived together for almost three
years, the only things I ever learned about him were physical facts. He had a fine singing voice. He was a better-than-
average cook. He had a hernia. Aside from these and other
equally superficial observations, I cannot describe him at all.
I don't even know if he liked me. On reflection, I doubt if
he did, since the only real relationship we had was as master
and slave.

*   *   *

One evening during the first week of my first term, Falk
Padgett came over to my rooms to study with me, and after
that he started coming twice a week. These visits became a
pattern, and accounted for some of the pleasantest hours of
my college career.

Falk's education had progressed erratically since Elam
Yates began to tutor him in the back room of the store. He
could read and write very well, could do his sums, and knew
his multiplication tables. Of geography and natural science
he was almost completely innocent, and his knowledge of history was a mosaic of awareness and ignorance that reflected
Elam's own highly specialized interests.

Falk and I were both fond of popcorn, and we would sit at the table in the parlor with a huge bowl of it between us, freshly popped and buttered and salted. Like as not, I would be struggling with Cicero's irregular verbs, and Falk would have a world atlas propped up on the inkwell in front of him. "Come on, Hasty, let's do Italy," he'd say. Grateful for the momentary interruption, I would agree, and he would close the atlas on his finger. "Papal States, Tuscany, Parma, Lucca, Modena, Lombardy, Venetia, Genoa — and the Kingdom of the Two Sardines!" He grinned proudly.

"No, no, Falk, you're mixing two of them up together. There's the Kingdom of Sardinia, and then there's the Kingdom of the Two Sicilies, which is down in the south end. It's ruled by the Spanish Bourbons."

"You reckon they're as tasty as the Kentucky bourbons?"

"Falk, if you don't buckle down, you're going to stay as ignorant as an old hound dog all your days! Now hush up and let me work!" And I'd seize a handful of buttery popcorn and return to the Roman Senate.

My busy and comfortable routine insulated me from the war fever, which was abating anyway. I remember hearing we had taken California, and Taylor had fought another battle, at Monterey, but neither of these events seemed as important as an approaching trigonometry quiz.

Right after the first of the year came word that Cassius M. Clay and most of the Lexington Light Infantry had been captured by the Mexicans at a little town called Encarnación. Apparently the Mexican officer in charge had ordered all the gringos executed; Clay had stepped forward and presented his chest to the officer's pistol. "If your sense of honor allows you to take the lives of unarmed soldiers," he said scornfully, "take mine — but spare my men!" The officer rescinded the order. Later, on the grueling prisoners' march to Mexico City, Clay insisted on sharing his horse, the only one in the group, with the enlisted men of his company. For a day or two everybody in Lexington was singing the praises of C. M. Clay.

"I declare, human beings are almost as entertaining as a flea circus, if you can keep from losing your sense of humor," Josh Brain said one afternoon, over a glass of hot punch in the taproom of the Phoenix Hotel. (I was drinking fragrant apple cider, spiced with lemon, cinnamon and raisins.) "When you hear them gabbling like geese about Cash Clay's exploits, it's instructive to remember that not so long ago they wanted his head on a pike and his giblets on toast." He paused to light one of the twisted Havana cheroots to which he was addicted, took a deep puff, and went on reflectively, "After he gets back with all his medals, and after the testimonial dinner and the band concert and the presentation of the engraved saber, how long do you reckon it will be until they're out after his hide again?"

"I guess that depends on how much agitating he does, and I suppose most people figure he won't be doing much. After all, he is supporting the war."

"So is Bob Todd's son-in-law up in Illinois. So is Henry Clay. So are most of the Whig Party, except for a handful of 'Conscience Whigs' in New England. It's the old 'My country right or wrong' spirit — and incidentally somebody ought to take a good hard look at *that* chestnut some day! But cast your speculations ahead a year or two, Hacey. What's the slavery situation going to be after the war?"

I thought a moment. "Pretty much the same as it was before, I guess."

"Wrong. It's going to be *worse,* a devil of a lot worse. You don't believe me? I'll prove it to you." His voice took on the pompous and orotund tone it always acquired in the courtroom. "Your Honor, I'd like to place these two documents in evidence. The first is a map of the North American continent. The second is the docket of this Court.

"Let us look at the map first. Here, from the Atlantic coast to just past the Mississippi River are the thirty States of the Union, counting Wisconsin, which will be in any day now." He sketched an invisible map on the tabletop with a sausagelike finger. "Fifteen of them are slave states and fifteen are free. A perfect balance, right? Wrong again! Because look: When Henry Clay got the South to agree to the Missouri Compromise, they decided that if Missouri was to come in slave, from then on, any other new states north of the southern border of Missouri — in other words, any other states even with her on the map — would come in *free*. Back in 1820 the Southern politicians thought they had gotten the best of the bargain, because they already had their eyes on Texas and New Mexico and California, and Oregon was blocked off from the North by the agreement with England for joint occupancy, and most of the territory in between was plains and deserts they didn't figure could ever be inhabited by white men anyway.

"But since then the picture has changed a mite, Your Honor. In the first place, the population of the North has increased twice as fast as the South's. That means that although there are still an even number of senators on both sides, there are a whale of a lot more congressmen from the free states. Next, it don't look as though slavery is going to work out in any of the new western states, even if it's allowed, because cotton won't grow there — and for some reason, the only places where slavery pays off is where you grow cotton. And as far as those supposedly uninhabitable deserts go, why, it's a damn shame how inhabitable they've turned out to be for Yankee sodbusters. And to top it all off, Eng-

138

land went and agreed to let us have Oregon all to ourselves up to the forty-ninth parallel, and that means more free states as sure as God made goldfish. So what it all amounts to is that war or no war, Texas or no Texas, the South has painted itself into a corner and can't get out. There just ain't going to be any more slave states than there are now."

The rotund lawyer emptied his glass and smacked his lips. "This pleading is thirsty work, Your Honor. And even though we're discussing the approach of Armageddon, there's no reason to be uncomfortable while we're doing it. Boy!" he called to a passing darky waiter in a new white jacket, "I'll thank you to recapitulate the synthesis of these libations with maximum celerity. In other words —"

"I know, Mr. Brain. You all want some more drinks." He went off briskly to fill the order. Brain was a good customer.

"Sometimes the speed with which the subject race advances toward mental parity awes me," he mused. Then, in another tone entirely, he added, "And that's a pompous Old Massa remark if I ever made one. Hacey, when everything in society conspires to convince you that you are a superior creation of the Almighty, it's hard to keep reminding yourself that you're just another berry on the vine — but it's worth your undying soul to forget."

We sat in silence until the drinks came. Then Brain assuaged his thirst and resumed his plea. "Your Honor, you'll remember I placed two exhibits in evidence. I'd now like to move to Exhibit B — the docket of this Court.

"If you will leaf through the pages of this book and jot down all the crimes committed by Negroes against whites this year, you'll find the list is half again as long as a similar list for last year would be — or indeed, for any previous year. Poisonings, with rat poison, toadstools and ground glass, infants suffocated with pillows by faithful old nurses,

horsemen breaking their necks because grooms cut through
the bellybands of their saddles with razors, ladies of fashion
burned to death because a maid "accidentally" touched a
lighted candle to a petticoat — pick any clandestine kind of
homicide you like, and I'll show it to you on the list! Nobody likes to talk about it, Hacey, but since so many of the
young men left for the Mexican War, the blacks are losing
the docility which many of us have always confused with
contentment. You remember that poisoning trial you were
so interested in back in 'forty-five?"

"Yes, sir."

"It was a seven days' wonder then — on opening day you
could hardly find a seat in the courtroom. Today it wouldn't
draw enough spectators for a game of whist. It's common-
place; 'Another nigger murdered his master, I see. Ho hum,
what's the news from Frankfort?' "

He interrupted himself to order another glass of punch,
and relit the cold stump of his cheroot, which did nothing to
improve its aroma. "Hacey," he resumed, "do you know
what a maroon is?"

"I guess it's somebody who's marooned on a desert is-
land."

"That's one meaning. Another is a fugitive slave. Right
now there are thousands and thousands of maroons right
here in the South, great gangs of them, armed and living in
their own outlaw towns hidden away in swamps and forests.
I've heard that there are better than a thousand of them in
just one camp in the Dismal Swamp in North Carolina, and
there are camps in practically every slave state except Kentucky. Sometimes they get out of hand and start pillaging
and raping and burning down outlying plantations, and it
usually takes a regiment of militia to put them down."

"I've never heard about that, Mr. Brain."

"No, you wouldn't, unless you made an effort to find out. It's another subject the master class doesn't like to talk about. But it's true, nonetheless. Why, do you know that during the Seminole War down in Florida there were hundreds of nigger maroons fighting right alongside the Indians, and the soldiers who fought them said they were crueler and cunninger and more bloodthirsty than the Seminoles themselves? How well do you think you'd sleep at night if your plantation was on the edge of Okefenokee Swamp?"

"Not too well."

"Not too well is a considerable understatement." He turned the glass in his fingers, watching the liquid bead on the smooth inner surface. "Let me sum up the evidence that has been produced from our two exhibits, Your Honor, and we'll see if we can read the handwriting on the wall.

"The slave-owning South is committed to an economic system which cannot successfully be planted in any new states. It is doomed to see itself becoming an ever-smaller percentage of the American Empire, as the population of the North and West leapfrogs upward, as factories multiply, as railroads join both oceans and speed the bounty of free agriculture to the cities.

"Morosely watching all this, the planter becomes aware that the slaves themselves are moving toward insurrection. They are fleeing to the Free States, building fortresses in swamps, putting arsenic in the baby's milk. The unfairness of it! For they are his property — it was because of them that the whole beleaguered edifice of slave-owning society was built. How can they be so ungrateful?

"Since he's a man and not an angel, the planter concludes it's because some damned outsider has seduced the simple souls from their natural loyalty. It's the abolitionist, of course. If it wasn't for him, things would still be like they

141

used to be — happy niggers singing in the cotton fields, love-able "Mammy" and "Auntie" and "Uncle" koochy-kooing gurgling white babies, and the planter taking his ease on the veranda, surveying all he is lord of.

"It really never was that way, even in the beginning, but you can't tell him that. He can't see anymore — his eyes are too full of blood. All he can think of is, he's going to stop those damned agitators from stirring up his niggers, and he's, by God, going to *keep those niggers in their place!* Even if he has to kill half of them and sell the other half down the river to do it.

"And so a spiral is formed, something like the funnel of a tornado. The planter increases the pressure of discipline on the Negro. The wretched Negro, made more wretched than before, makes increased efforts either to escape or to fight back. If he escapes, he tells his story up North, and a new crop of abolitionists is born. If he fights back, he's either killed or hounded into hiding, and either way is used as an example to justify even more repressive measures. Meanwhile the power and wealth of the Free States increase. The North and West are wrapped around the South like a python, and freedom for the black is only the width of a river away . . .

"Your Honor, what do *you* think will happen when this war's over and the young Southron soldiers take off their uniforms and address themselves to solving the problems on the plantations they expect to inherit in a few years?"

He emptied his glass, sighed in acknowledgment of the pleasure it afforded him, crossed his legs and patted his belly, and regarded me with bright questioning eyes. I took a few seconds to get my thoughts in order.

"It sounds like you said — that things are going to get worse. Even more than that, it sounds like things are hopeless, and there's nothing anybody can do about it. Is that really what you think, Mr. Brain?"

"Thou sayest, Hacey, thou sayest." He got to his feet a trifle unsteadily, left some money on the table for our drinks, and led the way out of the taproom. Our discussion for the day was finished.

XI

---·•·---

"Choice Stock"

It was about this time that I took my first tentative steps onto the dance floors of life.

Every two weeks Madame Mentelle's boarding school, which my sister Rosalie attended, played hostess to the young gallants of Lexington at a ball. These "Fortnightlies," as they were called, attracted many of my classmates from Transylvania, including a certain Danford Ranew, on whom my sister had developed a furious schoolgirl crush. To ensure that Ranew continued to attend all Fortnightlies faithfully, Rosalie decided to teach me to dance so that I could bring him with me every alternate Saturday night. It was a struggle for both of us.

The arena was the drawing room at Hazelwood, and the time was every Saturday afternoon. Mother would play waltzes on the harmonium and Rosalie and I would spin around the floor determinedly. My main problem was that in Lexington society at the time the waltz was danced with both partners rotating counterclockwise only. It was as if you kept winding yourself up all the time and never got a chance to let your works run down. After two or three minutes of it, my *"one*-two-three, *one*-two-three" had degenerated into a drunken stumble, and like as not I had taken the first step or two up my sister's ankles.

"Mama, don't you see? He's just not trying," she would cry. "Hacey, you're a clumsy clod, and I hate you! I really don't know why I go on trying to help you like this."

"I reckon you're a victim of your own generous nature," I would reply.

"Hacey, you mind your manners," Mother would say. "Your sister is only trying to keep you from becoming a social pariah. Now dance." And around we'd go again.

In a matter of a few weeks I was dubiously judged proficient enough at what my sister called, in my case, "Tripping the Light Ridiculous" to be ordered to collar Danford Ranew and drag him to the Fortnightly. Not that this was difficult. The fellow seemed as attracted to my sister as she was to him. I couldn't understand it, but I figured everybody has a right to be a plain damned fool in his own way.

I suppose Ranew was considered quite a catch, particularly for a girl like Rosalie, whose people were neither rich nor prominent. Ranew and I weren't close friends, but we got along well enough, until a certain evening in the late summer of 1847.

Ranew's family was kin to the Wickliffes, and he'd always had too much money for his own good. Also he had an unusually poor head for whiskey for a seventeen-year-old Kentuckian. When he appeared at my rooms one night about eight, both of these flaws were in evidence. Jubal gave me an oblique look as he held the door wide and Ranew lurched in.

He was wearing skintight riding breeches and boots, a tailcoat and a frilled shirt, all considerably the worse for wear. He looked like he had fallen into the mud on the way over. His face was flushed, his mouth foolishly agape.

"Hacey, you're a good old boy, you son of a bitch, you.

Love your sister. Angel. How son of a bitch like you could have such an angel for a sister, can't understand it. But going to do you a favor, because you're her brother. Good old boy. Give me a drink."

"Come in here, Danford. Jubal, take Mr. Ranew's hat, and then see if you can find that bottle of applejack Falk Padgett brought over last week."

"Applejack!" Ranew swayed on his heels indignantly. "You expect a Kentucky gentleman to drink applejack? Bourbon, sir!" he shouted. "Bourbon!"

"If you want a drink, you'll drink applejack, because that's all I got. Now sit down before you fall down." I steered him to a chair and seated him. Jubal appeared with a glass of home-brew applejack, and Ranew took a noisy pull at it. "What's the big favor you're going to do me, Danford?"

"Favor?" He looked at me blankly for a moment, then remembered what had brought him. "You and me, men of the world, Miller. Understand each other. Know about how men are. Rosalie wouldn't understand. Angel. Got to protect her. Two kinds of women, Miller. Kind you bed and kind you marry. You understand."

"If you came over here to take me to a whorehouse, Danford, then I'm sorry you wasted your time. I just don't happen to want to go to those places, that's all. I've had plenty of chances, but I just plain turned them down." This was completely untrue, of course. I had never turned down an opportunity to go to a whorehouse, because I'd never been offered one. I'd seen the blowsy drabs soliciting from their windows down by the railroad tracks, and the modicum of desire they kindled in me was overmatched by a large amount of fear and disgust. So it wasn't hard to refuse his offer — or what I thought was his offer.

He shook his head indignantly. "No, no, Miller, not whorehouse. You don't understand. I'm talking about Robards' Choice Stock!"

I gasped in surprise. In every way, Robards' Choice Stock was a horse of a different color. Lewis C. Robards was the most famous "nigger buyer" in central Kentucky. A few years earlier, he had rented the old Lexington Theater on Short Street and begun using it for his slave auctions, and within a short time more black livestock passed under his hammer every week than was sold at the public auctions on Cheapside.

Next door to the theater was a modest two-story building, well-kept, with brightly painted shutters and flowers in the narrow garden that bordered the street. This was where Robards had his office, and also where, as every white male in Lexington over the age of ten knew, he kept his "Choice Stock" — his most desirable, his most voluptuous, his lightest-complexioned women. To their rooms he reputedly conducted qualified buyers — men who could afford to spend $1800 to bring a little extra enjoyment into their lives — who were then allowed to conduct private examinations of the merchandise. But only up to a point. Robards drew the line at a shopworn inventory.

"Robards' Choice Stock?" I said unbelievingly. "How in tarnation would you get in to see Robards' Choice Stock?"

"Father," he said owlishly. "Father bought six thousand dollars' worth of niggers from Robards today. Robards invited him to come over tonight, look over good stuff. Only Father had to go back home. So I get to go instead. You and me, Hacey, you good old son of a bitch." He giggled and reached out to punch me on the arm. I moved away and he missed, almost falling out of his chair and slopping applejack down his fawn-colored coat.

I had mixed emotions. On the one hand, I was tired of being "son-of-a-bitch-ed" by this loose-mouthed young souse and could hardly wait to see his back going out the door — and on the other hand, I confess I had a powerful curiosity to see the inside of Robards' parlor.

So I procrastinated. "Jubal," I called, "get some coffee for Mr. Ranew."

"Coffee, hell," cried Ranew in outrage.

"Look, Danford, you're in no damned condition to go to Robards' or anywhere else. Now here's what we'll do. You drink yourself a cup of hot coffee and clean yourself up a little — maybe Jubal can brush some of that mud off your coat — and then in a half hour or so, if you still feel like it, we'll go over." I figured the chances were fifty-fifty he'd fall asleep in the chair. Then I'd move him to the sofa and let him sleep through the night. The alternative was that he would be sufficiently sobered by the coffee to manage the visit to Robards' little house. It was in God's hands.

God must have blinked about then, because in half an hour Ranew had drunk three cups of black coffee and was apparently considerably sobered. His coat brushed and his cravat retied, he was eager to be off, and I agreed to accompany him.

We passed the darkened mass of the Lexington Theater and turned into the gate of the house that adjoined it. We rang, and the door was opened by an extremely dignified old darky in a blue claw-hammer coat with brass buttons. "Mr. Ranew and Mr. Miller," Danford told him. "We were invited by Mr. Robards."

"Certainly, sir." He bowed and stepped to one side. "Won't you follow me to the parlor, gentlemen? Mr. Robards is engaged, but I'm sure he'll be free to welcome you directly." He led us across a small hallway and, pulling open a pair of sliding doors, showed us into the celebrated Robards parlor.

It was an attractive room, furnished in a handsome though heavy style I later learned was called Empire. The mantel was of gracefully carved rose marble, and above it was a large gilt-framed painting of the abduction of a group of nude women by a gang — or herd — of centaurs. An inlaid desk stood in one corner. The wallpaper was hand painted, and a rich oriental rug covered most of the brilliantly waxed floor.

While I was admiring the sumptuousness of the appointments, the Negro asked if we would care for a drink while we waited. Ranew answered for both of us, and soon we were each holding a brandy balloon half-filled with the most dulcet bourbon whiskey I had ever tasted. To this the old darky added an inch or two of cool, clear limestone water, nothing else. With whiskey like that, only a savage would alter the flavor.

We must have waited for Robards for fifteen minutes, and during that time Ranew finished his drink and had another. He was holding his glass out for a third when the doors slid open and Robards entered.

He was a middle-aged man with gray hair, a high color, a pitted face, and cold blue eyes, dressed all in black except for his snowy white dress shirt. He bowed his head quickly but formally. "Good evening, Mr. Ranew. Even though your father has disappointed me, I'm delighted you and your friend could visit us." He nodded toward me inquiringly. "Mr. — ?"

"Present my friend, Mr. Miller," said Ranew thickly. With misgivings I realized that he had more than lost all the ground he had gained at my rooms; he was thoroughly and lumpishly drunk.

Robards raised his eyebrows a fraction of an inch, then leaned forward to shake my hand. "Delighted to make your acquaintance, sir. I hope Fortune will provide me with the opportunity of serving you and your family some day. Until then, it's my pleasure to have you inspect my establishment."

"Thank you, sir, it's a pleasure to be here," I replied, dry-mouthed.

"And now, Hannibal, why don't you summon our four nymphs to the parlor? Meanwhile I think I'll pour myself a soupçon of that good bourbon and branch water. And may I refresh your glasses, gentlemen?" His eyes flickered from Danford, slumped in his armchair, his gaze turned to some inward vision, to me, nervously cupping my snifter in both hands.

"No, thank you, Mr. Robards, I'm still drinking this. It's very good," I hastened to add, as if his feelings might be hurt that I was drinking so slowly.

He mixed himself a drink and then engaged me in small talk — where I went to college and what I was studying, who my people were — he didn't know my father personally, but was well acquainted with Cousin Whitney Ledyard. He was courtly and polite, and made me feel he was really interested in my answers to his questions. I was actually sorry when we were interrupted.

For about one second.

Four young women came into the room together. In age I would guess they ranged from seventeen to twenty-two, in color from warm café au lait through olive and the palest flush of copper to an alabaster white shadowed with violet, in shape from compactly rounded to statuesque. They were gowned as for a formal ball, and groomed to the very height of fashion. They were the most beautiful women I had ever seen.

The first girl to enter stepped into the middle of the room, while the remaining three stood grouped by the door. Robards rose to meet her and took her by the wrist, turning her slowly as he spoke. Danford Ranew's fuddled brain came back from wherever it had been, and he leaned forward in his seat.

"Gentlemen, allow me to present Cathy for your approval. This lovely creature is, to the best of my calculation, one-sixteenth black. She was raised in gentle surroundings, in the home in which her mother was a maid. Her father was one of the largest landowners in the western part of the state, a widower with no legitimate children, and he spared no expense on his dusky daughter's education. She speaks French, is adept at needlework, and performs creditably on the pianoforte. Her nature is docile and loving." The girl, whose face was white as mine, except for a faint shading of copper where the light struck highlights, stared expressionlessly at the walls as Robards turned her until she was in profile to us. She stood straight and motionless as he cupped one firm breast in his hand. "As you see, she is handsomely endowed . . ." He lifted the breast slightly, then let it drop back against his palm. ". . . and eager to lose her sweet innocence . . ." He slid his hand down her belly. ". . . and break the back of some lucky stud. Aren't you, my dear?" His hand slipped between her legs, and I could see his fingers moving against the fabric of her dress. My mouth tasted of brass.

Danford Ranew began to struggle to his feet. "Taking her to her room for private examination," he said thickly.

Robards gauged his condition with one quick glance. "I'm

afraid I can't allow a private examination tonight. Perhaps some other day, when your father is with you. Just keep your seat and allow me to present Melissa."

"Hell with that. Said I wanted a private examination of this bitch."

"I'm sorry. I'm afraid you're not going out of this room with her."

"Then I'll do it here — I don't give a damn." He grabbed Cathy by the arm and pulled her toward him. He fell back in his chair and jerked her down on his lap. Robards' face turned pasty white. "Let her go, Ranew," he said icily.

"First thing, let's examine those tits," said Danford. Using both hands, he ripped her dress open to the waist, exposing two firm round breasts, with nipples of palest pink. Cathy tried to cover herself with her hands, but Danford seized her wrists, twisted her arms behind her and buried his face between her breasts.

Robards stepped quickly across the room and pulled open a drawer in the desk. The three other girls began to scream. "Danford, for God's sake stop it," I shouted. "Let her go, do you hear? Let her go!" I grabbed his shoulder and tried to pull him away from the girl, whose lovely face was as empty of emotion as though she had been drugged.

Then Robards was beside me, a riding quirt in one hand, a silver-mounted pistol in the other. He struck Ranew savagely across the back of the neck with the quirt, then a second time, then a third. The skin parted on the third blow, and blood lay glittering between hair and collar. Only then did the pain reach Ranew's torpid brain, and he raised his head from the girl's bosom and shook it stupidly as he tried to understand what was happening to him.

Robards pressed the muzzle of the pistol against Ranew's left eyeball. "This is a pistol, and it's loaded," he said in a low flat voice. "I'd hate to blow your brains all over my parlor, you drunken swine, but I'll do it in two seconds unless you take your hands off that girl. Now!" The last word cracked like a whip, and slowly Ranew's hands opened, releasing Cathy, who rose to her feet and pulled the torn dress together across her breasts. "All right, Cathy, you and the others go back to your rooms." Cathy backed away from us, her gaze never leaving the pistol pressing against Ranew's eye. As she reached the door, she spoke for the first time.

"Kill the white trash, Mr. Robards," she said in a genteel but husky voice that made a tingle run through my whole body.

The slave trader laughed. "If I killed everybody who wanted to diddle my girls, I wouldn't have any customers left, would I? Now go to your rooms." After a moment's hesitation, Cathy followed the other three from the room, and old Hannibal closed the sliding doors behind them.

Robards withdrew the muzzle of the pistol from Danford's eye, smiled down at him coldly and turned to me. "Mr. Miller, I have nothing against you but the company you keep. So I'm prepared to do you a favor. If you don't want your charming friend here cowhided with this quirt and marked for life, get him out of here right now."

"Sir, I wouldn't call him a friend of mine, not any more. But I'll take him home. I wouldn't want to see him all scarred up." I took Ranew by the arm and pulled him up from the chair. He was unresisting and seemed dazed. I led him from the parlor into the entrance hall. "I'm sorry he behaved like that, Mr. Robards," I said politely — and then blurted out, "but it was the way you treated that nigger girl that made him do it. I think you're worse than he is. At least he was drunk."

"Goodbye, Mr. Miller," he answered laconically as he

opened the door. "I don't expect I'll ever see you here again. Please don't surprise me."

I never did.

I took Ranew back to my rooms for the rest of the night, and the next morning told him I wanted him to stop his attentions to my sister. He tried to argue, but when I threatened to tell the entire story not only to Rosalie but to our classmates at Transylvania as well, he had no choice but to acquiesce. I watched him as he descended the stairs, the new scab on the back of his neck scowling up at me like a second mouth.

Rosalie couldn't understand why he stopped coming to the Fortnightlies. But soon she had other beaux, and in a month or two she had forgotten Danford. I envied her that. It must be wonderful, I thought, to be a beautiful and desirable girl, with no thoughts in your head except boys and clothes.

Then, remembering Cathy, I amended the thought: But only if you are *sixteen*-sixteenths white.

XII

———•———

A TIME TO PLANT

CASSIUS M. CLAY returned to Lexington in November of '47, and received the hero's welcome Josh Brain had predicted for him. Everybody turned out to see it. Robert S. Todd delivered the oration, the Light Infantry Band played patriotic airs, and a five-year-old girl presented him with an armful of flowers and received a sound kiss on the cheek for her reward.

Clay and Todd passed only a few feet from me on their way to their carriage. On an impulse I pushed through the crowd. "Mr. Clay! Mr. Clay! Welcome home," I shouted.

Clay heard me, and for a second a puzzled look crossed his face. Then he placed me and put out his great paw to shake hands. "Why, if it isn't Elam Yates' friend — Hacey, isn't it? Hacey Miller? You've done some growing, boy."

"I'm glad you got back all right, Mr. Clay. We were worried about you."

"Thank you. I was a bit worried myself. Are you living in Lexington now?"

"Yes, sir. I'm going to Transylvania College and reading law."

"Well, come by Thorn Hill some afternoon, and we'll

catch up on old times over a glass of root beer." He gave my hand a final squeeze and continued through the crowd, exchanging greetings and shaking hands with scores of spectators.

It was two weeks before I took Clay up on his invitation. During the interim I had started to walk up North Limestone a number of times, only to turn off before I reached Fifth Street and Thorn Hill. "He didn't really mean that about paying him a visit," I would tell myself. "What would he want to talk to a young sprat like you about? Can't you tell when somebody is just being polite?" But finally the day came when my admiration and my curiosity overcame my shyness, and I knocked on his door.

He opened the door himself, and his heavy features brightened with a smile when he recognized me. "Ah, my friend Hacey Miller, come for his root beer — and about time, too. Come in, young fellow."

He took me into his study, offered me a worn and comfortable armchair and rang for a servant. "Bring this gentleman a big cold glass of our justly famous root beer, Timothy — unless your dissipated college tastes incline toward something stronger, Hacey?"

"Oh, no, sir — root beer's fine."

"And a cold toddy for me," he added. He sat down in a chair facing mine and brushed back the shock of black hair that had fallen nearly to his eyes. "Now tell me about yourself. What are you planning to do with your life, Hacey?"

"After I finish at Transylvania I figure to go into Mr. Brain's law office and get admitted to the Bar."

"You mean Josh Brain, here in Lexington?"

"Yes, sir, he's a friend of my father's."

"I know him. He's as good a lawyer as there is in the

Bluegrass. So you want to spend your life practicing law, do you? You must enjoy it."

"Well, from what I've seen of it, I don't enjoy it all that much," I admitted. "But I want to be in politics, and Father and Mr. Brain say that's how to do it."

"Oh, there's more than one way to skin a cat. But why are you so anxious to enter politics?"

I hesitated a moment, because I felt awkward answering the question. "To try to get rid of slavery — like you do, Mr. Clay."

He smiled slightly. "Yes, I rather suspected we had a convert in you. Tell me, does your family know your convictions?"

"No, sir." I looked down at my hands, feeling like a sneak.

"Your father's a Democrat, I imagine. I wonder how he'd feel if he knew you were planning on dedicating your life to destroying the 'peculiar institution'?"

"I guess he'd feel bad about it, sir. But he's not like some of them — he doesn't claim that slavery's a good thing, or the natural state for black people or any of that flapdoodle. He admits it was a mistake to start it in the first place, but he doesn't think there's anything that can be done about it now."

"I know, Hacey. Lots of people feel that way, and they might just as well be slave breeders, for all the good they're doing to solve the problem." He smiled at me sympathetically, to take the sting out of his words. "If the only people we had to fight in this life were bad people, it would make everything a lot easier. But I ask you again — what about the way your father and mother will feel?"

I looked up and met his eyes. "I know they will feel bad,

and I'm sorry. But not so sorry that I can be something I'm not, just to please them. It seems to me I've just got to do what I think is right."

He looked at me for a moment without speaking, and I had the feeling that his dark brown eyes were penetrating well beneath my skin. Then he asked, "How do you like the root beer?"

"It's fine."

"Like some more?"

"No, thank you, sir."

"Very good." The amenities accomplished, he leaned forward in his chair. "Hacey, the Mexican War's as good as over, except for the peace treaty. We've got Texas and New Mexico and California, and Oregon to boot, and the question is, what kind of states are we going to carve out of them? Slave or free? That's the national question, and it's what all the hooraw about the Wilmot Proviso is about. The local question is, how can we put an end to slavery in the states where it's already entrenched — in Kentucky particularly, as far as you and I are concerned. To do it, we'll have to rewrite the state constitution. That's going to be the biggest job since fumigating the Augean Stables. But I have a hunch that fight won't begin until after next year's national election — which I have very little interest in anyway — so I think I'll sit back and enjoy my newfound popularity for a few months."

"Why don't you care about next year's election, sir?"

"Because I don't expect it will prove anything or change anything. If that wretch Polk were running again, I'd be campaigning day and night to stop him — but he's pledged himself not to try for a second term, and I don't see how even he can wiggle out of that. So the Democrats will nominate some other paragon of proslavery prejudice, without a humane idea in his head. If my cousin Henry were running on the Whig ticket I'd campaign for him — although they tell me I didn't do him much good in 1844 — but I don't think he'll get the nomination. I'd guess that either Zachary Taylor or Winfield Scott will wrap the American flag around himself and win hands down — and neither of them cares a tinker's curse about ending slavery."

He rose from his chair and crossed to the front window, where he stood looking out at Thorn Hill's well-kept yard. "All that being the case, the next year or two seems a good time for traveling and attending to personal business. Building up strength for the days ahead. Or, in your case, attending to your studies with diligence, while you still may."

I felt a twinge of disappointment, as if I had presented myself at a recruiting station, only to have the sergeant advise me to return to mother. "Of course I'll be doing that, sir — but isn't there something more I can do at the same time? Something that will help — when the time comes?"

"Yes, you can be reading. Reading the kind of stuff that builds a head of steam inside your boiler. Read Rousseau, read de Tocqueville, read John Locke and Tom Paine. And here —" he stepped to the tall bookcase that ran across one wall, and selected one book, then another. *"Narrative of the Life of Frederick Douglass,* and William Lloyd Garrison's *Thoughts on African Colonization.* Take these with you, and bring them back when you've finished them, and I'll give you some more to stoke up on."

Sensing that my visit had run its appointed length, I rose and took the proffered books. He put his arm around my shoulders as we left the study. "Ecclesiastes says, 'To everything there is a season — a time to plant, and a time to pluck up that which is planted.' This is planting time, Hacey. Don't worry, harvest time comes soon enough."

In the months that followed I visited Thorn Hill every few weeks, each time carrying away a book or two. And all during that time my admiration for Cassius M. Clay and my belief in his cause kept growing. No feudal squire ever prepared to follow his armored knight on a quest with more awe for the one, more resolution for the other. Of course I was setting myself up for a crisis of loyalties, and it happened in the early fall of '48.

I was starting my third year at Transylvania, and my brother Boone had just begun his education at the medical college there. He was sharing my rooms. It was a pleasant arrangement. We were both basically "home bodies," and the barrooms and stews of Lexington held no appeal for us. Jubal saw to it that we were well enough fed and groomed. Boone paid no attention to my studies — I'm not sure he knew who William Lloyd Garrison was — and I was less than fascinated by his interest in *materia medica.*

One Sunday morning as the church bells were ringing, Boone burst into our sitting room. "Hacey, get out of those churchgoing clothes and get into your boots and britches," he said excitedly. "We got some riding to do."

I yawned and looked around the dresser top for my pearl stickpin. It had been a late evening at the Fortnightly, which was why Boone and I had stayed in Lexington rather than riding back to Hazelwood. "What in the world are you talking about, Boone?"

He was pulling off his good gray dress trousers. "Nigger uprising out near Paris. They say there's a hundred or more, and they're armed, and marching for the Ohio River."

I could hardly believe my ears. "A nigger uprising? In *Kentucky?*"

"Well, I'm not talking about Paris, France!" He pawed through the clothes in the closet, looking for his riding breeches. "The marshal is swearing in a posse comitatus at the courthouse in twenty minutes. Dang it, Hacey, have you seen my britches?"

"Jubal probably put them with your riding coat. Look, Boone, slow down to a trot and tell me about this. What happened? Has there been any killing? When did it start?"

"Nobody knows any details yet. It happened before dawn this morning. Niggers from farms out on the Paris Pike stole guns and lit out. Somebody must have planned it, and there's a rumor it was a white man. I don't think anybody's been killed yet — but there sure is going to be!"

"If nobody's been killed, how come you call it an uprising? It sounds like an escape to me."

"What difference does it make what you call it? It's a bunch of niggers with guns!" He pulled on one boot, then the other, grunting with the effort. Then he noticed I was still dressed as I had been when he came in. "Hacey, I told you the posse was going to be sworn in twenty minutes. You got to get out of those clothes."

"No, I don't, Boone," I said slowly, and with an empty feeling of finality. "I'm not going."

"What do you mean, you're not going?"

"Just what I said." I sat down with a sigh. "I'm not going, Boone. I'm not going to get a gun and a horse and go riding after some niggers who only want to be free."

He stared at me as if he had never seen me before. "But Hacey, they're *slaves!* They've got no right to be free! It's our duty to stop them!"

"Boone, can't you understand? *I'm on their side.* I hope they get away. I hope every slave in the South gets away."

We looked into one another's eyes, and each saw pain and pleading in the other. I hoped against all reason Boone would understand my feelings, and Boone, I know, was praying that somehow I could heal the wound I had caused to his loyalties. Neither got his wish, of course.

My brother turned away from me and pulled on his plum-colored riding coat. "Reckon I better be getting over to the courthouse," he said. There was a quiver in his voice. "I wouldn't want folks to think that neither of us knew what his duty was."

"Goodbye, Boone," I said.

"Goodbye, Hacey," he replied, and left the room.

For three days the Bluegrass was turned upside down as the hunt for the fugitive Negroes continued. There were no classes at the College, since almost every student with a horse had joined the posse. People milled around on the sidewalks and exchanged wild rumors of arson and rape. By Monday morning we had a fair idea of *what* had happened, but even two days later nobody had any idea *where* the absconders were.

Apparently the plot had been organized by a Centre College student named Patrick Doyle, reputedly a Northern abolitionist. Working through cadres he painstakingly selected from among the field hands on ten or so farms in northeastern Fayette County, he prepared about seventy-five Negroes to make the break for freedom. On the night of the escape, obviously with the connivance of many house Negroes, they armed themselves from their owners' arsenals and made their way to a rendezvous point between Lexington and Paris. From there they just disappeared.

It had been no Nat Turner affair, no bloody carnival of murder. Not a single white person had been harmed during the escape.

All day Monday and all day Tuesday, the posse covered the roads from Paris to the Ohio River like a seine, but to no avail. Tension increased in Lexington. Could the blacks have doubled back? Could they have eluded their pursuers and headed southwest — back toward us? Many a property owner whose house was on the northeast side of town brought his family into Lexington and checked into the Phoenix Hotel.

Finally, on Wednesday evening, word came to us that the fugitives had been found and surrounded in a hemp field outside Cynthiana. When ordered to throw down their arms and surrender, they refused. The posse opened fire, and, after a number of Negroes were killed, including some women and children, the survivors surrendered.

Friday the prisoners were marched into Lexington and jailed. The crowd that lined the street was ugly, even more ugly than the mob that had gathered outside the *True American* office three years before, because this crowd had been afraid, and despised itself for having been afraid, and detested the people who had made it afraid. Patrick Doyle, the instigator of the escape attempt, was barely recognizable as a white man under the dirt and dried blood that covered his face. He was loaded down with chains, his shoes were broken, and he walked like a man who has been kicked between the legs. As he passed me I looked into his eyes and saw they were unfocused, unconnected with the mind behind them. The crowd screamed, cursed, jeered and spat on him. Its malevolence was as tangible as the clods of mud and manure it rained upon him and upon the Negroes who walked beside him.

I returned to my rooms. Boone was there, packing his things. It was the first time I'd seen him since Sunday. He looked tired and sad. "Hello, Boone. You figure on moving out?" I asked.

163

"I reckon it's the best thing for both of us."

"I'm sorry you feel that way. I don't suppose there's much sense in talking about it, is there?"

"Talking about things is what causes most of the trouble in this world," he said in a dry, sour voice. "If folks would forget about talking, and just do what they're supposed to do, we'd be a sight better off."

"Where you going to be living?"

"Figured to move in with Pritch over on Walnut Street." Pritch was Alan Prichard, a friend of ours from Frankfort. Boone finished his packing and he and Jubal manhandled the heavy trunk down the stairs and into a waiting wagon. Then, while Jubal stayed with the horses, Boone came back upstairs to pick up one or two pieces of hand luggage. We shook hands awkwardly.

"I don't suppose we need bother Mama and Papa with our problems, do you? I'll just tell them we were too crowded here, and Pritch had extra room and everything. All right?"

"All right, Boone." By common consent we had both avoided mentioning the posse and the fugitive slaves, but now, as my brother started down the stairs, he paused and turned back to me. "Oh, by the way, Hacey — you know, we didn't catch all the niggers in that gang."

"Oh?"

"No, there was one of the ringleaders who got away — he's probably across the Ohio by now. He was Doyle's number two man, they say. A coal-black buck with a peculiar scar on his forehead — shaped like a star." He looked at me levelly from under lowered brows. "Did you talk about things a lot with him, Hacey?"

I didn't answer, and after a moment he continued down the stairs.

* * *

I was lonely after Boone left. During the few weeks we had shared rooms, I had come to enjoy his quiet presence a great deal, and now that my beliefs had caused me to forfeit it, there was an emptiness in my days.

The presidential election afforded little interest. As Clay had foreseen, Zachary Taylor "wrapped himself in the American flag" and won, with the unintended help of the new Free-Soil Party, whose activities in New York denied that state to the Democrats.

My studies at the college palled, and more than ever I felt that the practice of law might not be for me. It was an autumn of discontent, and I took my misgivings to Cassius Clay.

"Hacey, I can only congratulate you on your lack of enthusiasm for the practice of law," he told me. "Notice I said the *practice* of law, not the law itself. I yield to no man in my respect for the law — I believe it represents our major advance from barbarism. I have never broken it, nor advised others to, even when it seemed to be temporarily out of harmony with humanitarian ideals. Civilized people may work to *change* the law — they may not disobey it.

"But the *practice* of law — that's something else again. Often it seems to encourage cynicism, cunning and the use of petty technicalities at the expense of justice. No, don't expect me to pull a long face when you tell me you don't have the call, Hacey. All that means to me is that you have too much respect for the law to practice it. So let's move on to the next question. What do you want to do now?"

"I don't know, Mr. Clay. I still think the same way — I still want to help fight against slavery — but what I'm doing seems pointless, and I don't know what else to do instead."

He looked at me speculatively. "How would you like to preach? Or teach? Or write? Or all three?"

"Do you think I could?"

"I think you could — if you wanted to enough, and if you prepared yourself."

"Writing and teaching — I think I'd like that. But preaching — I don't know about that. I'm not what you'd call real religious, Mr. Clay."

"There's preaching and preaching, boy, and not all of it's done in church. Hacey, I think you ought to go East next fall."

The idea was breathtaking. "East, sir? You mean to a college in the East?"

"That's right. Harvard or Yale, I should think. Harvard, probably. Yale was my alma mater and I loved it, but Harvard's closer to Boston, and Boston is where things are popping today. I can give you letters to Garrison and Phillips and Hosea Binder — you can stop off in New York to visit Seward and Beecher — maybe we can get you in to meet Martin Van Buren —" He was up and out of his chair, pacing the room vigorously as he listed name after fabled name. "And in Washington you'll want to meet Sumner and Charles Francis Adams and that wild man Thaddeus Stevens —"

"Mr. Clay," I interrupted dizzily, "please sir — I don't know if my father could afford to send me to Harvard, let alone having me go gallivanting around the country!"

"You'll never know unless you ask him, will you? And I shouldn't think the money would present an insurmountable problem. If your father doesn't have the ready cash put by, I think I could arrange a loan at, say, two percent per annum, without undue strain on my exchequer."

"I don't know what to say, sir."

"Then don't say anything. Think of how you're going to put it to your parents, instead. Remember, you want to be on the train for Boston in August."

I left Thorn Hill that afternoon with my head in a whirl and went straight to my father's store. Father was going over the stock with a salesman from a Cincinnati hardware company, and Elam was waiting on a customer. I stood around until Elam was free and then told him about my conversation with Clay. He was dubious about my chances of getting Father to agree.

"Somehow the mental picture of your father tying you up with a bow and sending you to William Lloyd Garrison, prepaid, don't seem to want to form in my brain," he said.

"Gosh all hemlock, Elam, if it's a matter of money —"

"Most things are a matter of money one way or another."

"— then Mr. Clay said he'd lend me enough, at two percent interest."

"Did he now?" Elam thought a moment, and a faintly malicious smile crossed his monkey face. "Well, that might be what it takes. Yes, sir, that just might be what it takes."

"You mean Mr. Clay's money?"

"What?" He looked at me in alarm. "You just don't mention Mr. Clay's money, Hacey. You pretend you never heard about Mr. Clay's money, hear? If you want to go to Harvard, act like your papa's the only chance you got. And don't be discouraged if he turns you down to begin with."

Which Father did, in terms and tones of deep moral outrage. Over the past year or so he had become aware of my admiration for Clay — "seduction" was the word he used — but he had had no idea it had progressed to the point of corrupting my political values, turning me against my people and making me a pawn of the leprous abolitionist jackals of Boston. And so on.

During the following two weeks it seemed hopeless. Each weekend at Hazelwood Father would return to the subject, as if he hadn't yet supped his fill on the horrors of the serpent's tooth and the thankless child. And then gradually a new element entered his diatribes and grew in intensity until it became his dominant complaint: Cassius Clay was trying to embarrass him by making him look cheap.

I realized that Elam had leaked the information about Clay's loan offer in such a way that Father felt his solvency was in doubt. That was a mortal attack, and Father had been a businessman too long not to respond to it. Unfortunately his only possible response was to show he *could,* by God, afford to send his son to Harvard. As time passed, this attitude took root, and by spring it was accepted in the family that I was going East in the fall.

I was sorry to have to tell Josh Brain that I doubted I would ever be a candidate for admission to the Bar, but he was as understanding as I had hoped he would be. I remember one thing he said. It reminded me of something Cassius Clay had said on the same subject a few weeks before.

"You believe in absolutes, Hacey, and that's fine, you should. You're a young man, and young men need absolutes. The law is an absolute, so you can believe in it. Anybody can believe in it — except lawyers. Lawyers are positively prevented from believing in it, because they have to make their living out of it. I have a deep affection for the law, like a kind-hearted procurer might have for the talented whore who has kept him in silk shirts for twenty years. But God! Imagine how it would be if I loved her!"

XIII

The Third Argument

Cassius M. Clay had been right when he predicted that the 1848 presidential election would be dwarfed, both in importance and in excitement, by the election of delegates to rewrite the State Constitution.

In February the State Legislature issued a call for a Constitutional Convention in Frankfort on October 1. Suddenly the antislavery faction awakened to the desperate situation that had developed. In passing the bill calling for the Constitutional Convention, they had opened Pandora's box. Unless they could gain control of the Convention, it would shape a new constitution more favorable to slavery than the old one — a constitution which might make the eventual disappearance of slavery impossible.

The proslavery faction in Fayette County nominated two members of the Wickliffe family as delegates to the Convention — Robert N. Wickliffe and Aaron Wooley, the Old Duke's son-in-law. The emancipationists nominated Reverend Robert J. Breckinridge and Samuel Shy. Concurrently, Robert S. Todd ran for a second term in the State Legislature, on a generally antislavery platform. Cassius M. Clay strapped his bowie knife under his arm and returned to the hustings, and his popularity as a Mexican War hero melted as the snows of yesteryear.

I finished my studies at Transylvania at the end of May, and so was free to attend political meetings to my heart's content. Almost every day during the first two weeks in June there was a barbeque or a military muster somewhere in the Bluegrass at which one or more of the candidates spoke. Invariably the sentiments of the crowd were proslavery, and often there were disorders apparently organized by hired bullies. It was not uncommon to see posters and placards promising death to all abolitionists and "nigger-agitators."

On the 19th of June a meeting was scheduled at Foxtown, the settlement two miles from Hazelwood, where we had gone to grammar school. Squire Turner of Richmond, who was running for Delegate from Madison County, was announced as a speaker, and Cassius Clay had said he would be present for rebuttal. The Turners were known as a hotheaded family, and I thought I could sense the thrill of anticipated violence in the air as I arrived at the open field where the meeting was in progress.

Squire Turner, a short, square-built man with a grating voice, was speaking. Cash Clay was standing on the fringe of the crowd with three companions, listening to his opponent's remarks. He seemed serenely unmoved as Turner cried, "How would you describe a man who basely attacks everything his people and his race hold dear? Cassius M. Clay is a traitor, an assassin, a blackhearted, conscienceless thief in the night who would steal away our homes, our property and our sacred honor! I tell you, a hound bitch who devours her own young is like the fragrant honeysuckle compared to such a moral pismire!"

"A trifle purple, but still he's in pretty good form today," I heard Clay say quietly as I joined the group around him.

"I wonder if he knows a pismire is an ant. Good morning, Hacey, I'm glad you could join us."

I said good morning to him and the others. One was his eldest son Warfield, whom I knew by sight, but had never spoken to. The other two were brothers, Wyatt and William Wilkerson, who had recently attached themselves to Clay's faction, and had the reputation of being handy fellows in a fight. The five of us waited for the Squire to finish his calumny.

It took him the better part of an hour to find a stopping place. After he had worked Cash Clay over for twenty minutes, including selected readings from *The True American,* he moved on to Reverend Breckinridge (fifteen minutes) and Robert S. Todd (ten minutes) and finished up with ten minutes on Henry Clay and the Whig Party.

Cassius Clay waited for the cheers and hand-clapping to die down before he pushed his way to the platform. As he took his place behind the speaker's table and surveyed the sullen faces of the suddenly quiet crowd, and threw his head back and brushed the hair away from his eyes, I realized that underneath his calm manner he was as angry as I had ever seen him. Squire Turner had gotten under his skin.

He opened his speech with a flourish I had seen him use on previous occasions, but today his quiet fury made it seem more ominous than before.

"Good friends and neighbors of Madison County, for those of you who believe in the laws of the land, I have this argument." He reached into his left coat pocket and pulled out a bound copy of the Constitution, and laid it on the table before him. "For those who believe in the law of God, I have this argument," and he pulled a copy of the New Testament from his right coat pocket and laid it beside the other book on the table. "And for those of you who believe in neither the laws of God nor of man, I have this argument," and he whipped out his bowie knife from its shoulder sheath and held it glittering in the sunlight for a moment before laying it across the two books in front of him. The crowd muttered.

From then on, Clay made no attempts at oratorical devices. His speech was a bitter and devastating personal attack on Squire Turner — on his hypocrisy in public life and his venality in private, on his moral imbecility and criminal genius, his miserliness in good works and prodigality in bad. It was a documented indictment which, even for those days, was uniquely destructive.

Three of Turner's sons were in the audience, and the moment soon came when they could no longer bear Clay's abuse. The eldest, Cyrus Turner, pushed his way through the crowd until he stood directly in front of the speaker's platform, and shook a burly fist in Clay's face. "You're a Goddamned liar," he shouted.

Clay was off the platform in a second, his face suddenly flushed with rage. In one flowing motion, he carried the momentum of his leap into a furious blow with his right arm, smashing Turner on the side of the head below his left ear and dropping him to the ground as though he had been pole-axed.

Instantly Clay was surrounded by twenty men or more. Our group was at least forty feet from the speaker's stand. "Jesus," I heard Warfield Clay yell, "he left his knife on the platform." As one man, we pressed forward through the milling crowd toward the focus of the action.

Many hands seized Cash Clay and held him. Believing that they were peace-makers, simply trying to stop the fight, he ceased struggling in their grip. Then Turner's second son, Alfred, stepped up to him and drove a knife into his lungs.

Clay stood for a second, frozen into immobility, bound by

the hands of his captors like Laocoön bound by the marble coils of the sea snake. Then, a froth of blood on his lips, he convulsed his muscles and burst free, to stand swaying with the hilt of the knife sticking out from his chest.

Cyrus Turner was on his feet again. He reached out and seized the hilt of the knife his brother had planted, and pulled it from Clay's body with a twisting motion. But before it was quite free, Clay's fingers closed over the bloody blade, and the two wrestled for possession of it, with Turner's hand gripping the handle, while the sharp metal cut through Clay's flesh and tendon to the bone.

At that moment Squire Turner's third son, Thomas, pulled out a six-shot repeating pistol, leveled it at Clay's head and pulled the trigger. It misfired, and he cocked it and tried again, and it misfired again, and then a third time. Then the Wilkerson brothers, Warfield Clay and I reached the scene, and before young Turner could try a fourth time, the brothers had borne him to the ground.

Cash and Cyrus Turner were still grappling for the knife, and their two hands and the knife itself had lost detail under the bright red coat of blood that covered them. Warfield dashed in like a terrier at Turner's heels, and Turner smashed him to the ground with one backhand blow. Clay's eyes were glazed, and showed no recognition of his son's attempted assistance. I was a step or two behind Warfield, and before I could reach the combatants, two strong arms grasped me around the chest and waist, and a voice said in my ear, "Whoa, there, boy! You just better stay right here, less'n you want to get hurt."

Unable to move, I watched as Clay and Turner strained and groaned over the knife. The crowd around them was deathly silent. They were watching an epic fight, and they didn't want to miss a second of it.

173

As the endless seconds ticked by, Clay's hand slowly moved to a position of advantage, and Turner's wrist was twisted into an increasingly awkward angle. In a few moments, it had reached a point where only by releasing the knife could he prevent his wrist from being broken. His fingers opened, and Clay seized the handle, wrenching it from the other's grasp.

Turner must have known at that split second that he was a dead man, because he started screaming even before the knife slid into his lower belly and he felt the blade begin to move upward as Clay sawed it in and out.

Clay opened up nearly a foot of the abdominal cavity before Turner fell away from the knife, staggered backward three or four steps, hands pressed to belly in the futile attempt to hold himself together, and then crashed to the ground. Clay stood alone, swaying drunkenly in the sunlight, daubed with bright blood from head to foot, blood in his hair and his eyes, a froth of blood bubbles on his lips, his hands and arms slick with his own blood, and his shirt and trousers sodden with the blood from Turner's gutting. Then, slowly, with a sound somewhere between a deep cough, a sigh and a groan, he allowed himself to sink to the earth.

Clay and Turner were carried to the little schoolhouse we Millers knew so well, and laid out on benches. Both men were still alive, although it seemed obvious that neither would continue to be alive very long. In a few minutes a doctor arrived from Richmond and examined each of them. "Well, they really done for one another," he said, as he stepped out of the schoolhouse afterward. "Gut wounds and lung wounds — both of them is as certain as the final trump."

The next night, as predicted, Cyrus Turner died, his agony only slightly diminished by laudanum. But Clay wouldn't die. After a few days he was moved to his country home, White Hall, where he remained flat on his back for three months. Ironically enough, the fact that he was bed-ridden at White Hall instead of actively campaigning in Lexington during that period may well have saved his life.

When Josh Brain heard about the Foxtown fight, I believe he snorted and said, "A plague on both their houses." Whether he did or not, he should have, and I choose to remember him paraphrasing Mercutio over a glass of hot punch in the taproom of the Phoenix Hotel. It was the kind of grim jest he would have liked, for at that very moment the filthy gutters of Iristown were breeding the cholera germs that were to decimate the city of Lexington within the next two months.

The cholera epidemic of 1849 was the worst pestilence ever visited upon the Bluegrass. Scarcely a family was spared, and lamentations were raised in the mansions of the mighty as often as in the hovels of the poor. Business stopped, grass literally grew in the streets of Lexington, and — most incredible of all — for almost a month politics was forgotten.

Of Lexington's four candidates for Delegate to the Constitutional Convention, three had the cholera by the middle of July, and the fourth, Reverend Breckinridge, was so busy conducting funeral services — at the height of the epidemic there were fifty deaths a day — that he had no time for politicking. Robert S. Todd had it. Henry Clay had it. John Hunt Morgan had it. Elam Yates had it. Half the Ledyard slaves were down with it — and then one day I didn't feel so well myself.

Early in July Rosalie and Boone and I had all moved back to Hazelwood at the insistence of my mother. Father had instructed Elam and Falk to close the store for the duration of the epidemic, and then when Elam came down with the disease, had both of them move in with us. Falk nursed Elam, and slept close to him in the guest bedroom, while the rest of us tried to keep our distance from both of them.

One evening we were sitting on the veranda watching the flicker of heat lightning across the skies to the north. Every so often there would be a distant rumble in the air. The night was as still and oppressive as sulfur smoke in a low-lying fog. "Listen to that thunder," said Mother. "Sounds like it's going to rain in Lexington."

"That's not thunder, Mama," said Boone. "That's the cannons. They've got a hundred cannons in the parks and spread out in a circle around town. They're from the U.S. Army artillery. They're going to be shooting every night from now on until the plague's over."

"My lands, whatever for?"

"The engineers and doctors think it will help clear the air of the cholera. All night long they shoot off a volley every fifteen minutes."

"Salvo, not volley," I corrected automatically — and suddenly felt a contraction of my bowels that threatened to force a voiding from both ends before I had time to reach the privacy of the water closet.

The symptoms of the disease were well enough known by all of us so that my stumbling dash from the porch was not for a moment misconstrued. "Hacey's got it!" cried Rosalie, and she and Boone and Father and Mother all raced after me in my embarrassed flight.

That flight is the last thing I remember clearly for more than two weeks. During the next twenty-four hours I was racked by diarrhea and vomiting, and was so weakened I couldn't attend to my own needs. My mother, Boone and

Aunt Hessie divided the unpleasant responsibilities. Then my fever went up and I began to suffer a nightmare of wrenching cramps in arms, legs and torso. I must have cried and shouted a good deal from the pain, but I have no recollection of anything except the pain itself. My mouth and skin were dry as parchment and it didn't seem there was any moisture left in the world. Somehow I felt if I could just make water, things could begin to mend — but I couldn't make water, there was no water to make, no water anywhere, in me or out of me.

Remembering it now, the voiding time was bad, the cramping time was worse, but the dry time was an infinite bit of hell, and the few days it lasted were forever.

Coming out of the cholera was a slow, golden Thanksgiving. Gradually my gratitude broadened to include, not just my nurses and the members of my household, but the animals of our farmyard, the birds in the trees outside, the murmuring woods beyond the fence, the dew of the morning, and the big, low-riding moon at night. It was a return to a life of rich variety — and to the freedom to enjoy it.

*   *   *

By the beginning of August the cholera had loosened its grip on the Bluegrass. The toll was overwhelming. Robert S. Todd was dead. Wickliffe's son-in-law, Aaron Wooley, was dead. Whigs and Democrats had been cut down impartially by the scythe of pestilence. Between fifteen hundred and two thousand souls had been returned to their Maker, and hundreds of others were so weakened they would fall prey to other ailments before the year was out.

And so — as it always must in Kentucky — came the election. It brought overwhelming success to the slavocracy. In Fayette County there were proslavery majorities in every precinct. The delegates to the Constitutional Convention would be free to rivet the shackles of slavery onto Kentucky so securely that no abolitionist sentiments could ever challenge it again — they thought.

By the end of August I was beginning to get my strength back, and was looking forward to my journey to Cambridge. One morning Mother brought me a cup of cold bouillon and sat beside my bed.

"Well, you're coming along, Hacey. In another two weeks I expect you'll be able to leave us."

"I expect so, Mama."

"You'll be meeting all those terrible people Mr. Clay told you about — Garrison and Phillips and those other Yankee abolitionists."

"Yes, ma'am."

"I could wish you were a little more selective in your friends, Hacey. In this world a man is judged by the friends he makes. As far as abolitionism goes, I believe it's a snare and a delusion, and no good will ever come of it."

"Yes, ma'am."

"However, in my family we were brought up to believe in freedom of conscience. Speak the truth and shame the Devil. So I want you to know that as long as you are following a course you believe is Christian, you won't get any criticism from me. I may think you're addled, but I won't fault you for it."

"Thank you, Mama. I appreciate that."

She rose from her chair briskly. "Well, I have work to do — unlike some people, who can spend their time lollygagging in bed." She started to leave the room, then paused. "Oh — you don't have to mention what I said to your papa. It would only get him more upset than he is now."

A day or two later Father came to my room one evening

after dinner. "Well, the fledgling bird prepares to spread his wings and leave the nest, eh, son?" he began jovially.

"I think I'm about ready for the trip, Papa."

"Harvard College," he mused. "Now who would have ever thought we'd be sending a boy of ours to that abolitionist pesthouse? Your friend Clay really snuck one over on us there."

"Oh, I don't think it's as abolitionist as all that. I understand they've got all shades of opinion there."

"They've probably got one Democrat — stuffed and under glass in the museum, so all the little abolitionists can learn to identify the enemy." He snorted and addressed himself to the glass of Madeira he had brought with him from the table. "Hacey, I'm afraid you have fallen among thieves. If you had only let me know the way your thoughts were tending when you first came under the baleful influence of that scoundrel, I might have been able to pluck you out as a brand from the burning. But now —" He left the sentence uncompleted, and it hung dolefully in the air.

"I'm sorry if you think I was dishonest, Papa."

"No, not dishonest, never dishonest. Immature, innocent, ignorant, but certainly not dishonest. That's why I can't find it in my heart to blame you as I no doubt should. Hacey, even though I have strong principles, I have always been able to see both sides of a question. That's why I know that some abolitionists, though misguided, are not entirely evil. Now don't ask me which ones they are; I just said there are *some*. There have to be. God in His infinite wisdom wouldn't allow the entire population of New England to exist without some saving grace. Look what he did to Sodom and Gomorrah." He stood up, walked back and forth across the room, took another swallow of Madeira and sat down again.

"Hacey, my boy, all I want to say is this: even though I think you're a damned fool, and even though everybody in Fayette County agrees with me, if you think you're right, you go ahead and do what you've got to do. I believe you are old enough and smart enough to know the difference between good and evil — and I'm prepared to back your play." He glared at me.

"Thank you, Papa. I appreciate that."

"Just wanted you to know. By the way, son — your mother is a wonderful woman, but you couldn't expect her to show the tolerance and flexibility of mind that characterizes the stronger sex. So I wouldn't mention this little conversation to her, if I were you."

*   *   *

And so finally, one bright September morning I stood at the railroad station waiting for the train to Cincinnati to be ready for boarding. Mother, Father, Boone and Rosalie were with me. Jubal was storing my two huge portmanteaux and my horsehair trunk in the baggage car. In the letter box under my arm were letters of introduction from Cassius M. Clay to Wendell Phillips, William Lloyd Garrison, Theodore Parker, Henry Ward Beecher and a number of other gentlemen of like beliefs and almost equal notoriety.

The train whistle blew its summons. I kissed my mother on the cheek, pumped my father's hand, punched Boone on the biceps, hesitated a second in front of Rosalie, not knowing what to do, and then, to our mutual surprise, kissed her on the cheek too and hurried up the steps and took my seat in the coach where I was able to wave to them for the few remaining seconds before the train began to move.

It was taking me to Boston — one stop farther along a route that had begun in Fayette County Courthouse the day I first met Cassius Clay, and would not end, I was determined, until I had put my weight into the balance in the fight against slavery.

Thinking large thoughts, I watched the rolling Bluegrass hills jerk by, and unwrapped an Old Ham sandwich.

XIV

———•—•———

WENTWORTH

THE REVEREND HOSEA BINDER had four daughters, named, in descending order of seniority, Faith, Hope, Charity and Prudence.

The effect of names on personality is a subject too little explored. In the case of the Binder girls, the four biblical virtues with which they were tagged seemed to have a profound effect on their behavior. Faith, for example, pointed her bony nose in the direction of the church at every opportunity; Hope stared at each passing young man with slightly goitrous eyes from which the spark of a forlorn hope was never absent; Charity buried her unfulfilled desires in a flurry of good works; but Prudence tempted every boy she met to indulge in the most imprudent actions.

In the spring of 1850, when I had been at Harvard five months, she tempted me into as imprudent an action as I can imagine — starting an argument with Frederick Douglass, the Negro abolitionist. It was a day I will never forget, for also on that day I began my friendship with that great man Thomas Wentworth Higginson — a most rewarding friendship that has now lasted for more than half a century.

I had arrived in Boston in the middle of the previous September, and immediately enrolled as a graduate student at Harvard. As I had no firm professional aspirations, I was allowed to study "at large," a not infrequent privilege in those days. I had chosen to take a room at the college and eat in the Commons rather than chance the food at any of the nearby boardinghouses frequented by the students. This was probably a wise decision, for although the fare at Commons was hardly at gourmet level — it tended to emphasize turnips, squash, potatoes, cabbage, beans and yams, with small portions of meat every other day — still it was both wholesome and cheap. My room was on the third floor of the dormitory called the Old Den, and provided a pleasantly pastoral view of the Yard.

In a week or so I was comfortably settled in, had met my neighbors in the Old Den and had struck up acquaintance-ships with some of my classmates. I decided it was time to begin presenting my letters of introduction. I chose first the Reverend Theodore Parker, probably the most outspoken enemy of slavery in Boston, with the exception of Garrison himself.

I presented myself at his home one Sunday afternoon, only to discover that he had left Boston for a lecture tour of Pennsylvania and Ohio. Since I had gotten myself all primed to meet a clergyman, I looked through my letters for another likely candidate and found an envelope addressed to the Reverend Hosea Binder.

I knocked on the door of a modest but well-kept brown-stone a few steps off Beacon Street, and was shown into Reverend Binder's study. He shook my hand warmly, asked me to take a chair and then began to read the letter I handed him.

Watching him as he read, with his lips shaping inaudible comments and his eyebrows rising and falling apparently at random, I thought he was one of the ugliest men I had ever seen. His fleshy nose looked boneless, and the pores of his face were very large, many of them displaying their own individual hairs. His protruding ears dropped their lobes below his jaw line, and his chin seemed to disappear into the folds of wattled skin above his collar. And yet there was an engaging quality about him that was immediately apparent.

He spoke in a mild but surprisingly deep voice. "Cassius Clay. Goodness gracious. I haven't heard anything about him since he put out that newspaper in Lexington, what was it called? *The True American*. They suppressed it. Dear me. How is he, Mr. Miller?"

I replied that I believed he was as well as a man could be who had recently been stabbed in the lungs with a bowie knife.

"Violence, violence. Clay has always had such violent proclivities. When he was a student at Yale — it must have been almost twenty years ago — he would speak in the most alarming manner about what he intended to do to any slave-owner who tried to prevent him from expressing his opinions. I gather he has carried out those intentions more than once." He shook his head sadly. "Those who live by the sword —" he began, then checked himself. "Well, Mr. Miller — or may I call you Hacey? Odd name, Hacey, don't believe I've ever encountered it before." He paused for a moment as he searched his memory for my namesakes. "Well. Welcome to Boston, Hacey. I hope you'll visit us often. I have four unmarried daughters whom you may consider inducements." His eyebrows leaped toward his hairline and he puckered his mouth in an arch expression. "An unexpected bonus, hey?"

"I hope I'll have the pleasure of meeting them soon, sir."

"Why not this evening? We have musical evenings every

other Sunday, and we have one planned for today. There will be a number of young people here, as well as a few dilapidated specimens of my generation. Eight-thirty. May we see you?"

"Thank you, sir. I'll certainly be here." And shaking his hand again, I took my leave.

Musical evenings at the Reverend Binder's home always followed the same pattern — and I must have attended at least fifty of them. Guests arrived from eight-thirty to nine, and were greeted by the preacher, his wife, and his four daughters, given a cup of "temperance punch" and directed into the parlor, where there was general conversation. Usually there were ten or twelve guests, at least six of whom were young men whom Reverend Binder had brought together in the hope of discovering a possible son-in-law. The other guests included some of the most famous reformers and antislavery agitators in New England. For in spite of his mild speech and pacifistic beliefs, our host was a devoted soldier in the abolitionist army.

Faith, Hope, Charity and Prudence were the center of the young people's group — more precisely, Faith, Hope and Charity were dutifully attended by one young man apiece, while the rest of us clustered around Prudence like bees around a hollyhock. By unspoken agreement, those of us who were "regulars" at the Binders' musical evenings each took our fair share of the Faith, Hope and Charity detail, even though in our minds they may have appeared as the three weird sisters who hocused Macbeth on the heath. It was worth it to be allowed to worship at Prudence's feet another day.

After fifty years, I can look back on Prudence Binder as a piquantly pretty girl with a second-rate intelligence and an overpowering vanity that fed on the adoration of young men.

But at the time, her snub nose, white teeth, small red mouth and large brown eyes spelled the sum total of female loveliness to me.

A little after nine o'clock, Reverend Binder would say to Mrs. Binder, "Isn't it about time we proceeded to the music room, my dear?" and she would reply in a small, piping voice, "I believe it is, Mr. Binder." Then they would lead the way from the parlor down the hall to the music room at the back of the house. There we would find seats, and the musicale would begin.

Reverend Binder played the flute, his wife played the piano, and Faith, Hope and Charity performed on the violin, viola and cello, respectively. Prudence sang, in a small, clear voice and with great emotion. Generally the program was made up of individual pieces featuring each of the instrumentalists, two or three songs of contrasting moods for Prudence — such as "Oft in the Stilly Night" and "Camptown Races" — and a flute quintet for a finale. Then back to the parlor for more temperance punch and conversation, and finally we took our farewell at eleven o'clock.

It was in March or April that Frederick Douglass was a guest at a Binder musical evening. Ever since Cassius Clay had loaned me his copy of *Narrative of the Life of Frederick Douglass* when I was at Transylvania, I had admired that dauntless ex-slave from afar. The opportunity of meeting him in person had rendered me completely inarticulate, and as I shook his hand I babbled silly remarks.

Prudence swept up and wrinkled her pretty nose at me. "Merciful Heavens, Hacey, what's the matter with you? You certainly did look a fool with Mr. Douglass."

Since I knew her observation was correct, it maddened me. "Oh, you think so, do you? Well, it just so happens I intend to have a long conversation with Mr. Douglass after the musicale."

"Oh, la! What would you have to talk to Mr. Douglass about?"

"You just wait and see. Maybe I'll set him straight on a few points."

"You?" She laughed in a tinkling, artificial manner. "La! If you ever got in an argument with him, he'd eat you up in one gulp, and have room for a sandwich besides." And before I had a chance to reply, she turned her back on me and put her hand on the arm of a young man I fancied to be my deadliest rival.

The Binder musicales never seemed short, but that one seemed interminable. Oblivious to any of the performances, I rehearsed conversational gambits in my mind, but found all of them wanting. Finally I resolved to abandon a preconceived plan and trust to my native wit to involve me in a conversation with Douglass which would reflect credit upon me.

When we returned to the parlor after the music, Douglass was immediately engaged in conversation by our host and another guest, a young man of twenty-seven or -eight, with a slender build, a long face and sensitive features. I had been introduced to him earlier and remembered his name as Higgins.

Their conversation seemed to be about the proposed new Fugitive Slave Law which was one of a number of proposals recently introduced to the United States Senate by Henry Clay, who had returned to Washington for just that purpose, to try to create peace between North and South "for the next thirty years" with an omnibus package of compromises.

"I understand the law would allow magistrates to turn

over Negroes to slave-catchers on the word of the slave-catchers alone — would require no supporting evidence, and would exclude testimony of the Negroes," said the sensitive-looking young man.

"Frightful, frightful," said Reverend Binder. "It must be made a dead letter."

Douglass, a short, stocky man with Caucasian features and middling dark skin, grinned wickedly. "The only way to make a law like that a dead letter is to make half a dozen dead kidnapers right off."

I thought I saw my chance. "You don't believe in supporting the law of the land then, Mr. Douglass?" I asked.

All three of them looked at me in surprise. Douglass's eyes traveled over me from head to toe as if he were cataloguing me. "That's right, young man — I regard a law as illegal when it contradicts a higher law."

"Mr. Clay would disagree with you, I believe." I meant Cassius Clay, of course, but everyone assumed I meant Henry.

"Oh, you mean the President," said Douglass.

"Sir?" I asked, confused.

"Henry Clay — President of the American Colonization Society. I think we should always honor him with his presidential title, because it's the only one he'll ever get!"

This cruel joke was greeted with considerable laughter from the listening guests, and even brought a smile to the lips of Binder and the slender young man beside him. Where I came from, the reverence due Henry Clay was second only to that due George Washington, and I flushed hotly at such ridicule.

"You are in error, sir. I was not referring to the Senator from Kentucky, but to his kinsman, Cassius M. Clay. You may have heard of him. He's freed a number of your people."

Binder's eyes opened a little wider, and Douglass's slitted as he said, "Yes, I've heard of him. I admire the way he supports the law of the land — by sticking knives in the bellies of his enemies."

"He has never once broken the law, Mr. Douglass. He has on occasion acted in self-defense."

"Sure he has. And you, Mr. — Miller, is it? — Mr. Miller, you're a great supporter of C. M. Clay, I can see that."

"Yes, sir," I said proudly.

"You share his views on slavery, then?"

"Of course, sir."

"You abhor the idea of human beings in bondage as much as he does?"

"Yes, sir."

"And naturally you have refused to live in any home where slavery is practiced? Naturally you have declined to eat any food grown by the sweat of black field hands and prepared by the skill of black kitchen slaves? Naturally you have saddled your own horse and brushed your own clothes and shined your own shoes and made your own bed, ever since you arrived at your laudable convictions about the evils of slavery?"

"I —" suddenly I had no more words. I remembered the soft hands of Aunt Hessie as she nursed me, the cool competence of Jubal in our rooms at Transylvania. How could I have failed to realize that they were slave labor as much as the wretched coffles of shackled blacks shuffling through the streets of Lexington?

"I would imagine that some people might call C. M. Clay

a hypocrite," the ex-slave went on remorselessly. "It's a word that's sometimes used to describe people who claim to respect the law and then go around breaking the Sixth Commandment. But there's one kind of hypocrisy no one's ever accused him of — and that's preening himself as an emancipationist while he's living like Ol' Massa' on the labor of others."

I felt my face flushing beet red, and I could think of no word to say. I might have been a ten-year-old schoolboy, caught by my teacher as I practiced some act of secret obscenity. For a long moment nobody in the parlor said anything. Then the tall, slender young man coughed in a diffident manner and spoke.

"Surely, Mr. Douglass, if our Father's House is the antislavery movement, it has room for many Mansions. There are those who accept violence, but respect the law — like our young friend's hero, Mr. Clay. There are those who willingly break the law, but refuse to resort to violence — like Mr. Garrison and the Quakers and the whole Underground Railroad. And there are those, like you and me, who countenance both violence *and* law-breaking in the service of the cause. It takes a wide roof to shelter such divergent beliefs, I think. Don't you agree?"

Douglass flicked his angry eyes from me to the slender young man, and as I was freed from his gaze, a weight of oppression seemed to disappear. "And if I agree?"

"Then, can't we allow Mr. Miller a place under that roof as well? Surely there are not so many of us that we can turn a well-wisher from the door."

Suddenly Frederick Douglass smiled, and the smile lit up his dark face like a beam of sunshine on a cloudy day. "Of course, Mr. Higginson — I'm glad to shake the hand of every enemy of slavery." He stepped across the floor and put out his hand to me. "I've enjoyed our conversation, Mr. Miller," he said, giving my hand a paralyzing squeeze. "I'll look forward to a resumption of it at a later day." He made a formal little bob of his head, then turned back to his conversation with Reverend Binder and my savior.

A few minutes later, after I had pulled myself together and endured a brief taunting by Prudence Binder, I was able to speak to the tall slender young man alone. "Hacey Miller, sir," I said. "I made a champion fool of myself, and I want to thank you for saving me from what I had coming."

He smiled, and the gentleness of that smile was belied by the ironic laughter in his eyes. "Thomas Wentworth Higginson, sir — Wentworth to my friends, of whom I hope I may count you a recent and valuable addition."

"How valuable I hesitate to say," I replied ruefully. "Judging by tonight's performance, I'm destined to be more of an embarrassment to my friends than my enemies."

"Oh, fiddle — when I spoke to Douglass about our Father's House having a wide roof, I wasn't just making pretty phrases. It *has* to have a wide roof, to shelter me!" He paused, drumming his fingers on his bony knee. "I'm not sure I've done a single thing of real importance since I finally had the courage to break the umbilical cord and leave my rooms in the Old Den!"

"The Old Den? Did you live there? That's where I live!"

"Really? Whereabouts?"

"On the third floor. Northeast corner, facing the Yard."

"Really? Not the corner room!"

"No — second from the corner."

"Too bad — mine was the corner. There was a Lodge where you are — one of the less intelligent Lodges. He used to have marvelous high teas." Higginson paused, as if remembering the cakes and cookies and hot buttered scones. He had the look of a man who hasn't eaten as well as he might have during the recent past.

"When were you at Harvard, Mr. — Wentworth?"

"Aha. When *wasn't* I at Harvard is the question. I started there in 'thirty-seven, at the age of thirteen — spent four years skating, swimming, playing football and reading a lot, and graduated in 'forty-one. Hadn't an idea in my head about what I wanted to do except form countless deep sentimental relationships with young ladies who couldn't be bothered. Spent two years as a pedagogue, at which I was an utter failure. Was able to finagle my way back into Harvard as a graduate student in 'forty-three. Studied at large because I still didn't know what I wanted to be —"

"That's just what I'm doing now," I cried excitedly.

"Yes — the last refuge of the free spirit. You have the look. To continue, after three years of floundering around, I received what I like to think was The Call, and joined the senior class in the Divinity School — an odd group of mystics, skeptics and dyspeptics if there ever was one — in time to graduate with them in 'forty-seven. With an uncharacteristic outburst of energy I took a wife and a pulpit the same summer, became the Unitarian Pastor of Newburyport. It took me exactly two years to preach myself out of the pulpit. Hope the wife will last longer."

"What have you been doing since then?" I asked, fascinated by my new friend's rapid-fire reminiscences.

"Looking for another church — where the congregation isn't happy to serve God as well as Mammon just so long as Mammon gets the first slice of pie. You see, Hacey, I don't believe a Christian church can include people who own slaves or support slavery. If a single whiff of slave-breeder, slave-owner, slave-trader or slave-catcher comes in the door,

Christ goes out the window. That's what I preached in Newburyport, and that's what I'll preach from my next pulpit,
and it just may have something to do with why I'm not be-
sieged with offers."

"Courage, Wentworth — be not cast down in the Lord's
work," said Reverend Binder, who had just joined us. "Who
knows? Within a few years Mr. Miller here may be joining
the ministry and — ahem — taking a wife, even as you did.
When that time comes, we wouldn't want your words of dis-
couragement ringing in his ears."

"If I get discouraged, Reverend Binder, it won't be because of anything Wentworth said. It will be because I did
some tomfool thing like I did tonight. I really want to apologize about saying what I said to Mr. Douglass."

"Nothing to apologize for, my boy. Actually, I think
Frederick would like to apologize, but he's too proud, of
course. Have another glass of temperance punch and confound the Devil." He pushed a cup of the innocuous bever-
age into my hand and beamed at me as I swallowed some of
it.

"Wine is a mocker, and strong drink is raging," quoted
Wentworth piously, with laughter dancing in his eyes.
"You've come a long way from the Bourbon whiskey of
Kentucky, Hacey."

"I certainly have, Wentworth," I agreed regretfully, "I
certainly have."

*   *   *

At the end of my first academic year at Harvard, I returned home via New York City, where I was able to present
my letter of introduction to Dr. Henry Ward Beecher of
Brooklyn. I'm sorry to say that I thought he was a pious
fraud, insincere and self-serving, and I've never had reason

to modify that opinion. Doubtless he suffered by comparison with the Parkers, Binders and Higginsons of Boston, especially as I was conscious of enduring a surfeit of godliness for the past few months.

The Bluegrass was restorative. My sister had announced her engagement to Charles Truesdall of Georgia, the son of a wealthy planter, who had been in the class ahead of mine at Transylvania, and there were parties and balls for the happy couple all during July and August. During the long summer days Boone and I rode and hunted in the woods, or I visited friends at the college, or shared a sociable glass of punch — *real* punch — with Josh Brain at the Phoenix Hotel, or roamed the streets of Lexington with Falk Padgett. I wasn't able to spend any time with Cassius M. Clay. He was not in Lexington that summer, but we continued the correspondence which we had begun when I entered Harvard.

By tacit agreement everybody avoided the subjects of slavery and abolitionism. My sister's wedding took place at the end of August, and I was back in Cambridge by the end of the first week in September. I barely had time to begin my new studies when the news arrived that Congress passed the Fugitive Slave Law — and Boston exploded.

This unspeakable law — which I had heard Frederick Douglass and Wentworth Higginson discussing the previous spring — was the blood money Henry Clay paid the South in order to get his Compromise of 1850 enacted. By its terms slave-catchers were guaranteed the right to seize any Negro they claimed to be an escaped slave, on their testimony alone. They then brought the Negro in front of a special Commissioner, who decided whether the captive was to be returned to slavery. Commissioners were compensated ten dollars for each Negro they returned, but only five dollars for each Negro they freed. Accused fugitives were denied the right to jury trial and were not allowed to testify in their own defense. Marshals and deputies refusing to execute warrants were liable to $1000 fines, and citizens interfering with the arrest or transportation of fugitives were also subject to fines of $1000, as well as imprisonment for up to six months, and civil damages of $1000 for each fugitive lost.

At the time there were more than 600 fugitive slaves living in Boston, many of whom had been valued members of the community for a decade or more. The prospect of allowing them to be whisked away by mercenary bullies, under the aegis of a cynical law, whose only justification was as a quid pro quo to persuade Southern Congressmen to let California and New Mexico join the Union as free states, was more than the people of conscience in Boston could bear. As a man who was still unknown to the world, John Brown wrote to his wife; "It now seems the Fugitive Slave Law is to be the means of making more Abolitionists than all the lectures we have had for years."

Wentworth Higginson knocked on my door one morning in mid-October. "Just passing by and thought I'd drop in and look over the old stamping ground," he said blithely. I asked him in and offered him a glass of sherry, which he refused, not on grounds of temperance, but, as any good New Englander should, because the sun wasn't yet over the yard-arm. "It's a day for clear heads, Hacey. The slave-catchers have come."

"Well, we expected that. What's happening, Wentworth?"

"You know that Theodore Parker is Chairman of our Vigilance Committee, and in charge of all resistance? Well, yesterday he found out that two wretches by the names of Hughes and Knight had arrived in town and were making inquiries about William and Ellen Craft, a fugitive couple who have lived here almost five years. Craft is a carpenter, and an excellent one. They are industrious, friendly, skillful people, harming no one, an asset to Boston. They're now to be taken back to Virginia in chains. Parker forestalled the kidnapers by removing the Crafts and hiding them."

"Good for him!"

"Hughes and Knight countered by crying to one of our ten-dollar Commissioners that they were being interfered with in the performance of their duty. The Commissioner apparently got in touch with Washington and now there's a rumor that six hundred soldiers have been ordered here to enforce the law."

"Soldiers — in Boston? Don't they remember what happened when the British tried it in seventeen seventy-six?"

"Apparently our government remembers on July fourth and forgets on the other three hundred sixty-four days. Well, come on — get your coat."

"Where are we going?"

"Calling on two slave-catchers. Parker wants a large group."

"Wait a minute, Wentworth. If this is a mob you're talking about, I don't want any part of it. I've seen mobs in action, and I'd rather let the slave-catchers alone than stop them that way."

"Hacey, Hacey, what must you think of us? Do you think Theodore Parker would countenance mob violence? No, this is merely a demonstration of solidarity which we hope may have a cautionary effect on Hughes and Knight. Now stop shilly-shallying and come on."

The slave-catchers were staying in a third-rate commercial hotel near the railroad station. When we arrived, there were thirty or forty men on the sidewalk in front of the entrance. "Where's Parker?" Wentworth asked a well-dressed man with a suspicious bulge in his pocket that marred the drape of his coat.

"He should be here in another five minutes or so," the man replied.

"Are our friends still inside?"

"The desk clerk says they haven't left their room all morning."

I tugged at Wentworth's sleeve and whispered to him, "What is this? That fellow has a revolver in his coat pocket, and if most of the other men here aren't armed too, then I'm a Dutchman. You told me this wasn't going to be a mob."

"I wish you'd stop talking about mobs all the time. We're here to accompany a friend on a social visit — ah, I believe I see him now. Good morning, Theodore."

"Good morning, Wentworth," said the new arrival, whom I recognized as the famous Congregationalist preacher. "Shall we proceed?"

"After you," said Higginson politely. "The room number is two hundred and fourteen."

Parker entered the hotel and climbed the stairs to the second floor, closely followed by at least fifty armed men, who now produced their weapons and held them openly in their hands. I was shocked to see that my friend was holding a derringer, of the kind known as a "belly gun" and favored by gamblers. Noting my astonished expression, he smiled blandly and said, "In this uncertain life it is best to be prepared for all eventualities."

Parker stopped in front of room 214 and rapped on the door. A moment later it was opened by an unwholesome-looking man who, seeing the crowd in the hallway, immediately attempted to close it again. Before he could do so, Parker pushed his way into the room, and a dozen or more of us followed.

The two men in the room stared at us open-mouthed. "What the hell is this? What do you people think you're doing?" one of them managed to squeal. "You can't just break into a private room."

"I didn't. I knocked," replied Parker. "My name is Theodore Parker, and these gentlemen are my friends. We came here because we're worried about you."

"What do you mean, worried?"

"Worried for fear we can no longer ensure your safety. You see, ever since the good people of Boston discovered your purpose in visiting this city, there has been a certain restlessness in the air. Now, with the report that you have requested troops be sent here, tempers have risen alarmingly. Frankly, we're no longer sure we can defend you against our fellow citizens."

"*Defend* us? Why, you low-down abolitionist snake —"

"Therefore, it is my recommendation," continued Parker imperturbably, "that you both be on the train for New York City this afternoon. I believe we can fend off violence that long — but not for any longer. The train is at two-thirty, gentlemen. I think that's all." He bowed courteously, turned and stepped back through the door. For a few seconds the rest of us in the room stared at the two slave-catchers, and they stared back at the guns so much in evidence. Then Wentworth put his derringer away and left the room, and the rest of us followed. The last one out closed the hall door behind him, and we all trooped silently down the stairs and out into the street.

"Well, that should suffice, don't you agree, Hacey?" asked my friend cheerfully.

"Maybe — but I'm not at all sure it was the right thing to do. It smacks of intimidation to me."

"*Smacks* of it! Why, I should hope so. And now, if your

offer is still open, I believe the sun is definitely over the yardarm." And arm in arm, we made our way down the sidewalk until we found a carriage to take us back to Cambridge. Sure enough, the two slave-catchers were on the two-thirty train, and were never seen again in Boston. The Crafts returned to their home and William resumed his trade. No soldiers were sent into the city. Higginson and his fellow abolitionists were jubilant; they believed their action had paved the way for making the Fugitive Slave Law a dead letter in New England. I couldn't agree. For one thing, the illegal nature of it had disturbed me. For another, it had been too easy. I simply couldn't believe that the Wickliffes of the South, who had the power to force such an iniquitous law on the country, would allow a handful of Boston altruists to balk them.

Unfortunately I was right. During the following years, the slave-catchers came back — not Hughes and Knight, but others, more determined and more resourceful. Higginson was in the vanguard of the resistance on each occasion. In 1851, trying to arouse a mass meeting to march on the courthouse and free a fugitive named Sims, he made a speech which was so inflammatory that Wendell Phillips said later he had thought it put us "on the eve of revolution." And in 1854, in the most famous case of all, it was Thomas Wentworth Higginson, by then Pastor of the Free Church of Worcester, Massachusetts, whose shoulder forced open the jail door and who was wounded in the head in the attempt to rescue the fugitive, Anthony Burns.

These were stirring days, but in between them were many ordinary days on which I continued my studies, roamed the fascinating back streets of old Boston, and enjoyed musical evenings at Reverend Binder's. I had long since ceased to think of myself as one of Prudence's suitors, as it was apparent that she was unwilling to trade a covey of admirers for a single husband. In consequence I was able to enjoy an easy and undemanding relationship with the whole family, for which I have always been grateful.

In 1852 I decided to enter Harvard's Graduate College of Education. Ever since Cassius Clay had suggested that I might like to "preach, or teach, or write — or all three," I had been toying with the idea of becoming a teacher. Everyone I discussed it with thought I would be good at it, and the longer I lived with the possibility, the more logical and natural it seemed. So I was well on the way toward winning a Master's degree in Education to go along with my Master of Arts certificate, when I received the most fateful letter of my life.

XV

———•———

A Larger Hope

My dear Hacey,

I trust this finds you in good health, and as good spirits as can be expected in these dark times.

In your last letter you mentioned that it is now your intention to become a teacher. Sometimes I am forced to the trite conclusion that Providence does indeed move in mysterious ways, for it may be that a good teacher will be the most valuable man in Kentucky during the next few years.

I know how impatient you have been with the role assigned to you before you went East. It was as if you feared our "peculiar institution" would dry up and blow away before you were able to take up arms against it. Well, it has not dried up — and the time you have been preparing for may have come.

Let me explain. Among my real estate holdings is a considerable tract in the southern part of Madison County, about two miles from Boone's Gap. In it is a tiny settlement called The Glades, where twelve or thirteen families, all of good mountain stock, make their home. The Glades is literally the doorstep to the mountains, which begin only a mile or so to the south and west. It is the natural portal for all traffic from the Cumberlands to the Bluegrass; in other words, *from the free South to the slave South.*

It has long been my belief that the mountain folk, as Southerners who own land but do not own slaves, could become the vanguard of the emancipationist army. They share no economic interest with the planter class, are highly individualistic and freedom-loving, and are bitterly resentful of the unwarranted contempt in which they are often held by Tidewater and Bluegrass aristocrats.

They are also extremely God-fearing, and a few months ago representatives from the little community approached me, as the major landowner in the vicinity, and asked my assistance in starting a church in The Glades. I assured them of my support, and as a first step volunteered to seek out a minister for their approval.

I knew a preacher named John G. Fee, who had recently started churches in Bracken and Lewis Counties, on the Ohio River. Fee is an avowed enemy of slavery, even to the point of excluding all slave-owners from membership in his congregations. He had prepared and had printed an anti-slavery manual, a copy of which had chanced to come into my hands. Greatly impressed, I wrote him asking for additional copies, for distribution among those residents of The Glades who could read, and Fee immediately responded with a boxful. I had them delivered, and a few days later asked the good people whether they would care to have Reverend Fee as their guest for a series of meetings this summer. They assented enthusiastically. I then wrote Fee offering a most cordial invitation, and assuming the expenses of his journey. He accepted, and indicated he will arrive at The Glades in July, for a month's visit.

At the outset, my hope was simply to find a vigorous anti-slavery preacher for one small community. But as I have thought about it over the past two months, a much larger hope has begun to grow in my heart. With a man like Fee to build around, and with the unique location of The Glades at the edge of the mountains, I believe it would be possible to start a school there — possibly even a college — to train the young men and women of the Cumberlands in the arts and sciences of the nineteenth century, as well as the ideals of Christian antislavery. The effect this might have on Southern politics can scarcely be exaggerated. An estimated two million people live in the mountain areas of the South. Almost all are *potentially* emancipationist in their views, but their isolation and ignorance combine to make them politically impotent. Imagine the effect of introducing these proud (and quarrelsome!) egalitarians into the seats of the mighty.

This then, my young scholar, prompts my letter. I need a Kentuckian who combines youth, antislavery zeal, discretion and the qualifications of an educator — in a word, you, Hacey Miller — to represent me in day-to-day relations with Reverend Fee at The Glades this July, toward the ultimate goal of establishing a school for mountaineers. I will, of course, see that you suffer no financial loss if you agree to do this.

It has been said more often than need be that great oaks from little acorns grow. Examine this acorn, and send me your answer soon.

Impatiently, your friend,
C. M. CLAY

April 30, 1853

The letter exploded in my life like a bomb. When I received it I was studying for my oral examinations, and for the next few days all thoughts of academic subjects flew out of my mind. I went from room to room in the Old Den, soliciting the opinions of my classmates; I buttonholed my professors for their opinions; and of course I consulted Reverend Binder and Wentworth Higginson.

Higginson was buoyantly enthusiastic; Reverend Binder considerably less so. "You must remember to beware of adventurism, Hacey," warned the latter over teacups in his study. "I believe I have detected in your personality a certain tendency toward — ahem — the impulsive and unconsidered action, which is no doubt a result of your admiration for Cassius M. Clay. I don't mean to imply that Clay is not in many ways admirable, but I would hesitate to follow his lead uncritically in all matters, if I were you." He shook his head from side to side to emphasize the negative nature of his words, causing his drooping earlobes to swing like fat little pendulums.

"I can't agree," countered Wentworth. "Whether or not we approve of Cassius Clay's sometimes overly exuberant tactics is hardly the point, is it, sir? Generals may choose their aides, but aides don't choose their generals. Hacey has been chafing at the bit for years, complaining to anyone who will listen that he's not *doing* anything. Well, this is his chance to do something."

"You believe this — ah, opportunity — offers him the scope he might find elsewhere? To me it seems — forgive me, Hacey — modest at the outset, problematical in development and quite possibly dangerous in its potentialities." He shook his head again, and refilled all three of our teacups.

Wentworth, his mouth not entirely free of toasted muffin,

cried excitedly, "Of course it's a gamble, sir — so was Thermopylae! But Clay's right — there are great issues at stake here. And it just may happen that this little clearing in the foothills will turn out to be a crucial battlefield in Man's war against injustice! Hacey, I envy you the chance to serve there."

It was on this note — with Wentworth's enthusiasm, undimmed by Reverend Binder's apprehensions, buoying my spirits — that I took my leave from both of them.

Prudence Binder was sewing in the front room, and I stayed to chat with her for a few moments.

"So you've really decided to disappear into the wilderness forever, have you, Hacey Miller? Well, I'm sure it's very noble of you," she said tartly, pausing in the middle to take the pins out of her pretty mouth.

"Yes, I thought I'd do that," I replied nonchalantly. "I hope it's not wormwood and gall to you. Try to remember that there *are* other men in the world."

"That's something I've never been in the least doubt about. But you did help swell the multitude. It's too cruel of you to take yourself off without even asking my permission."

I smiled at her, and her eyes twinkled back at me. Since I had given up any romantic interest in her, we had become friends. "You're quite the prettiest thing I'll be leaving, Prudence," I told her.

"Thank you. Just for that, you may kiss me on your way out."

"I'm on my way out now." I bent over and kissed her pink, pursed lips. She smelled fresh and sweet, like a flower garden in late spring. After a few seconds I said, "It's too bad we didn't start this some years ago."

205

She sighed. "Good luck, friend Hacey. Take care of yourself."

"Goodbye, Prudence. You're the prettiest girl I know."

During the next two weeks it took all my will power to force myself to study for my examination, and I passed it with considerably lower marks than I might otherwise have received. Then Commencement, farewell parties, goodbyes to friends — all of it seemingly irrelevant in the light of the exciting future ahead.

For I was done with Boston now, I felt — done with the North, done with beans and squash in the Commons, done with musical evenings at the Binders'. I was going back to Kentucky, to the Bluegrass and the mountains, to fight the good fight with Cassius M. Clay.

I had just turned twenty-one years old.

XVI

———•❦•———

The Glades

THE MORNING AFTER my return to Hazelwood I saddled Sacajawea myself — even after two years, the gibing words of Frederick Douglass were still a burr under the blanket of my brain — and rode over to Clay's country home, White Hall. I tied my horse to the hitching post outside the handsome portico and knocked on the door. It was opened by Timothy, the ancient Negro servant who had been with Cash Clay since he was a boy. "Good morning, Timothy, how have you been?"

He squinted his old eyes fiercely. "Sir?" he demanded.

"It's Hacey Miller, Timothy. I expect you better get yourself a pair of spectacles."

His face lit up with a gratifying smile, and he swung the door wide. "Sakes alive, Mr. Hacey, how you been? What you talking about, spectacles? I knowed it was you, only I just wanted you to fret a minute, on account you been such a stranger. Mr. Clay be mighty glad to see you."

"Thank you, Timothy. You just tell me where he is and I'll find my own way."

But he insisted on showing me to Clay's study himself, and announcing me with a flourish. Clay rose from his easy chair and greeted me warmly. Of his bout with death four years ago there remained no sign; he was as dynamic as I remembered him to have been at Foxtown, or, for that matter, in the office of *The True American,* four years before that.

He put an arm around my shoulders affectionately. "Hacey, confound it, you're a man!" he said in his resonant deep voice. "Don't you know it's a terrible thing to present yourself to your older friends as a man grown? It makes them face the fact that a fair amount of water has flowed under the bridge since they first saw you. *O lente, lente currite, noctis equi.*"

"That's the first time I ever heard a Kentuckian pray for a horse to run slow."

Clay gave a rare chuckle. "First and last time, I hope. Timothy, I think some refreshment would be in order. I'm afraid we don't have any root beer to offer you today, Hacey —"

Remembering my consumption of countless gallons of temperance punch in Boston, I answered, "I think I'll follow your lead and have a cold toddy, Mr. Clay."

"Good fellow! Make it two, Timothy — and use the twelve-year-old bourbon."

Timothy shot an aggrieved glance at his employer. *"Of course* I use the twelve-year-old bourbon! You think I want to poison him with that four-year stuff?" He shuffled from the room, muttering in exasperation.

A few minutes later, frosty drinks in our hands, Clay and I were talking about abolitionist Boston and the Fugitive Slave Law. Clay reacted to my account of Parker's and Higginson's calculated defiance of the law with mixed feelings.

"The law is the law, and it must remain inviolate. You

can change it, yes — that's what a government of laws is for. But break it wilfully? Never — because that's anarchy. And much as I admire your friends — particularly Higginson, the way you describe him — I believe the road they're following can lead only to anarchy. Hacey, remember this — laws are made by men, and they can be changed by men. All you ever need to amend a weak or vicious law is a bare majority of honest and informed citizens who are not obliged by self-interest to uphold it."

"But what if you can't get a majority?"

"Then you shouldn't change the law!"

"Even though it's a bad law, Mr. Clay — as bad as the Fugitive Slave Law?"

He closed his eyes for a second and brushed the hair back from his brow in an automatic gesture. Then he replied soberly, "That's where the plow hits the rock, boy. But, yes — even though it's a bad law — even though it's the worst law in the world. Even then — you obey the law or you change it. One or the other. But you don't break it. Or if you do, you're a criminal, and deserve to be treated like one."

Silence hung between us for a few seconds, as I cast about for a way to change the subject. "The people in the mountains, though — you think there's a chance of adding them to the emancipationist forces, to create that 'bare majority' you mentioned?" I asked.

"I do. Under the right circumstances, I believe they can take and hold the balance of power in the nation. They can put an end to slavery within our lifetime, and do it legally, and with fair compensation for the slave-owner."

"And you think that this Reverend Fee can become the catalyst for all this? I'm sorry, Mr. Clay, but I don't understand how. There have been antislavery preachers around here for years — some of them really famous, like Reverend Breckinridge — with no discernible effect, as far as I can see."

"That's true, of course. But Hacey, I believe that for the first time we may see the right man at the right place at the right moment. The right place is The Glades, for the reasons I told you about in my letter; it's the doorstep to two million free Southerners. The right moment is now, while Cousin Harry's Compromise still holds up, and the hands of the clock are stopped at five minutes to twelve.

"And the right man is John G. Fee.

"Let me tell you a little about this man. He's utterly dedicated and utterly fearless. He's been clubbed, stoned, bushwhacked, whipped — for years he's lived every day with the knowledge that his wife and children were hostages to the prejudice of his neighbors — but he's never backed down an inch. He was raised a Presbyterian and graduated from a Presbyterian seminary — but when the Synod told him he wasn't allowed to exclude slaveholders from his church, he quit without a moment's hesitation!"

"I'm sure he's a great preacher, Mr. Clay. But in your letter you wrote about starting a school as well as a church. Why do you think Fee would be interested in that, or be any good at it?"

"Since he left the Presbyterian Church, Fee has been supported — in a very modest way — by the American Missionary Association. This is a Yankee group that believes in civilizing the heathen, and takes the enlightened view that the heathen start at the Ohio River. Fee sees himself as an educator as well as preacher, and in the past he's occasionally been assisted by young students from Oberlin College, who've spent their summer vacations teaching illiterate children to read and write."

"And is that what you want me to do?"

"Hold your horses, Hacey — we've got to learn to crawl before we can begin walking. When Reverend Fee comes to The Glades next month, it will be for the sole purpose of holding a series of meetings with the people of that community. What will come of it, only time will tell. I happen to think that mighty important things may come of it. But we're fishing for big fish, and I'd hate to jerk the line before the hook is set."

"You mean you don't want to talk to Fee about your ultimate hopes?"

"That's right. I don't want to talk to him about them, and I don't want *you* to talk to him about them, either."

"Then what am I supposed to do when he gets here?"

"You go with him wherever he goes, see that his needs are satisfied, advise him on local questions, drive his buggy for him — and make sure he doesn't get hurt." He reached over to his desk and pulled open a drawer. "I don't suppose you've ever learned to use a bowie knife, have you?"

"No, sir. Not so's you'd notice it."

"Too bad. A bowie knife is always loaded, and it never misfires. However — you'd better take this along with you." He took a pistol from the drawer and handed it to me. I recognized it as one of the type known as "pepperboxes," with five revolving barrels. Clay rummaged in the drawer again and produced a small cloth bag. "Here are some percussion caps. Don't drop them — they're fulminate of mercury, and they'd blow a leg off you. There are some balls in there, too. I trust you know how to load them."

Stung, I answered with some asperity, "I may not be a virtuoso with a bowie knife, like some people, Mr. Clay, but I'm a moderately accurate pistol shot."

"I'm gratified to hear that," he said dryly. "Mr. Fee

seems to attract the attention of persons of a not overly pacific type, so I hope you'll stand ready to demonstrate your moderate skill at any time."

I stood up and slipped the pistol into one coat pocket and the percussion caps into another. "I trust I don't prove a disappointment to you, Mr. Clay," I said with what I hoped was chilly dignity.

"Oh, Hacey, don't get up on a high horse. I didn't mean to hurt your feelings. It's only that I've learned never to take anything for granted where self-defense is concerned. When trouble starts, there's no margin for error. You stay alive because your reactions are a split second faster than the other man's, or because your powder is drier than his, or because you put in a fresh percussion cap ten minutes ago, or because you remembered to leave your coat unbuttoned. I don't really expect you to be involved in any gun fighting, or I wouldn't ask you to take on the job — but you have to know that it *is* possible. This man Fee inspires high feelings, and I wouldn't want anything to happen to either of you."

Ashamed of my brief exhibition of petulance, I replied quietly, "I'll try to do everything you and Reverend Fee expect of me, sir. When do you think he'll arrive here in Madison County, and when do you want to see me again?"

"He promised to come to White Hall the first Monday in July. I don't suppose he could get here much before evening. Why don't you figure on coming over sometime after dinner that night to meet him? Plan to stay the night here, and the next day we'll all ride down to The Glades together."

"I'll be here," I said, and shook his hand as we made our farewells. Old Timothy showed me to the front door. "Tell me the truth, Timothy," I said to him as I was leaving. "Would that four-year-old bourbon really have poisoned me?"

"You just remember what I said, Mr. Hacey, and don't you mess with it," he replied dourly.

*   *   *

My parents were concerned about my professional future. Although I couldn't think seriously about anything beyond the coming summer, I made application for a teaching position at both Transylvania and Centre College in Danville. After a number of personal interviews with whatever functionaries were available during the summer vacation, I was tentatively promised an instructorship in philosophy at Transylvania, beginning the following fall. Thus resolving all doubts about whether or not I was capable of earning my daily bread after a total of seven years in college, I felt free to relax and enjoy myself until Reverend Fee arrived.

The placid June days swam by as I renewed old friendships, briefed myself on another year's worth of tangled Bluegrass politics, and, two or three nights at least, drank myself into a happy fuddlement. I attended a Fortnightly at Madame Mentelle's, where I was much the most worldly and sophisticated fellow on the floor, and where I watched with brows ironically raised as my brother Boone waltzed Robin Ledyard through the evening.

Boone was now in his senior year at Transylvania Medical School, and doing well. He had been promised the opportunity of going into partnership with Dr. Miles Renfro, one of Lexington's leading doctors, upon his graduation. His future looked bright, and he seemed to feel it was time to give some thought to the taking of a wife.

I had mixed feelings about Robin as a sister-in-law. She was attractive enough, certainly, with long black curls that hung to her shoulders, a well-rounded little figure that stopped just this side of being plump, and a dark and roving eye. A bit flirtatious, in fact, but most girls were in those

213

days. What bothered me was her Ledyardism. I had gotten into the habit of thinking the Ledyards represented all the worst in Southern culture: the assumption of superiority based on blood rather than intelligence or character; the callous disregard for the feelings of people below one's own class; the quarrelsomeness that masquerades as a high sense of honor; the blind uncritical eye that values counterfeit European work over honest American. If Boone married her, I would have to try to modify my prejudices, and I didn't really want to.

I discussed it one night with Falk Padgett, over a half gallon of corn whiskey. Falk couldn't afford decent bourbon, so he patronized a nefarious Iristown peddler of "moon." He insisted he liked it better than aged sour mash, but I think that was just natural mountain contrariness.

"Aw, hell, Hasty, I don't think you got much of a problem," he said, hooking a finger through the loop on the neck of the jug and tilting it over his forearm. "It's always easier to be prejudiced against your in-laws than against strangers. Look at it this way — you ain't losing a brother, you're gaining a whole passel of aristocrats."

"You always were a comfort," I said bitterly. "Pass over that pop-skull before you drink yourself stone blind." I took a swallow and shuddered.

"Good squeezings," Falk said complacently. "Now what was you saying about that settlement in Madison County?" Before our digression on in-laws, I had started to tell him about Reverend Fee's approaching visit to The Glades, and to explain something of Clay's hopes for a bridgehead into the mountains.

"You say Old Cash is fixing to start a school for mountain folk? A sure-enough college?"

"Well, that's what he told me. Of course, that's years in

the future. For now, we're just trying to see if Fee likes The Glades and The Glades likes him."

"A college for mountain folk," mused Falk quietly. "You know, if there was such a place as that, why, people could go there and get enough learning to go home and teach other people. And then those other people could teach another batch of other people — and it could keep going on and on forever."

"That's right, Falk. The mountains would never be the same again."

He looked at me shrewdly. "And I reckon that ain't the only thing that would never be the same again, is it?"

"What do you mean?"

"I mean after a while the Bluegrass wouldn't be the same as it was, neither. Old man Wickliffe wouldn't be able to lead them Frankfort politicians around by the nose the way he does now, would he?"

"I suppose it might have some effect on the slavery question, yes."

"Like eating a plate of beans might have some effect on the farting question. And don't look at me so disgusted — I'm just trying to get things straight in this little old woolly brain of mine." He addressed himself to the jug briefly, then wiped his mouth with the back of his hand. "Hoooo — that's what you call mellow! You know, it occurs to me that there's a considerable number of people around here who ain't going to be as friendly as four in a bed, when they find out what you and Clay are up to."

"You reckon?" I opened my eyes wide and blinked them innocently.

"As a matter of fact, I wouldn't be surprised if you were buying yourself more trouble than Old Cash got into with his newspaper!"

"I declare," I said with a Delta accent. We sat in silence for a moment, and then a smile curved up one side of his mouth. "A college for mountain folk. Now wouldn't that be something! Hasty, I got me a little sister — I ain't seen her for years. She'd be about fifteen now. You reckon she'd be able to go to that college before she gets too old?"

"Shucks, Falk, I don't even know if there's ever going to *be* a college, let alone when. Now pass me over that embalming fluid, and be ready to catch me when I fall."

I seem to remember that after some more passing of the jug we took the remains of the "moon" with us and paid a call on two friendly young ladies of Falk's acquaintance. While it certainly wasn't a commercial transaction, I thought it might not be inappropriate to present a small monetary gift to the ladies, and their gratitude was heart-warming.

Later, after we had returned to Falk's room in the back of the store, I was just beginning to fall asleep when I heard him say, "If that don't beat all!" Expecting a spicy footnote to our evening's adventures, I asked him what he meant.

"A college for mountain folk. God damn! If that don't beat all!"

*   *   *

The first Monday in July, Clay sent a message to me at Hazelwood confirming Fee's arrival that evening. After dinner I packed two saddlebags with enough necessities so I wouldn't need to come home for two weeks, and rode over to White Hall. Timothy showed me into the study, and I had my first glimpse of John Gregg Fee.

He was in his late thirties, rather below middle height, with a large head and a slender body. He was clean-shaven, and his hair was reddish brown. His expression was solemn, and his large, eloquent eyes seemed reproachful, although I was to discover that his face could light up with joy when the occasion permitted it.

He and Clay rose as I entered the room, and Clay introduced me. "Reverend Fee, I'd like you to meet Hacey Miller — a young man, but an old friend in the emancipation movement. Hacey's just come down from Harvard, where he took a Master's degree in Education."

"How do you do, Brother Miller," said Fee in a high, piping voice, putting out his hand to take mine.

"It's a great pleasure to meet you, Reverend," I answered. "I've geen looking forward to your arrival ever since I got back to the Bluegrass."

"While he was in Boston," continued Clay, "Hacey managed to meet a good number of the leading antislavery people: Parker, Garrison, Phillips, a young preacher named Higginson . . ."

"And were you encouraged with the progress of our Northern brethren?" Fee interrupted.

"Yes, sir — but I couldn't help wishing I had more brothers down here and fewer up there. Sometimes in Kentucky you get to feel like an only child."

Fee searched my face for signs of levity, and finding none, replied, "None of us is alone, Brother Miller, remember that. The Spirit is with each of us, and without the Spirit, all else is as sounding brass or a tinkling cymbal."

"Amen, Reverend," said Cassius Clay. "And now I wonder if I might offer you a bit of refreshment before you retire — teetotal, of course."

And out came the famous C. M. Clay root beer. I accepted it philosophically, for I had already faced up to the fact that I wouldn't taste alcohol again while I was in the company of Reverend Fee. And it really *was* good root beer.

The next morning Timothy woke us early, and after a substantial but brief breakfast, we were on the road to Richmond and The Glades. Fee had arrived on horseback, but Clay decided the preacher would be more comfortable if he had the use of a buggy as well. So the two of them rode in the little four-wheeler Clay insisted on lending Fee, pulled by a high-stepping gray mare, and leading their two saddle horses. I rode beside them on Sackie.

We went through Richmond by eleven o'clock, and were at The Glades by early afternoon. The last two miles of road we traveled hardly deserved that name; at the thought of what it would be like after a rain, the mind boggled. All of us realized that the buggy was an impractical idea in such country, but nobody said anything about it, because Fee and I also realized that Clay didn't want to be bothered taking it back to White Hall over the same road that afternoon.

The Glades was a settlement of a dozen or so rustic cabins in a saucer-shaped depression that might have been a prehistoric lake bed. Just to the south of the settlement, the ground sloped gradually upward to form a ridge a hundred feet high, then leveled off into a plateau that ran for two miles and ended at the foot of the mountains that reared abruptly skyward. The Ridge — which was the land Cassius Clay owned — and the tableland behind it were uncut by any roads and were covered with almost impenetrable underbrush.

Ahead of us, to the south, lay the gap in the mountains through which Daniel Boone first glimpsed the verdant richness of the Bluegrass. Beyond that gap were the Appalachians, ten different ranges, 150 miles deep, 500 miles long. Two million people lived there, Cash Clay had said. Two million Southerners with scarcely a slave among them — damned up as though behind a dike.

A sudden tingling excitement played over my body like a

chilling wind. *Is this where the dike will burst?* I asked myself.

We rode down the wretched dirt trail into The Glades and stopped in front of a large but graceless building built of hand-hewn logs. Most of the mud that had been packed between the logs had fallen out, and through the small window at the front we could see large holes gaping in the crudely shingled roof.

"This is Glades Meeting House, Reverend," Clay said. "A bit worse for wear now, but I'm sure the good folks here will help you and Hacey get it into shape."

Fee walked slowly around the outside of the building, then around the inside, taking careful note of all that needed to be done before the meetings could begin. By the time he was through, a small crowd of residents had gathered around us. They were a poor-looking lot, I thought — what the Ledyards would have called "trash." The men and boys wore overalls, mostly without any shirts under them. The women were dressed in drab-colored dresses of homespun, and many of their heads were concealed in their poke bonnets. The children were silent and dirty and barefooted. One little boy had lost all of his hair from a vicious case of impetigo, leaving his scalp covered with scabs. He was protectively holding the hand of a little girl two or three years his junior, whose unfixed gaze and open mouth testified that she was "touched."

Clay knew all the people there, and spoke warmly to each of them. "Mrs. Boatright, ma'am, I'm proud to see you again. And is this little Caleb? Why, I never would have known him! Caleb, boy, you know you've *grown!* Mrs. Boatright, let me introduce you to the preacher, Reverend Fee. Reverend Fee, I'd like you to meet Mrs. Nester Boatright and her son Caleb. Why, howdy, Mrs. Kinnard, you're

looking mighty fit. Howdy, John! Are these your youngsters? Now, don't tell me, let me sort them out myself. This
is Boag, and this is Burritt — Lordy, boys, how you've
grown —"

One by one he went through the whole crowd that way,
passing them on in turn to Reverend Fee. When they'd all
been introduced to the preacher, Clay gave a wave of his
hand toward me. "Folks, this is Hacey Miller from over on
the other side of Richmond. He's come to help out Reverend
Fee any way he can."

Everyone looked at me with the carefully neutral look
that mountain people use on you until they've found out
something either for you or against you. I smiled and
nodded my head, wondering if I looked like a "swell" to
them in my worn broadcloth suit. "Howdy. Pleased to meet
you all," I said, and they nodded gravely in return.

Clay then addressed himself to the question of accommo-
dations for Fee and me. The family with the largest house in
the settlement — two large rooms with a full loft above, and
only one child — claimed the preacher. The bidding for me
was considerably less spirited; after two or three home owners allowed as how "we might squeeze him in with a couple of
the young ones for a night or two, if he can't find no place
else," it was decided I would sleep at the Swinglehursts'.
Apparently there was room enough in little Andrew's bed,
if Ann Eliza slept with her ma and pa. Little Andrew was
the boy with impetigo, and Ann Eliza his unfortunate sister.

For the next week I worked harder than I had ever
worked before. Since most of the men in The Glades were
employed on neighboring farms, the only help I could count
on regularly was Reverend Fee, and he had a frail physique
and very little manual dexterity. Each day I started before
seven o'clock, after a breakfast of corn bread and sorghum

and hog belly stewed with greens, and with all of it sitting uneasily an inch or two under my heart. Chinking the logs took two days, repairing the roof took three more, for I had to split my own shingles. Then, once the meetinghouse was weathertight, I had the problem of repairing all the slab benches inside, and building a platform six inches higher than the packed dirt of the floor, to serve as a pulpit. When this was completed, there only remained the job of white-washing the inner walls of the meetinghouse, and the Church of The Glades was ready for services.

As soon as the whitewash was dry, the word was passed around the settlement and the neighboring farms that Reverend Fee was going to preach that night after supper. It was a joyous meal in The Glades, a real church supper, the first one most of those folks had ever had in their own settlement. The men set up tables on the ground outside the meetinghouse, and the ladies piled them up with fried chicken and fresh pork, crackling and gravy and corn pudding, greens sharp with the flavor of vinegar and bacon, and thick slices of fresh-baked bread still warm from the bake oven, richly spread with sweet churned butter.

I don't know where those poor people got all that food. Each household must have contributed the better part of a week's supply of victuals, and the very best they had in their larders, at that. But it couldn't have been better spent. The women were so proud of themselves for laying out that spread they were near to bursting, and the men and the children kept looking from one dish to another in happy incredulity.

The Glades had its church and its preacher — and by God, now it was going to eat supper!

After everybody had eaten everything he could stuff down, and the ladies had cleared away the remains, people began to arrive from the surrounding neighborhood. One I recognized was a farmer named Rawlings, who lived over toward Richmond, at least five miles away. He was a tall, lanky, weather-beaten man with a jutting beak of a nose and hooded eyes of milky blue. He had a soft voice and a humorous way of turning his mouth down at the corners that had caused me to like him on sight.

I nodded a greeting to him, and to a few other arrivals I knew, but what I was really watching for were troublemakers. There were bound to be some in attendance, since Mr. Fee's antislavery principles were no secret. Although I didn't expect any trouble that night — if it came, it would come later, after a warning — I was carrying the pepperbox in my side pocket, and it bumped my leg uncomfortably each time I took a step.

The bully boys weren't difficult to identify when they arrived. For one thing, they were the only people present who were not well scrubbed and wearing their Sunday best. For another, they carried themselves with the ostentatious arrogance that generally masks an inner nervousness. They didn't seem to have anything to say to anyone else, but stood together on the fringe of a group, conspicuous in greasy jeans and work shirts, either in silence or talking to each other. Their names were Lafe and Barney Tuttle.

I decided not to mention my suspicions to Reverend Fee, but to stay close enough to them to prevent any unpleasantness while they were at The Glades. When the two of them found seats on a bench in the meetinghouse, I took a place on the bench immediately behind them. A moment later a man squeezed past the people at the end of my bench and took a seat beside me. I glanced up and saw it was Mr. Rawlings. I smiled a greeting and started to speak, but he silenced me with a shake of his head. Then he pointed with a bony,

leather-skinned finger, first at me, then at Lafe Tuttle's fat
back directly in front of me, then at himself, then at Barney
Tuttle's skinny back directly in front of him. His meaning
was unmistakable, and I felt a kind of muscular sigh go
through my body at the discovery that I had an ally in the
meetinghouse.

When everyone had found seats and the youngsters had
been quieted, Fee stepped on the platform and looked over
his congregation. We looked back at him, and in the silence
I felt like a naughty child brought before a stern father for
righteous punishment. Then a gentle, almost a bashful smile
lit up his features, and he began to sing, in a pure, high
tenor:

> We are climbing Jacob's Ladder —

The congregation joined in, tentatively at first, then with
more confidence:

> We are climbing Jacob's Ladder,
> We are climbing Jacob's Ladder,
> Soldiers of the Cross.

It was the first time I heard the familiar hymn sung the way
Fee sang it. I wonder how many times I have heard it since
— two thousand? five thousand? And yet each time my
heart leaps upward with every musical step up that ladder to
Heaven.

Fee started us out on melody, and once we were pounding
along satisfactorily, he began singing harmony with us, and
some of the more daring singers in the congregation followed
him. On each rung of the ladder, his harmony got further
away from our melody, until, on "Soldiers of the Cross," he
would come back to join us in ringing unison.

It made my back hair stand up.

After "Jacob's Ladder" he led us in the Lord's Prayer. Then we sang "Rock of Ages." Then it was time for the sermon.

As Fee read the lesson from the Scriptures, the Tuttle boys leaned forward and paid close attention. It was Deuteronomy XXIII, 15 and 16. "Thou shalt not deliver unto his master the servant which is escaped from his master unto thee," he read in his high, penetrating voice. "He shall dwell with thee, even among you, in that place which he shall choose in one of thy gates, where it liketh him best: thou shalt not oppress him."

It didn't take a biblical scholar to know that this reading had some application to the fugitive slave problem of the day, but Fee didn't leave anything to chance. He spelled it out, clear and unmistakable. Slavery was against the law of God. Therefore it was the duty of every Christian not only to free his own slaves, but to assist anybody else's slaves to escape if he had the opportunity. No slave-owner could possibly be a Christian, and therefore no Christian church could admit a slave-owner to membership. And only when no man remained a slave or a slave-owner could the United States consider itself a truly Christian nation.

He quoted Scripture to back up every statement he made. He spoke in a calm manner, but with great earnestness, and no one who heard him could fail to realize he not only believed every word he spoke, but was also willing to follow that belief wherever it led.

Schooled as I was in the difference between abolitionism and emancipationism, I realized that Fee represented abolitionism of the purest Boston strain. I wondered if C. M. Clay knew how cheaply Reverend Fee held the law of the land, when he felt it contradicted God's law.

He spoke for close to an hour, and after he finished, the Tuttle boys could barely wait through the singing of "Onward, Christian Soldiers," to be off and make their report to whomever was waiting for it. As they pushed their way through the departing crowd, Mr. Rawlings looked at me with a deceptively sleepy expression, pulled the corners of his mouth down, and said, "They was in such a hurry to leave you wouldn't reckon they was planning on coming back, would you?"

"I'd reckon they were planning on coming back, sir," I answered.

"Would you? Well, come to think of it, I'd reckon they was too," he said reflectively. "I'm just a hog about good preaching. Figure to be over here at The Glades every night while the Reverend's holding his meetings. Was you planning on being around too?"

"Yes, sir, I'll be here every night — it's sort of my job. I'm glad to know there will be two of us."

"Oh, I expect there might be more than that, if there was to be a need for them." He smiled and touched one leathery finger to his snowy white hat brim and took his leave. The next night he was back, and every week night and Sunday that Reverend Fee preached.

But as it happened, neither Mr. Rawlings nor my borrowed pepperbox were called into service during the meetings that July. Nonetheless, Lafe and Barney Tuttle and their friends were heard from.

The morning of the first Sunday Fee preached — it must have been about the fifth day of the meetings — we found a proclamation nailed to the door of the meetinghouse. It was signed "Madison County Law and Order Committee," and it served notice that the law-abiding citizens of the county had discovered that criminal abolitionism was being advocated at The Glades by one John Gregg Fee of Bracken County, a notorious demagogue who had been expelled from the Presbyterian Church for his illegal and atheistic views. The patience of the good people of the county could not be expected to last indefinitely, and if Fee were permitted to continue at The Glades, or if he were allowed to return, the blood would be on the misguided heads of those who supported him.

The following Sunday was the last day of the meetings, and after services a delegation of the residents of the little settlement called on Reverend Fee and formally asked him to live among them and be their preacher. He replied that his duties in Bracken and Lewis Counties would keep him occupied for the balance of the year, but that next spring he would be proud to move his wife and children to The Glades and join them.

We had taken our first short step toward the Dream.

XVII

---•---

THE SCHOOL

THE GREAT COMPROMISE of 1850 — that omnibus of balanced libertarianism and injustice, which was sure to preserve harmony in the Union for thirty years — was overthrown less than four years after its passage. In January of 1854, Senator Stephen A. Douglas introduced his Kansas-Nebraska Act for the organization and admission of the two territories as states on the basis of "Squatter Sovereignty," with each state to come in free or slave depending on the choice of its inhabitants. This spelled the death of the Missouri Compromise, and the Great Compromise of 1850 which had incorporated it, for now there was no Henry Clay to enter the lists in its defense; the Sage of Ashland, slowly dying all during his last year in office, had laid his burden down more than a year before.

I was living in Lexington and teaching at Transylvania when the debate on the Kansas-Nebraska Act began. I kept my views to myself, since I saw no virtue in trying to argue with the entire Bluegrass. But I was lured into honest disputation once, and it almost resulted in tragedy.

One weekend in early spring, my brother Boone's roommate, Alan Prichard, invited some friends to a house party at his home on the Kentucky River near Frankfort. At the same time his sister invited an equal number of her friends, and by a happy coincidence her friends turned out to be just those young ladies in whom his friends were most interested. In my case the young lady was Miss Arabella Moore, to whom I was attracted primarily because of her resemblance to Rebecca Gratz Bruce — recently married to John Hunt Morgan — the most ethereally beautiful woman I had ever seen.

The house party began with a luncheon early Saturday afternoon, then moved out-of-doors for boating on the river and croquet on the lawn. Boone and Robin Ledyard and Arabella and I were just finishing a game of croquet, when the next foursome came along. It consisted of our host, "Pritch," my old friend Danford Ranew, and their two young ladies.

My feelings toward Ranew were unchanged since the time I had warned him away from my sister after his disgraceful behavior with Robards' "Choice Stock." The looks he leveled at me during our infrequent meetings indicated that he reciprocated my feelings.

Boone had just asked me if I didn't feel that the Kansas-Nebraska Act might not solve the slavery question once and for all, and I replied that I certainly hoped so.

"I declare, don't you boys have anything else to talk about but politics?" Arabella asked with a winsome toss of her head.

"No, wait a minute, 'Bella," said Pritch, who was serious-minded about his politics, although not overly bright about the subject. "You said you *hoped* so, Hacey, not that you *think* so. Don't you think so?"

"Well, who knows, Pritch?" I replied, still trying to avoid

228

a direct answer. My ball was squarely in front of the last two wickets, in line with the stake. "I haven't got my fortune telling cards with me, so I pass the question." I made my shot, and the ball headed through the wickets, straight toward the brightly striped stake.

Ranew, rattling the ice in the julep he was holding, put out his foot and deflected the ball to one side and backward, leaving me with an impossible shot. "He passes the question because he hasn't had a chance to ask Cash Clay or his preacher friend if the law's going to help abolitionists to steal our niggers," he said, in a voice that showed the effects of more than one julep.

"Come on, Danford," said Pritch warningly. "No, seriously, Hacey — I'd be interested in hearing your views on the subject."

"*I* wouldn't!" said Arabella, pouting.

Annoyed with all of them, I replied shortly, "All right. It's a bad law. It's already wrecked whatever perilous stability we got from the Compromise. It gives the slave power the foolish hope they can extend slavery into the territories. Now they'll keep on trying, and it will mean fighting everywhere they try it." I walked over to my croquet ball and picked it up and placed it back in front of the two wickets. "I'll take that shot over, if there's no objection."

"Hell, we don't mind a little friendly cheating," Ranew replied. Nobody said anything as I made my shot and hit the stake. Boone's face went dead white.

I picked up my ball and turned to Ranew. "The trouble with the lard-heads who like to think of themselves as the Southern Aristocracy," I said deliberately, "is that they keep getting what they *want* mixed up with what they can get. For instance, Danford, some of them would like to see Rob-

ards' Choice Stock available in Kansas as well as Lexington.
Now you have to admit that's just plain jackass stupid, don't
you?"

He stared at me for a second while he sorted out the meaning of my words. Then he took a step toward me and said,
"You're no gentleman, Miller. You're a damn poltroon. Give
me satisfaction or I'll have you cowhided."

"Like Robards threatened to do to you?" I jeered. I had
been sure he intended to call me out, and I was exhilarated
by his challenge. Cassius Clay's words to John Hunt Morgan on the courthouse lawn rang through my mind, and I
modified them to fit the circumstances. "Ranew, I have no
intention of setting myself and my beliefs as a target for the
bullies and assassins of the slavocracy. But I am always
willing to defend myself against attack — no matter how
cowardly."

I turned from him and gave a nod to Arabella, feeling that
Junius Brutus Booth could hardly have played the scene
more dramatically, or acquitted himself better. But I had
failed to remember how differently my brother Boone and I
looked at things — as I realized when I heard the slap of a
hard hand against a flabby cheek.

Suddenly sickened, I didn't need to turn around to know
what had happened. Boone, ashamed because, in his eyes, I
had failed to act as a man of honor should, had determined to
save the family's good name by calling out Ranew himself.
It was as idiotic as it was inevitable.

"Oh, Jesus, Boone —" I began.

"Hacey, would you act for me in this matter?" he interrupted levelly.

Ranew stared incredulously at Boone for a moment, and
then said, "All right, you son of a bitch, if I can't kill your

brother, I guess I'll have to kill you instead. Pritch, second me, will you?"

"The sooner we do it the better, Ranew," said Boone. "Hacey, arrange it for tomorrow morning." He turned to Prichard and said, "Sorry, Pritch," gave a little bow to the girls, and walked away from us into the house.

Prichard and I agreed that we wouldn't make any arrangements until both of us had talked to our principals privately and tried to dissuade them from such a desperate and foolish adventure. Swearing the four girls to secrecy — and knowing how much good *that* was going to do — we separated; he took Ranew off for a walk in the garden, and I went to find Boone.

He was in his room, writing a letter to our father and mother. He looked up as I burst through the door. "Hacey, would you see that ma and pa get this letter, if anything happens to me tomorrow?" he asked politely.

"Boone, you don't need to write any letter. There's not going to be any duel tomorrow."

"Oh? Did Ranew apologize?"

"No, he's too stupid to apologize. But that's not the point. The point is, this doesn't make any sense. You and Ranew don't have anything to fight about. It's me he was after, not you. Why the hell did you stick your nose into it, anyway?"

"I didn't figure I had any choice, Hacey," he said mildly.

"Christ, Boone, don't you know that this whole dueling business is a swindle to allow wasters and bullies like Ranew to kill anybody they want and get away with it?"

He smiled. "Yes, I know that's often true."

"Then why in the world would you fall into the trap? Do you *want* to get your brains blown out?"

"Hacey, you're older than I am, and smarter. You've

231

been East to college, and I'm sure you know a lot more about most things than I ever will. But there's one thing I figure I know a little more about than you do. And that's what we owe to our family and our family name."

"Boone, don't be more of a fool than God intended for you to be. Do you think Mama and Papa will be happy you defended the family name when you're brought back to them with a pistol ball in your head?"

"Maybe not happy, but prouder than they'd be if they heard their other son wasn't man enough to accept a challenge!"

"Do you really believe that?"

He sighed. "Hacey, I'm not right sure I know what to believe. I remember how we used to argue about niggers when we were children. I didn't understand how you could say some of the things you said, but I figured it was just talk and didn't really make any difference. I didn't understand how you could think Cash Clay was such a fine man, when Ma and Pa always said he was a troublemaker — but I didn't figure that was important either, compared with the way we felt about one another in our family. I mean, I never thought you could really be *disloyal*."

"But now you've changed your mind, have you?"

"I remember that day when the posse went out after that nigger mob over near Paris, and you wouldn't go. I knew then there was something really wrong with the way you thought about things. And now, today, not accepting Ranew's challenge after what he said to you in front of Pritch and Robin and Arabella — why, Hacey, it made me ashamed of having you for a brother!"

It was no use. Nothing I could say had any effect on him. He was going to save the family honor I had jeopardized, and that's all there was to it.

Pritch and I agreed to the details later that afternoon. The duel would be fought in a meadow overlooking the river, which was much used on such occasions. Pritch volunteered a handsome matched pair of silver-mounted single-shot dueling pistols. We arranged to have a surgeon from Frankfort meet us at the scene at six the next morning, and persuaded an elderly gentleman named Somers, who lived nearby and had had considerable experience in affairs of honor, to serve as referee.

Boone stayed in his room all evening, and took his dinner on a tray. I suppose he was writing his letter — I don't know, because he didn't welcome my company. Ranew was out somewhere drinking, and I confess I prayed he'd get such a skinful that his hands would be shaking like aspen leaves in the morning.

The mist from the river was still lying heavily on the meadow when Boone and I arrived there. It was damp and chilly, and the sun hadn't yet been able to cut through the pearl-gray air. The surgeon and the referee were waiting, and a minute or two later Pritch and Ranew arrived in an open carriage.

Everything had a dreamlike quality about it there in the mist as we went through the last formalities. Old Mr. Somers asked each of the principals if he couldn't agree that he had been misunderstood by the other. Neither could agree to that. Then they chose their pistols, and moved apart to load them. I made a final attempt to persuade Boone to drop the whole thing, as I was required to do in my capacity as his second, but he simply said, "Hush up, Hacey."

Then Mr. Somers called them together, had them stand back to back, and slowly counted off the ten steps.

Ranew pivoted with catlike grace, crouching with his right

233

shoulder raised and his right arm covering most of his chest and belly. Boone turned more slowly, with his pistol and arm extended. As each discovered the other's posture, each froze. Neither pistol was correctly aimed at its target, but neither duelist seemed to want to make the final irrevocable move of taking deliberate aim.

Then Ranew shot his arm out, lined up the sights, and pulled the trigger. He was very fast — too fast. His aim was faulty, and the ball whipped through Boone's coat and barely creased him across the stomach.

When Boone realized that Ranew had used his shot and missed, he drew himself up straight and took a long, slow sight down the barrel of his pistol. He drew a bead on Ranew's forehead, the muzzle of the weapon pointing unwaveringly at a spot directly between the other's eyes. For a long second he held that stance, then lowered the muzzle and pointed it at the ground and let the hammer fall. The sound of the shot was muffled by the mist.

"I am satisfied," Boone said. "Is the other gentleman?"

Without waiting for Ranew to answer, Pritch said eagerly, "Yes, sir, we are satisfied!" and old Mr. Somers said in a pleased voice, "Then I declare this affair concluded." And that was that.

On the way back to Prichard's, I congratulated Boone on the outcome of the duel, and he thanked me for seconding him. We both spoke briefly and formally, as though we were casual acquaintances. And this was the way we would continue to address one another — except on one occasion — as long as we both lived.

*　　*　　*

Toward the end of the spring term at Transylvania, I received a short note beginning "Dear Brother Miller" and ending "Pray for us, J. G. Fee." The preacher would be back in The Glades in early June, and hoped that, if I was not otherwise committed, he might have the pleasure of working with me again during the summer.

As soon as the term ended and I was free to leave Lexington, I went back to Hazelwood for a few days of relaxation. The third day I rode over to White Hall for a talk with Cassius Clay. I was lucky to catch him; he was planning to leave for Springfield, Illinois, within the week, in answer to an invitation to address the Free-Soilers and Anti-Slavery Whigs of that locality.

He told me he had signed over a ten-acre homestead on the Ridge to Fee, and given him $200 toward the cost of building a house there. He gave me another $100 in case of emergency and asked me to stay close to the man, as I had the summer before.

"And Hacey, about the school — it might be a good idea if you brought the conversation around to it every once in a while, in a subtle sort of way. You remember I once said it was the right time, because Cousin Harry's Compromise had stopped the hands of the clock at five minutes to twelve? Well, the Kansas-Nebraska Act has started the clock again, and now the time's running out. We need the school as soon as we can get it started — and Fee's the man who has to give the word."

"I'll do my best, Mr. Clay — but Reverend Fee isn't exactly what you'd call putty in my hands."

"Well, do what you can — I consider it of the utmost importance. And Hacey —"

"Yes, sir?"

"Do you still have that pistol I gave you last year?"

"Yes, sir." It was in my top bureau drawer, carefully wrapped in an oily rag, hidden beneath a layer of smallclothes and lying next to my carved cherrywood box.

"You better get back into the habit of carrying it with you. Unless I misread the signs, you may very well be needing it soon."

Reverend Fee generally accepted God's dispensations with a grateful smile, but I'm obliged to say that he was not overwhelmed with enthusiasm when he inspected the land Cash Clay had given him to build on. Fee and I, together with our friend Mr. Rawlings, fought our way through the dense undergrowth which gave the area its local name, the "Bresh." When we reached the appointed place, Fee looked sourly around him, and picked burrs off his trousers. It was a hot day, and had been a hard climb.

"It's a dreary place to bring a family to, and that's a fact," he said.

Rawlings, who had a great fondness for quotation, biblical and otherwise, replied, "Prisons would palaces prove, If Jesus would dwell with me there."

"Hmmmph. There's no water here, for man nor beast."

"Moses smote the rock and the waters gushed forth, Reverend Fee."

Fee began to look like he'd bitten into a lemon. "The heat is fierce up here. There's not a shade tree for a mile!"

"Remember that the Lord delivered his children out of the fiery furnace, Reverend."

Fee turned to Rawlings and cried out in exasperation, "A jackrabbit would have to pin his ears back to get through this Bresh! Now what does the Bible say about *that?*" And for once in his life Rawlings was stumped.

The next day we started clearing the ground, using axes and fire. When it was reasonably open, I rode to the nearest sawmill and made arrangements for logs to be delivered to The Glades. From there we had to use horses to snake them up the narrow trail to the clearing.

Building log cabins was no common experience in Kentucky in the eighteen-fifties, at least to folks who had been raised in the Bluegrass. I suppose I made every mistake possible and I was so exhausted every night that I could hardly stay awake until the Swinglehursts had finished their modest dinner and I could fall into bed with little Andrew (whose scalp, I'm happy to say, had improved).

While I was building his cabin, Fee was preaching. Sundays he would conduct services at The Glades meeting-house; then, from Monday through Saturday he would ride a circuit back into the mountains. I was apprehensive about that, because he went alone, with nothing but his horse and his Bible. But he pooh-poohed my fears, saying that neither he nor God had any enemies in the Cumberlands. And I guess he was right, because when trouble came it didn't come from that direction.

By the end of August my hands were one continuous callous, I had lost fourteen pounds, and my scalp itched. But the cabin was built, and Reverend Fee was satisfied with it.

"You've done the Lord's work, Brother Miller," he said, with his gentle smile. "I wish there were some way to repay you for the weeks of toil you've invested here. No doubt the Lord will find a way."

"No doubt He will. But there's a way you might anticipate Him a little, if you wanted to."

"Oh? How's that?"

"Reverend Fee, you know I'm a schoolteacher, and every time I see these children here — the difference between the way they are now and the way they could be — all I can think of is how much I'd like to get them into a schoolroom! I know you and Mr. Clay have discussed establishing a school here —"

His smile cooled, then gave way to a frown. I had observed that he was sometimes less than overjoyed at receiving suggestions from others. "Well, that's something we'll talk about a few years from now, I think. 'Sufficient unto the day —' "

"But why do we have to wait, sir? Your work here at The Glades has been so successful it's moved us way ahead of schedule! With all the people who come to the meetinghouse now, plus all those hundreds you've met with back in the mountains this summer, why, we've got the basis for ten schools!"

"Yes, the work is proceeding well, there's no doubt of that."

"Then why should we hold back? The mountain people are ready — you've reached them with God's message, and now we can begin to teach them skills they can take back home with them! As Shakespeare says, 'There is a tide in the affairs of men which —' "

He looked at me sharply. "I am familiar with the quotation, Brother Miller." He turned his eyes toward the hazy blue mountains to the south, and tapped his index finger against his front teeth. After a moment he asked, "Wouldn't setting up and maintaining a schoolhouse here in the Bresh provide quite a logistics problem?"

"Of course! But so did rebuilding the meetinghouse and building your house up here. It's the kind of problem you've been solving all your life."

He looked at me with an expression of mild distaste. "To persuade me to do the Lord's work, Hacey, it is not necessary to use *quite* so much soft soap," he said ironically. He paused, considering the alternatives. "I'll tell you what," he said decisively. "We wouldn't have time before winter to get the school built and give the students enough schooling to make it worthwhile. Also, as I remember, you have a commitment at Transylvania College for this fall and next spring. So why don't we do this: In the spring I'll send word to Oberlin that I need a young man who can both chop wood and teach children their sums. You come down as early as you can, and the two of you can build yourselves a school. You'll be in charge, and you can divide the responsibilities as you see fit."

"Thank you, Reverend Fee. I couldn't ask for more."

"Offer your thanks to the Lord, Brother. We are all but sailors on His ship, crossing dark waters and guided by a single star."

"Amen," I said.

The first week in September Fee rode off to Bracken County to move his wife, his three children and his belongings to his new home. At the same time I said goodbye for another year to the many friends I had in The Glades, and promised them that the following spring I would be back for good.

*　　*　　*

The winter of 1854–55 was uneventful. I can't remember anything that happened until February, when Robards, the slave-trader, was suddenly found to be on the verge of bankruptcy, leaving a number of creditors holding the bag. It developed that some of the most high-toned aristocrats in town had not been above making a few dollars "blackbirding." There were many red faces for a week or two. But one face that didn't turn red was John Hunt Morgan's; he calmly instituted a suit aganst Robards for $6100, which he won, destroying Robards in the process.

"Couldn't happen to two finer fellows," I remember Josh Brain saying, his gouty foot propped up on a chair in the Phoenix Hotel taproom. The rotund little lawyer was fatter than ever, and the affliction in his foot gave him considerable discomfort, which could be eased, he claimed, only by the Phoenix's hot punch.

"When thieves fall out—" I began platitudinously.

"Oh, don't fool yourself. Hunt Morgan's no thief. He's something a sight better or a sight worse. He's the kind of man who simply has never, not one solitary time, in his entire selfish life, ever given one smidgen of a thought to whether anybody else has any rights at all, if they happen to be in conflict with his whim of the moment. Under that dashing demeanor lives a hundred-and-seventy-five-pound baby who wants its tit and its rattle *now*, by God! Oh, give me a thief every time; I can live with thieves — I'm a lawyer, after all — the whole world's made up of thieves of one sort or another. But Morgan — he's Tamerlane, he's Genghis Khan, he's the boogieman, and frankly, my boy, he gives me the willies." He addressed himself to the steaming cup in his hand. "And you know who he reminds me of?"

"I suppose you'll say Cassius Clay."

"No. Cash Clay loves to see himself in a role of desperate derring-do, but to begin with, he casts himself in it because he really *does* care about what happens to other people. Then he's got this foolish respect for the law, which doesn't mean any more to John Hunt Morgan than the Vedas of the Hindus. And finally he is not completely insensitive to expediency. A man who has survived as many battles as he has obviously knows how to pick his battlefields."

"All right, Mr. Brain — if not Mr. Clay, then who?"

"Your friend Reverend Fee, of course." He smiled blandly at my surprised expression. "You mean the parallel has never occurred to you? Who else do you know who has spent so little time putting himself into the other fellow's shoes? Of course he thinks the other fellow is the Devil, but does that really change anything? Has he ever given one jot — one *tittle* — of a thought to whether the Devil has any rights at all?"

"Everything he wants and works for, he believes is God's Will!"

"Of course! God is his tit, and God's Will is his rattle. But don't you find the resemblance interesting?"

I didn't know how to answer. I was young enough and idealistic enough for the conversation to make me uneasy. "I'm afraid I don't see as much resemblance as you do, Mr. Brain," I answered cautiously.

"Oh, you will, Hacey," he said, raising two fingers to a passing waiter. "The watchword is 'Sedition.' Both Morgan and the Reverend are capable of it without a moment's hesitation. Clay is utterly incapable of it under any conditions. See if events don't prove I'm right during the next few years." He shifted his bandaged foot on the chair and groaned. "Oh, the joys of Cassandra! Where the hell is that drink?"

*   *   *

I received permission to leave Transylvania early (turning my students over to another instructor for their final examinations), packed my old horsehair trunk and made arrangements for it to be carted to The Glades. After brief visits to Hazelwood and White Hall I rode my venerable Sacajawea over to my new home.

I found Reverend Fee established in his new house with his wife and three small children. Mrs. Fee had made their home so attractive it was hard to believe it had been a raw and empty log cabin only a few months before. Mrs. Fee was like that, I was to find — a big, strong, capable and slightly horsy woman who could accomplish anything she put her mind to. She treated Fee as though he were made of china.

The Oberlin student the Reverend had promised had arrived two days before. His name was William E. Lincoln, and he was an Englishman, born and raised in London. He spoke a cultured, upper-class English that contrasted greatly with the drawling twang of the mountains, and yet his intelligence, eagerness and goodwill assured that he would be accepted into any company.

I appraised him as we shook hands, wondering how the two of us would work in double harness. I liked what I saw. He was big and strong-looking, with powerful shoulders. I resolved to let him have his fair share of the ax work.

He walked down from the Ridge to the Swinglehurst house with me, and we talked about where to build the schoolhouse.

"Six of one to a half dozen of the other, don't you think?" he said. "Wherever we put it, we'll have to clear the land and start from scratch."

"Yes, but if we do it at the southwestern end, the land we clear will adjoin Reverend Fee's land, and we'll end up with one pretty big piece of clearing instead of two little ones with the Bresh in between."

"Yes, that makes sense. And after the school's built, we can just keep moving outward from the cleared area for any other buildings we need, and the school grounds will expand like a balloon. Splendid!"

That's just what we did. During June and July, Bill Lincoln and I worked side by side, eleven or twelve hours a day, burning and chopping and digging out that damnable underbrush and then building a slab-sided one-room schoolhouse on the cleared site. When it was finished it was even more graceless than Reverend Fee's home or the meetinghouse. In its dim interior were a half-dozen benches for the students, a battered kitchen table and chair for the teacher, and, only out of pedagogic nicety, a slate blackboard carted in from Lexington and carefully mounted on the rough board wall.

Early in August we felt we had done as much as we could, and we asked Reverend Fee to come and see our handiwork.

"It's a fine beginning, Brothers," he said, smiling at the clumsy structure. "What do you propose to call it?"

"Why, the Glades School, I suppose, I hadn't thought," I said.

"There's a passage in The Acts of the Apostles that describes how Paul and Silas came to Thessalonica to preach the Word of Christ. There they were met by 'certain lewd fellows of the baser sort' who forced them to flee. They fled to another city, of which we learn that the inhabitants 'were more noble than those in Thessalonica, in that they received the Word with all readiness of mind, and searched the Scriptures daily, whether those things were so.' Do you happen to remember the name of that second city?"

Neither Bill nor I could recall it.

"Berea," Reverend Fee said. "It was called Berea. And I pray that the students and teachers of this school may be modern Bereans, ready to receive the Word of God and search the Scriptures for Truth."

Fee was moving in history that afternoon. Not only did he name the school, he also gave it its motto. A little later we were inside the single room admiring the blackboard. "Won't you write a lesson there, Reverend?" Bill asked. Fee picked up a new piece of chalk, thought for a moment, and then printed screechingly on that virginal black surface those words which have never been far from the mind of every Berean from that time to this:

"God hath made of one blood all nations of men."

* * *

Word of the opening of the Berea School traveled rapidly over the district, and soon we had students coming not only from The Glades and the mountains to the southeast, but also from some neighboring farms in the Bluegrass as well. By the end of the school year, we had fifteen students, ranging in age from eight to nineteen years. Each student came to us almost, if not completely, illiterate. Bill and I improvised teaching techniques never used at Harvard or Oberlin to stir their bright but uncultivated minds. We sang our multiplication tables to the tune of "Scotland's Burning" and our alphabet to "Now I Lay Me Down to Sleep." We held spelling bees and debates, and moved imaginary squirrels up geography trees, each branch of which was a state capital or a foreign country. Impatient to get them reading as soon as possible, we taught them to recognize whole words, even while we were teaching them the phonetics of the alphabet. We drove them hard, but interrupted the long class day often with hymn singing, outdoor games and short periods of manual labor — we had them all clearing the Bresh when the weather allowed it, or helping us finish our cabin when it was inclement.

Lincoln and I alternated as teachers. Generally one of us was riding the circuit with Reverend Fee while the other was in the classroom. We had decided to build a cabin for ourselves on the Ridge near the school, and whatever spare time either of us had went into that project. It was finished in early spring.

When we dismissed the children for their summer vacation at the end of May, 1856, three years had passed since Cassius M. Clay had written to me of his hopes for a bridgehead to the free mountain South. During those three years we had repaired one old building and built three new ones, cleared two or three acres of underbrush, preached a thousand sermons and taught fifteen children their alphabet.

There had been no single act of violence against Berea or the Bereans.

We must have incurred the displeasure of Providence by being too pleased with ourselves — for a little more than a month later our troubles began.

XVIII

Storm Warnings

On the Fourth of July, 1856, there was a celebration in the settlement of Slate Lick Springs, near Berea. Reverend Fee had been invited to speak, and so had Cassius M. Clay. The two speakers had never shared a platform before, and the day promised oratorical as well as pyrotechnic fireworks.

Clay was present when the Berea contingent arrived, and he greeted us warmly. Fee was gracious, but slightly constrained, as he often was in the dominating presence of his patron. The two men walked side by side to the platform — Fee's head at least ten inches below Clay's — and Mrs. Fee, Lincoln and I found seats under a shady oak tree.

The program of such municipal affairs never varied much. They opened with a band concert, then a preacher gave an invocation, a local dignitary read the Declaration of Independence, a visiting luminary made a patriotic oration, the preacher came back with a benediction, and the band concluded with the National Anthem. Then everybody ate and watched the fireworks.

At the conclusion of the musical program the local dignitary introduced himself, Fee and Clay. Of Fee he said, "His Christian views have made him well-known in emancipationist circles throughout the state." Certainly these were pallid words to describe a man as fearless and dedicated as John G. Fee, but they would probably have been deservedly forgotten if the speaker's introduction of Cassius Clay immediately following had not referred to him as "Indomitable . . . resolute . . . courageous alike in word and deed . . . the chief bulwark of emancipation in the South . . ." and considerably more of the same.

Fee would have been less than human not to be irritated — and Fee was nothing if not human. But other men might have concealed the wound. Not Fee. In his invocation he deliberately introduced the subject of the "Higher Law," which represented his major point of theoretical disagreement with Clay. Fee believed, just as Garrison and my friend Wentworth Higginson believed, that God's Law, as revealed by Christ's teachings, must be obeyed even when it contradicted the law of the land. Clay was unwilling to grant that any person, clergyman or layman, had the right to place himself above the laws that bound his fellow countrymen.

I remembered how Higginson, when he interceded to save me from the wrath of Frederick Douglass, had said that the antislavery House had room for many Mansions. Neither Fee nor Clay would have agreed that day.

Fee's invocation took twenty minutes, and consisted mostly of an attack against the "mouldy legalism" of those who questioned the doctrine of the Higher Law. When he finished, everyone in the crowd knew we were watching a historic encounter, and we squirmed restlessly during the reading of the Declaration, eager to hear how Clay would respond to the challenge.

Clay found himself in the novel position of arguing for the conservative view, but he argued it with all the passion he normally gave to the radical position. He described Higher

Law advocates as "glutted with vanity . . . insensitive alike to the hazards of their reckless course and the reproaches of their fellow citizens."

Forty-five minutes later, Fee had the opportunity to repeat all his points in the Benediction; the band struck up the National Anthem, and the program was over.

As the last notes of the music died away, I pressed through the crowd to the speaker's platform. I feared the debate had done us all serious harm, and I wanted to speak to Clay at once and try to minimize the damage. I saw him rise from his seat and cross the platform to the steps without a glance at Reverend Fee. I reached him as he stepped to the ground. "Mr. Clay, may I talk to you?" I asked earnestly.

"Why, Hacey, are you sure you won't be corrupted by my mouldy legalism? Apparently your associates are not so sanguine!"

"Mr. Clay, I pray you, don't lose your temper over this. It's a minor disagreement between two dedicated emancipationists. It would be a tragedy if we allowed it to harm the work you began at Berea."

"I don't see it as a minor disagreement, I see it as an outright challenge, as deliberate provocation. I believe in law, not anarchy, and I will not offer my support to any institution that teaches the opposite."

"But, Mr. Clay," I pleaded, "what does it matter compared to the creation of the bridgehead to the mountains? Those two million free Southerners in the Appalachians —"

Clay turned his leonine head and looked at me sadly. "Hacey, don't you understand? *I'm withdrawing my support!* The Berea School will have to get along without my help and protection. I wish you well — I even wish Fee well — but I simply cannot stand behind an institution that preaches contempt for the law of the land. The cause of emancipation is more important than any school or any preacher, and I won't see it jeopardized and compromised by irresponsibility. I made a mistake. There's no more to be said."

"What if Reverend Fee retracted?" I asked, clutching at straws.

Clay's heavy features were lightened briefly by an ironical smile. "Oh, Hacey, you know better than *that!*" he said, and then walked away to join a group of well-wishers.

And of course Fee was as intractable as Clay — more so; he refused even to discuss the situation. "Discussion is bootless, Brother Miller. God has revealed his Word, and it only remains to us to follow it." He and Mrs. Fee remained silent on the ride back to The Glades, and Bill and I were sunk in gloom and foreboding.

For the next few days, it seemed that our fears were unwarranted. But gradually a pattern of increased hostility toward the school began to emerge — mostly on the part of the loafers in Richmond and the tenants on a few of the neighboring tobacco farms. For the most part these were discourtesies and bits of minor vandalism, but as time went by the perpetrators began to gather courage and plan more ambitious persecutions. By September, when the second school year began, it was obvious how important the support of Cassius M. Clay had been, and how vulnerable we were without it. For although Clay hadn't publicly said a word against the school or against Fee, he had let it be known that he was no longer willing to come to our defense.

In October Bill Lincoln was pushed off the sidewalk into a mud puddle by a Richmond bully, and when he remonstrated, he was severely beaten. He came back to the school with two loose teeth, a black eye, and a pain over his heart that lasted for weeks.

Two nights later I surprised three farm boys dousing the walls of the schoolhouse with coal oil, preparing to burn us out. I tried to catch them and got a bruised jaw for my pains. As they disappeared down the path through the Bresh, I could hear them screaming, "Nigger-stealers! We'll get you nigger-stealers!"

Many of our students were removed from the school by their parents during the next few weeks, and others that remained reported they were jeered at and insulted by their neighbors.

Carters began to refuse to make deliveries to The Glades, and we were forced to drive our wagon into Richmond for every article we purchased.

Then one day as Reverend Fee stood outside the door of the schoolhouse, listening to the sadly diminished student body practicing its multiplication tables, his cheek was stung by splinters of bark from the log by his head, and he heard the crack of a rifle out in the underbrush.

A few moments later, as Fee stood fingering the fresh scratch on his face, and as the students in the schoolhouse tried to push around me and get out the door to see what was going on, a tobacco tenant by the name of Hemphill pushed through the undergrowth and came toward us, carrying a rifle under his arm. He was a fat, loud-mouthed man with a shifty eye, a friend of Barney and Lafe Tuttle.

"I declare, I pretty near winged you, didn't I, preacher?" he called out jovially. "I thought I seen me a coon up a tree, so I took a shot at him — but I guess my aim wasn't so good, eh?"

Fee looked at him expressionlessly for a moment, and then

replied, "It will have to improve if you expect to kill what you're shooting at."

"Well, you know what they say — practice makes perfect," Hemphill said good-humoredly.

"If you know what's good for you, you won't do any of that practicing around here," I said sharply. "Sometimes we take shots at coons and miss, too!"

The fat man turned toward me and squinted into the schoolhouse in an exaggerated manner. "Why, Mr. Miller — I didn't see you in there behind all them young'uns. Can't say as I blame you, though, since you ain't got Cash Clay to hide behind anymore."

I took a step out of the doorway and toward him. "Now do you think you could get at me without too much trouble?" I asked.

"I reckon," he answered, his voice still pleasant.

"Hacey, stay where you are," ordered Fee. "We'll have no violence here — don't you see that's what he wants? Mr. Hemphill, we accept your explanation. We can only ask you to be more careful when you're hunting near the school. Please remember there are children here."

"For the time being," said Hemphill.

"For the time being, yes. And now, good day. We don't want to keep you."

In the ensuing silence Hemphill looked from one of us to the other, apparently trying to decide if there was anything else he could do to increase the unpleasantness of his visit without an overt declaration of war. Not being able to think of anything, he shouldered his rifle and swaggered from the clearing.

Fee watched him go, a mildly puzzled expression on his face. "I never understand them when they act like that," he said in his piping voice. "So malicious, but so ineffectual. Somehow, once they screw up their courage to do *something,* I always expect them to do *more.*"

"Give them time, Reverend," I said dryly.

"Oh, certainly, in time they'll work themselves up to a higher level of efficiency. They always do. But just the same, the first few forays are always surprisingly clumsy. Almost as if they hate what they're doing and hope to fail at it." He rubbed his chin.

The children were milling around the schoolhouse, and I rounded them up and sent them back inside; then I asked Fee seriously what he thought we should do to meet the worsening situation.

"Why, just what we are doing, Brother Miller. And continuing to address our prayers to Almighty God."

"There are some other steps we might take, it seems to me, sir. We could call a meeting here of all the people we know are in sympathy with the school, and explain to them what's happening."

"I don't think our purpose would be served by trying to divide the community into two armed camps," he replied decisively.

"Then how about letting me ride to White Hall to see Cassius Clay? I'm sure he would be willing to offer us his protection, once he realized what —" My voice trailed off as I became aware of the expression on Fee's face. His mouth was pursed as if he had a mouthful of something he wanted to spit out but couldn't, and his eyes held an expression in which anger contended with deep sorrow.

For a moment he said nothing. Then, his emotions back under control, he replied with a simple "No."

This was the beginning of the period I always remember as the Dark Days. It was in some ways a state of siege, gradually increasing in intensity through 1857 and the early spring of 1858. The events taking place in national politics could only exacerbate our local problems. The Kansas war burst into full fury, elevating John Brown to national prominence, and inspiring my friend Wentworth Higginson to lead a group of armed settlers from Massachusetts to Kansas to relieve the beleaguered free state forces. He wrote asking if I would care to join him. It sounded like a memorable adventure — and turned out to be one — but the pressure of events in Berea forced me to decline.

During the last days of the spring term, the news of the Dred Scott decision reached us. Seeming to confirm in everlasting law the ultra-Southern view of the Negro as a subhuman piece of property with no natural rights of his own, this monstrous legal perversion incited the slavocracy and threw all emancipationists into deep depression. The Bereans — Reverend and Mrs. Fee, Bill Lincoln, myself and two new and valuable additions to our ranks, George Candee and Otis Waters — breathed easier with the children out of the settlement for the summer.

In June I left my fellow workers for a few days to attend my brother Boone's wedding. It was held at the Ledyards' great house, Redbird, and was quite a social event. Boone did not ask me to be his best man — Alan Prichard had that honor. He did ask me to be an usher, but I declined, feeling it might create some awkwardness. I attended the bachelor dinner in Lexington two days before the wedding, and felt as though I were walking on eggs the whole time. More than forty guests attended, including Cousin Whitney and his sons, Galt and Bryan. Everyone there seemed to have fairly virulent cases of Ledyardism. It's hard to say whether Boone was more uncomfortable with them or with me.

I watched my tongue and my drinking very carefully that

night, and so did most of the people I met, since my scan-dalous politics were well known by now, and nobody was anxious to embarrass the bridegroom on the eve of his wed-ding. Nobody but his prospective brother-in-law, that is.

Bryan Ledyard had never forgiven Boone for the excel-lent punch in the nose he had received the day his step-brother was beaten racing against John Hunt Morgan. He had never forgiven me, either, for garnishing him with a bowl of Brunswick stew in the kitchen of Hazelwood earlier that same year.

Flushed with drink, Bryan swaggered up to Boone and said, "You heard about Morgan's regiment, Miller?"

"No, I haven't, Bryan," answered Boone politely. "What about it?"

"Seems John Hunt Morgan has decided we need a new militia regiment in Lexington. Maybe he figures the Old Light Infantry was corrupted by that bastard Cash Clay during the war against the Mexes. Anyway, he's put out the word of all gentlemen of honor and patriotism to rally round the standard."

"Oh?" said Boone. "What's the regiment going to be called?"

"Lexington Rifles. Drill begins next Tuesday, at the Ar-mory. You going to be there?"

Boone smiled patiently. "I'm afraid I'll be off on my honeymoon, Bryan."

"Oh, that's too bad." He pulled a face. "I guess your family won't be represented. You'll be away, and your pa's too old — and there sure ain't anybody else in your family you could call a gentleman of honor and patriotism, is there?"

With a feeling of resignation, I took a step toward Bryan and opened my mouth to speak, but Boone was seconds too fast for me. Bryan had been standing with his back to a tapestried wall, and Boone moved smoothly against him, forcing him back against the fabric. Boone's knee was raised and pressed into Bryan's groin, and each of his hands held one of Bryan's hands pinned to his sides. Boone spoke in a harsh, almost inaudible whisper.

"You make any fuss here and embarrass my family, you dirty little piss-ant, and I'll push your balls so far up in your belly you'll think they're gallstones. You understand me?" Bryan's ashen face nodded quickly. "There are going to be no duels, remember that. *No duels!* If you want satisfaction later, after I come back from my honeymoon, I'll give you a chance to make your sister a widow then. Can you wait that long?" He pressed his knee in an additional inch and put a little more weight behind it.

"Ye — yesss!" groaned Bryan.

Boone suddenly moved away from him. "Hacey," he said in a pleasantly neutral voice, "I don't believe you have a drink. That will never do." As we walked together across the richly carpeted floor to the punch bowl, with his arm linked through mine, I felt awkward and embarrassed.

"Thanks, Boone, I'm indebted to you," I whispered.

He glanced at me from under level brows — that absolutely honest, utterly immovable look I knew so well. "I didn't do it for you, Hacey. I did it for the family and for Robin."

"All right — then I'm indebted to you for handling it so well for the family."

"You're welcome." As he reached the punch bowl, he took a cup from the officiating Negro and handed it to me. "Enjoy yourself," he said and turned away.

XIX

Ellie

No other untoward incidents marked Boone's nuptials. Three days later, riding my new mare "Jenny Lind" — named in commemoration of the unforgettable night when Wentworth and his wife and I attended the Swedish Nightingale's Boston debut, and replacing my beloved Sacajawea, who would spend her remaining days at grass — I returned to my cabin on the Ridge.

The next day Fee asked me to ride with him on a circuit he had never before traveled. It was to be the most ambitious journey he had ever undertaken — south and east into the Cumberlands, then east across the Licking River, north and east toward the Big Sandy, then, changing direction, a loop back toward Berea again. His main purpose was to preach the iniquity of slavery, but he wanted me to feel free to proselytize for the school among the mountain folk.

I remembered that Falk Padgett had told me many years before that his home was a few miles east of Paintsville, over near the Big Sandy. I recalled the incredulous way he had greeted my information about starting a school for mountain people, and how wistfully he had mused over the thought of his own little sister's having the opportunity of attending such a school. I resolved then and there that I would try to find the Padgett household and recruit a new student for the Berea School.

Reverend Fee and I rose early, breakfasted lightly, and were riding south on the trail to Boone's Gap before the sun was an hour in the sky. We took our luncheon cheese and biscuit in the saddle, and rode until four o'clock, when we reached a log cabin situated on one of the few level spots in that part of the precipitous Cumberlands. The barking of many dogs greeted us long before we came in sight of the house, and a platoon of youngsters poured from the door as we dismounted and secured our horses.

It was the home of Abraham and Zerelda Maupin, their seven children and Mrs. Maupin's aged grandmother. The house consisted of two rooms and a loft. In each of the four walls was a small window covered with oiled paper. The windows couldn't be opened for ventilation, of course — the door served that purpose.

I was destined to sleep in many homes of that type during the next three months — when I was lucky. The larger of the two rooms contained the fireplace, which was wide enough to roast a whole sheep. On either side of the fireplace was a bench, and there was a handsome and simple round cherrywood table between them; it was the only profession-ally made piece of furniture in the house, and had, no doubt, been brought through Cumberland Gap a generation or two ago. There was a bake oven and a skillet, an oil lamp on the table and a handful of cracked dishes on a shelf, along with a copy of the Bible and a book of sermons by some long-forgotten divine. Two beds were in the main room, two more in the smaller room adjoining, and three more in the loft. They were gay and inviting, with their colorful patchwork quilts and thick featherbeds. Beds were very important to the Maupins, for not only did they birth in them, mate in them and die in them, they also spent half their days in them during the winter, trying to keep away from the jagged mountain winds.

The walls were neatly whitewashed, and on them hung two rifles, powder horns, bullet mold, and leather bags for patches and balls. One of the rifles was an Army muzzle-loader from the War of 1812; the other, a handmade Kentucky Long with a welded barrel and a hickory ramrod, must have dated back to Daniel Boone.

The family supported itself by a combination of hunting, farming and livestock raising. They cultivated their land — less than an acre was arable — with a bull-tongue plow. Their stock consisted of a horse, two cows, two sows and a boar and some shoats, and fifteen or twenty sheep. They hoped to acquire some chickens some day.

Mountain folk are often described as a dour people, clannish and inhospitable to outsiders. Clannish they are for a fact, and possessed of an orneriness that sometimes comes close to matching that of the Rhetts and Hugers of the Deep South who look down upon them so — but no Tidewater planter has ever been more hospitable with his soft-shelled crab and French champagne than the Maupins and their peers were with their corn bread, bacon and coffee that summer.

Fee was eagerly received by the whole family, who had heard reports of his preaching from kinfolk in Rockcastle County. The old grandmother, bedridden and rambling in mind, was especially anxious to meet him; and he went directly to her and sat beside her, holding her hand, while he read her the Hundred and Twenty-First Psalm: "I will lift up mine eyes unto the hills, from whence cometh my help.

My help cometh from the Lord, Which made Heaven and Earth." He read with no dramatic flourishes, but his high, clear voice held absolute conviction. "The sun shall not smite thee by day, nor the moon by night. The Lord shall preserve thee from all evil: He shall preserve thy soul." The old woman's dry lips moved soundlessly as she repeated the words after him.

Meanwhile the children notified all the other families within a three-mile radius that the "Preacher" had arrived. After a simple but satisfying dinner of smoked ham, greens and bacon, corn bread and molasses, and a strong, hot coffee, we all trooped out under the trees, where the neighbors awaited us.

The sun was setting behind the mountain peaks to the west. Perhaps thirty people were assembled outside the Maupins' cabin — ten or twelve of them adults. Everyone was neatly and cleanly dressed in homespun, with an occasional store-bought shirt or bonnet visible. Adults were shod, children barefoot. They were all sitting in a semicircle, with the patient immobility they always maintained at such times, even the young ones. (Mountain children never seem to jitter or squirm.) As Reverend Fee took his place before them and introduced himself and me, a cool breath of air sighed around us in the trees. Then, as unexpectedly and yet as predictably as always, his clear sweet voice rose to lead them:

> We are climbing Jacob's Ladder,
> We are climbing Jacob's Ladder,
> We are climbing Jacob's Ladder,
> Soldiers of the Cross.

I joined my voice to his with a will, as did the congregation:

Every round goes higher, higher,
Every round goes higher, higher,
Every round goes higher, higher,
Soldiers of the Cross.

There, in those mountains, it was easy to feel you were closer to Heaven than the lowlanders, that it wouldn't be too long a climb, up Jacob's Ladder . . .

Fee gave them a strong antislavery sermon, and they responded warmly, with many Amens and Praise-the-Lord's. Then after another hymn, he introduced the subject of the Berea School, and asked me to describe its purposes and opportunities.

With more than a touch of nervousness, I began by talking about the value of Education. How Education prevents people from being enslaved, how Freedom is based on the Knowledge of the Enlightened Citizen, and so on. They listened to me politely but with expressionless faces. I realized I wasn't reaching them, had even begun to lose them. I decided to switch tactics.

"Let's pretend I've got a piece of paper in my hand, and I'm bringing it to you from the Government. You say, 'What's this all about?' And I point to a word and say, 'It's about your *taxes* — B-O-N-U-S — *taxes*. This paper tells how much you owe the Government in taxes.' "

I stared at them, and they stared back at me, without a single whole expression among the thirty of them. "So you look at this word, and you figure it spells 'taxes' like I said it did, and you either think, 'Well, I guess I got to pay it,' and get ready to hand over some money you can't afford, or you wonder if the Government would miss me if you was to put a bullet through me and drop me over into the creek bottom.

Right?" Still no expression. "Right," I cried, "except for one little detail: this word on the paper here — B-O-N-U-S — that word doesn't spell *taxes* — it spells *bonus!* The paper really says the Government is going to give you a *bonus* of two hundred dollars. But because you don't know how to spell, you believe me when I show you the paper and tell you to pay me the money for taxes. That's what education is about — to fix it so you'll know what you've got coming!"

An elderly man with a long jaw and a cast in one eye cleared his throat apologetically. "I reckon education is like the Saving Grace. The problem ain't knowing what it's good for — it's getting ahold of it."

"What I'm saying is the young folks can get ahold of it at the Berea School!"

"How they supposed to *pay* for getting ahold of it at the Berea School?"

"They don't have to pay a cent for it. We don't charge anything at all. The only thing a student has to worry about is learning his lessons."

"Don't you charge for victuals, neither?" asked a wrinkled woman of indeterminate age. " 'Cause if you do, there ain't many around here as could afford to send a young'un there."

"Oh, folks pay for their victuals one way or another. Those that can afford to, pay in money. Those that can't, pay in work, or in food, or in both. For instance, take your boy there — what might his name be?"

She put her arm protectively around the shoulders of a solemn-faced ten-year-old with adenoids. "Theron."

"Well, if Theron were to come to the Berea School, he might bring a sheep along with him for his share of the victuals. Or he might plant himself a few rows of vegetables and raise them. Or he might hire out to a tobacco farmer in the neighborhood, and give the money he makes to the school. It doesn't make any difference how he contributes, as long as he does."

"Where would he live if he was to go there?" another woman asked.

"So far, all the students who don't live at home are staying with families in The Glades. But next year we figure on building a new school building with a big loft over it, that should sleep maybe twenty youngsters."

"Boys and girls won't sleep in the same room, will they?" asked a sharp-featured woman in a poke bonnet. "I don't hold with any goings-on like that."

I assured her that the Berea School was not intended to be a hotbed of Free Love.

One after another they questioned me, and as I answered them I realized that the discussion had moved from the theoretical to the practical. In the case of at least three of the families represented, the question was no longer "What's the Berea School all about?"; it had become "How can I send Theron there?"

Then we got down to particulars: Mary Jane was good with stock, would there be work for her? Amos had worked a stretch blacksmithing, was there a smith at The Glades? George couldn't get away till October, because that was when his brother was getting out of jail. Was that too late?

For an hour or more we sat together there on the hill and planned how to get their children to Berea. By the time they trooped away home through the full moonless darkness, all three of the interested families had expressed a firm desire to send at least one child in the fall.

That first day and night was typical of our circuit that

summer. Each day was like the others; we rode, we ate, we preached and talked about the school, and we hoped we struck a spark which would grow into a steady flame to last a lifetime.

The days became weeks, then months, and one day we were over near the Big Sandy, and it was time for me to keep my promise to myself, and look for Falk Padgett's family.

I arranged a rendezvous with Fee for three days later, and rode off in the direction that seemed likeliest. At the first cabin nobody had heard of any Padgetts thereabouts. At the second, one old mountain man kind of recollected hearing the name, but couldn't rightly call to mind where they lived. At the third I was given specific directions. Two hours later, I arrived at the Padgett cabin at Head of West Hollow.

The Padgett family had undergone considerable change since Falk had described it to me in 1845. When he had left home — as he told me in whispers, both of us sweating under a tarpaulin in the back of the wagon on the Lexington pike — he had left behind six brothers and sisters, a brute of a father and an ailing mother. Twelve years later, the brute of a father had been shot with a handgun by one of his many ill-wishers, who was never identified, and thrown over the fence into a pigpen, where parts of his face and body were eaten before he was recovered for Christian burial. The ailing mother still ailed, in the manner of many wives and mothers who are provident enough to begin their ailing early in life. The eldest son had left two years after Falk and was reported dead. The next eldest son had left two years after that and was last heard of in St. Louis. The elder daughter had married a Callaway from the other side of Paintsville and came to visit the family one afternoon a year. That left the three youngest ones, Ellie, Armisted and Robert. Ellie was eighteen, Armisted thirteen, Robert eleven. The three of them, their mother and an uncle from the Padgett side who had come to visit them four years before and had stayed on, made up the Padgett family as I found them.

The uncle greeted me when I arrived. He told me his name was Lonnie Padgett, and that he was taking care of the family since there was no man on the place. His tone implied that he was making a considerable sacrifice. Falk's mother was in bed, and was friendly enough in a vague kind of way, although I was not certain she remembered Falk at all. The three children were out, fishing or hunting or checking their trap lines.

I talked to them for a few minutes about Berea, but it was unrewarding. Mrs. Padgett couldn't seem to keep her mind on it, and Lonnie sniffed around the subject as if he were trying to find some profit in it for himself, and then dropped it in disappointment. I sat with them uncomfortably, drinking coffee and trying to make small talk, for twenty-five uneasy minutes.

Then Ellie came in with the two boys.

She was small-boned and much too thin — she couldn't have weighed over ninety-five pounds — but she carried herself erectly and moved with vigor. Her hair was chestnut brown, and swirled around her shoulders like smoke. Her nose and chin were sharp and finely drawn, and her eyes were large and gray and slightly uptilted by her cheekbones. There was a dusting of freckles across her face. Her upper lip was a trifle long, and raised a bit by her front teeth, which were too prominent for fashion. Her breasts were small. I scarcely glanced at her two brothers.

"Ellie, this here's Hacey Miller, from over near Richmond," said Lonnie Padgett. "He's a friend of your brother Falk's."

She looked at me in surprise, and I was reminded of the

eyes of some wary animal looking out from a thicket. "Howdy," she said.

As I looked into those eyes, I found it suddenly difficult to speak. A cold spasm flickered through my body, and moisture disappeared from inside my mouth and magically reappeared in the palms of my hands. "Howdy," I replied in an unrecognizable voice.

"He's been telling us about a free school over in Madison County. Him and Falk figured as how you might get some book learning there, but I told him you couldn't spare the time for nothing like that," Lonnie continued.

Ellie looked at me intently before she said anything. Then she turned her head and said matter-of-factly, "I got to slop the hogs now. But you're welcome to come along and tell me what you got to say." She left the room, and, with a hasty nod to Mrs. Padgett and Uncle Lonnie, I followed her.

"Now what's this all about, Mr. Hacey Miller?" she asked when we were outside. "I don't know you from Adam's off ox, and Falk ain't as much as sent word he's alive since I was five years old."

As she moved briskly through her chores, I trotted behind her and explained the founding of the Berea School and how important it could be to mountain folk. "I told your brother Falk about it when it was still just an idea in Cassius Clay's head, and the first thing he thought of was what it could mean to you, Ellie."

"He did, did he?" She crossed her arms and looked at me angrily out of her big gray eyes. "And now you want me to run off with you and go to this Berea place, don't you? Except on the way we'll stop off at some house in Lexington for a couple of days, where there's this nice lady to take care of me, ain't that right?"

I was flabbergasted. "What are you talking about? A

day's ride from here is Reverend Fee! You think he'd have anything to do with that kind of thing?"

"How do *I* know who's a day's ride away?"

"Well, can't you just take my word for it? Gosh all hemlock, Ellie, I should think you could just look me in the face and see the way — what I mean is, how could you think I'd want to do you any harm?" I could feel hot blood pulsing in my ears.

"Just don't bother getting your pecker up over me. Plenty better men than you have tried." She turned away with a swish of her skirts and continued on her round of the farmyard, leaving me standing red-faced and furious.

I didn't try to talk to her again until dinnertime. The six of us sat around a plank table in front of the fireplace, Uncle Lonnie at the head of the table. I said grace, enjoying it more than usual because it gave me a reason to avoid Ellie's penetrating eyes.

But then, as we began to pass the food around, she started asking me questions about the school. What kind of things did folks learn there? Reading and writing? Ciphering? What else? Geography — what's that? And history? And science?

Soon the attention of Armisted and Robert was captured too. They were both quick-minded, although very laconic. I told them some of the things Berea might teach them when it became a college — agriculture and veterinary medicine and stock-breeding. "Think what you could do here, at Head of West Hollow, if you knew things like that!"

Armisted gave me an appraising look from eyes as gray as his sister's. "You sure-enough figure we could learn them kind of things?"

"I declare," said Mrs. Padgett vaguely, "it's enough to get a body all mixed up."

Ellie's face was animated with interest, and I noticed the livelier her expression became, the more sullen became that of her uncle. Finally he broke into the conversation.

"I don't hold with all this book-learning foolishness," he growled. "If the Lord had wanted us to go to the lowlands to learn that truck, He wouldn't have led our footsteps to the mountains."

"I don't claim to be able to explain the Lord's thinking, but Reverend Fee has been studying on the matter for years, and he hasn't any doubts," I answered a bit too flippantly. Lonnie gave me a look of pure dislike. He pushed his chair back, stood up, rubbed his stomach and belched.

"I don't reckon nobody around here's going off on any such wild goose chase," he said. "I'm going outside and have a smoke."

After he had left the cabin, the atmosphere was easier. Ellie and the boys were full of a hundred questions, and I tried to answer them all. Mrs. Padgett was often confused, but not unsympathetic. By eight-thirty, the family's bedtime, they had drained me dry.

Uncle Lonnie came back in after his smoke, trailing an aura of "moon." He climbed up the ladder into the loft, pausing at the top rung to look down at us and say, "Interesting talking to you, Mr. Miller. Sorry you're leaving first thing in the morning, but you know best." Then he took the last step up and disappeared in the room above.

There were two beds downstairs. I was to sleep with Armisted and Robert, and Ellie slept with her mother. Our ablutions were simple and quickly accomplished. With every attention to modesty, the boys and Mrs. Padgett were in bed, I was about to climb in myself, and Ellie, her contours lost in some indescribable night garment, was preparing to turn down and blow out the lamp. Suddenly she turned to me and seized my wrist; her fingers were cool, but her grip was demanding.

"What you said about the school," she whispered. "Was it all true? Promise me, was it all true?"

"Yes, Ellie, I swear it! Every word was true!"

For a moment her eyes probed mine, searching for additional reassurance. Then she lowered her head modestly and said, "Good night, Hacey Miller," and put out the light.

The next morning I awoke early, to find all the Padgetts except Uncle Lonnie already up. There was a smell of bacon frying, and coffee, and Robert was offering me an empty basin and a bar of homemade soap as I opened my eyes. "The pump's out to the side of the house," he said conspiratorially.

I pulled on my trousers under the blankets and then emerged to greet the day. I dowsed my face in ice-cold well water, scrubbed at my neck and ears and swished some water around in my mouth awhile. That waked me up fifty percent, and then the smell of the coffee waked me up fifty percent more, and when I returned to the fireside, I knew that things weren't normal in the Padgett cabin that morning.

Ellie was dressed in what was obviously her best dress, of bright gray-and-white store-bought gingham. Her hair, so softly shaped by the wind yesterday, was now severely pulled back and tied. There was a packed carpetbag on the floor by the door.

The two boys and Mrs. Padgett sat at the table, the boys saucer-eyed with excitement, the mother moistening her lips nervously as one arthritic hand tried to reassure the other.

"Have some breakfast, and get a move on," said Ellie briskly.

"Are you going — to Berea?" I asked, suddenly trembling all over.

"That's right." She dished me up a plate of bacon and grits, and then spooned bacon fat over the grits. "Ma and I talked it over last night. We reckon it's the kind of thing a body don't get the chance at twice."

"The hell you say," rumbled a voice above and behind us, and the sullen face of Uncle Lonnie appeared at the top of the loft ladder. "Ain't no girl of mine going off like the Whore of Babylon with the first young bastard that strings her a few lies, you hear?" He started down the ladder, and I stood up and faced him.

Mrs. Padgett cried in a frightened but defiant voice, "She *ain't* no girl of yourn. You got no claim to her."

"You hush up that old mouth of yours, now. I'm the man in this house, and I'm telling you what's going to happen. You, Ellie, you fix me some breakfast. You, old woman, you pour me some coffee. And you, Mr. Son-of-a-bitch-whatever-your-name-is, you get your ass outside and get it out of sight before I lose my temper. You hear me?"

My eyes met Ellie's. Hers were fearless — I don't think mine were. "Ellie," I said formally, "I believe you allowed you'd pay me the honor of riding to Berea with me?"

"I did," she answered.

"Then perhaps we better start." I gestured toward the door, and she stepped through it into the sunlight outside. I followed her, and hadn't taken two steps past the threshold when I heard an enraged roar behind me.

He hit me before I could turn to meet him. His knees struck me in the small of the back, and his arms wrapped around my neck. Since I had a second to prepare for the attack, I let his momentum carry me forward and over, in a roll. As Lonnie suddenly found himself on the ground with my weight on him, he released his grip, and I was able to leap to my feet and face him for a new beginning.

We circled one another in the opening movement of the mountain fight. It was going to be a stomping, of course, and Lonnie was very confident. I could tell by his smile. As we circled, it was as if we were both standing on a carousel, and the background went by as though it were painted on a moving strip of canvas. Behind him Ellie came into view. Her expression was intense and unafraid. For a second my eyes met hers, and I felt the commitment of her whole spirit to the outcome. Then Lonnie was upon me.

His attack was an alternation of wide, looping "haymakers" and kicks at my knees and shins. His fists were easy enough to avoid, and I was enjoying a moment of sudden confidence when a paralyzing kick struck my right leg, and I fell heavily on my hands and knees.

Immediately he gave me a jolting kick in the side and another on the pelvis — and I discovered that I was stretched out full length in the dust.

I heard his roar of triumph. I had perhaps two seconds before the stomping began — and once those heavy shoes began their work, I would lose all chance of survival.

I scuttled desperately, crabwise, away from him, at the same time pulling my knees under me until I was halfway to my feet. I rose quickly, which is why his kick caught me in the chest instead of in the face. I did the only thing I could do: I grabbed his leg with both arms, hugged it to my chest and buried my teeth in his thigh.

The exaltation I felt as his salty blood spurted into my mouth has ever since made me understand the true nature of the carnivore.

My teeth must have almost met in the great muscle of his thigh. He gave a wild, bleating scream, and began to pummel me ineffectually on the back and shoulders. Still holding tightly to his leg, I rose from my half crouch. He was carried off balance and fell clumsily on his back. I released my grip and threw myself full length upon him.

He drove his open fingers into my face, and one finger dug into my eye socket. Exploding bursts of pain went off like fireworks inside my head. I struck his hand away with one fist while I pounded down savagely on his face and neck with the other. I hit him on the forehead, the bridge of the nose, the upper teeth and the Adam's apple. Then I got to my feet and kicked him in the temple.

Ellie and Mrs. Padgett and Armisted and Robert and I all looked down at him as he lay there, blood oozing from thigh, nose and mouth. For a moment the only sound I could hear was my own labored breathing. Then Mrs. Padgett said, in a quiet voice that pleaded for understanding, "Don't kill him. It's so lonely out here in the Hollow."

I saddled Jenny Lind, and tied Ellie's carpetbag to the saddle, then watched while the little family made its farewells. Armisted and Robert assured their sister that they were big enough to handle Lonnie. Her mother kissed her goodbye, and I helped her up behind me. She put her arms tightly around my waist, and, with only one backward glance, we rode away from the cabin.

Her small, firm breasts pressed against my back — and the day was golden.

XX

———◆·◆———

NIGHT VISITORS

REVEREND FEE responded to intimidation as a horse responds to spurs. The pressure of our proslavery neighbors achieved what persuasion might never have accomplished: in January, 1858, the Berea School became Berea College.

When Fee sent for Dr. John Almanza Rowly Rogers, it marked his decision to shape our one-room schoolhouse into an institution of higher learning. Rogers was another Oberlin man, but with stronger credentials as an educator than his predecessors. He was the very finest type of teacher — patient, resourceful, buoyant in behavior and dedicated in spirit — and his wife Elizabeth was his match in all departments. I had thought Bill Lincoln and I had made great strides with our students, but Rogers surpassed our best efforts. I could tell by the progress Ellie made — and I saw enough of her to keep well posted.

But however much I saw of her, it wasn't enough. For I had fallen in love with her. The first time I realized it was when I found myself worrying about her safety at Berea. That was in late February, after Reverend Fee and I were mobbed, down by the Big Bend of the Kentucky River.

Fee had been asked to address a meeting at a little church

on the river south of Nicholasville. When we arrived, we were warned that some of the local bravos had boasted they would hang Fee if he tried to preach that day. He paid the threat no more attention than he would have given to a pleasantry about the weather.

I still carried the little pepperbox pistol Cassius Clay had given me four years before, and I unobtrusively shifted it from my saddlebag to my side coat pocket, where I could keep one hand on it. Then I took my seat in a pew near the pulpit.

Fee had just barely warmed up when the door burst open and three men swaggered down the aisle with pistols in their hands. "All right, nigger-stealer, we've come to get you!" shouted the man in front, a heavy-set ruffian with a scar on his chin, apparently the leader.

Fee took no notice of them whatever, and didn't stumble on a single syllable. When they realized he wasn't going to acknowledge their presence — that his high, penetrating voice would continue as if their mothers had never borne them — they rushed to the pulpit and seized him roughly. "God damn you," shouted the man with the scar, "when we say 'Stop,' you stop!"

I stood up and took my pepperbox from my pocket. "Hold it right there," I said loudly.

All three of them swung their guns toward me. Fee saw my pistol, and his eyes widened in shocked surprise. "No, Hacey," he cried. "No, I won't have it! Put that gun away!"

I crouched down so most of my body was screened by the pew in front of me. "Drop to the floor, Reverend," I shouted. The three bullies had pulled together behind him, and I didn't have a clear shot at any of them. Behind me I could hear women screaming.

But instead of moving, Fee shouted to me, "No, no! Throw the gun down! Obey the commandment of God."

Then one of them fired, and the bullet hit the edge of the pew that shielded me. I ducked down even farther, till only the top of my head was visible. "Reverend," I called desperately, "please get down! Do you want to get us both killed?"

And then, before I could get off a single shot, something hit me from behind, and I realized they had brought up reinforcements. Two men took me from the rear, and in a moment I was disarmed, with my hands secured behind me.

Fee and I were dragged out of the building. If any of the congregation were tempted to rescue us, they kept the temptation under tight control. Outside, a crowd of thirty-odd roughnecks waited. One of them held a rope with a noose at one end. The noose was fitted around Fee's neck.

"Now, you low-down nigger-stealer," said the man with the scar, "you promise you'll never come back to Jessamine County, and we won't hang you. Otherwise, we string you up higher than Haman."

"God's will be done," replied Fee.

"You ain't going to promise?" asked the man incredulously. Fee bowed his head.

"Let's drown them in the river," somebody shouted. The suggestion met with general enthusiasm, and we were dragged down to the water's edge. Once again the leader demanded a promise from Fee, and once again Fee ignored him. Then, baffled, the bully turned to me. "You, gun-boy, take off your shirt," he said. Seeing no point in resistance, I did as he asked. "Take him over to that tree and hold him against it," he directed two of his followers. I was made to face the trunk of a sturdy tree, and each man took one of my arms, pulled it around the trunk, and held it firmly. Then

the bully cut himself three limber sycamore branches, held
them together in his big fist and whipped me with them.

The first blow hurt so much I wouldn't have believed the
second could possibly hurt more, but it did. And the third
hurt more than the second, and the fourth hurt more than
the third, and on through ten strokes. After the tenth, the
men holding my arms released me, and I fell to the ground
beside the tree.

I heard the man with the scar speak to Fee as from a great
distance away. "I'll give you a hundred of those if you don't
promise me you'll never come back to Jessamine County
again!"

Fee's voice came from as far away, but lower down, as if
he were on his knees. "Then let my suffering begin now," he
said in his clear, flutelike voice.

"Don't whip him," cried someone I hadn't heard before.
"He's a preacher. You can't whip a preacher!"

"The hell I can't!" shouted the leader. But three or four
other voices joined the dissenter, and a general argument en-
sued. After some debate it was decided to escort us out of
the neighborhood, with renewed warnings of what would be
waiting for us if we should ever return.

Fee mounted his horse, and I was roughly pushed up on
mine, and we were escorted two miles along the road to
Berea. The ride home was a nightmare. Without Fee's gentle encouragement, I doubt if I would have made it. When I
finally reached my cabin, I retired to bed and slept for two
days and two nights.

*   *   *

Ellie nursed me. Actually there's not much nursing you
can do for somebody who has been whipped, except try to
keep anything from sticking to the scabs, but she stayed in

275

the cabin and made soup and sassafras tea, and provided me with something cheering to look at.

"You ain't got the brains God give a mule," she scolded. "Don't you never do nothing but get into fights?"

I protested that I almost never got into fights, but I didn't protest very hard.

During the week I was in bed, I tried to work myself up to telling her how I felt a hundred times, but every time I remembered how foolish she had made me feel back in Head of West Hollow, and rather than risk a repetition of that scene I kept my silence. Her manner toward me was friendly, cool and brisk, and if I fancied that once or twice I caught her watching me with something beyond friendliness, I wasn't sure enough to risk the sharp edge of her tongue.

I had barely regained my feet when rumor of a proposed attack on Berea reached us. There had been many such rumors during the preceding year, but this carried more credibility than most, since the unflappable Mr. Rawlings was one of the friends who reported it. To meet the threat, Rawlings and I organized our neighbors in the settlement into detachments of armed guards, and every night until midnight one detachment was on duty in the Bresh. Our job was complicated by the need to keep Reverend Fee in ignorance of our actions, for if he had known we were prepared to fight fire with fire, he would have forbidden us.

As the spring days lengthened and the weather gentled, tensions remained high. None of us was getting enough sleep. Ugly incidents were the rule every time a Berean went into Richmond for supplies. Groups of riders were seen in the vicinity of the college frequently. A number of our students were withdrawn by their parents, and, in spite of ourselves, we began to wonder how much longer Berea would last.

At that unhappy juncture I discovered that, unbeknownst to anybody at the college, Fee had turned Berea into a station on the Underground Railroad.

* * *

I would never have found it out if I hadn't returned very late from a Sunday visit with my family at Hazelwood. It must have been after one in the morning when Jenny Lind and I trotted slowly up the road to Berea. Clouds covered the waning moon, and the darkness was almost impenetrable. I was half-dozing in the saddle when I became aware of something in the road ahead of me — a cart or wagon, by the sound of it — creaking wheels, the jingling of harness, the sibilant nickering of horses. I pulled Jenny Lind in and listened. It *was* a wagon, perhaps fifty feet away, moving up the trail that led to Berea Ridge — to my cabin, Fee's and the schoolhouse.

I waited a few moments until the sound of the wagon subsided and blended with the night noises around me. Then, feeling sure this was the onset of the promised attack, I felt about in my saddlebag until I found my pepperbox and thrust it under my belt. Then I followed the wagon at a walk. I had just begun the slow ascent of the Ridge when there was a sudden flash of light ahead, as if a lantern had been uncovered and then swiftly covered again.

It came from about where I calculated Reverend Fee's house to be. I was immediately filled with apprehension. My back was wet with sweat, and I could feel the drops running down over the barely healed scars of my whipping. I continued up the trail as quietly as possible. The sounds ahead changed, as if the wagon had stopped and people were moving about in the darkness.

Suddenly Jenny Lind whinnied and shied, as an invisible hand seized her bridle. Simultaneously, bright light stabbed

277

into my eyes, as a lantern was opened close by. Other hands gripped my legs, and then a voice whispered, "Hacey Miller!" It could only have belonged to Reverend Fee.

"Is that you, Reverend? Are you all right?"

"Yes, yes, Hacey, everything's all right," he whispered irritably. "Just go to your cabin, and don't worry about anything!"

Then another voice, the voice of a Negro, spoke from the darkness. "Who this man, Reverend?"

"A friend. He works with us at the school. Nothing to be upset about."

"I surely hope you're right. Wouldn't want to come all this way just so some buckra could send me back again."

This time there was an edge to Fee's voice. "I said it was all right, didn't I? Hacey, get on to your cabin. I'll see you in the morning."

"Yes, sir, Reverend Fee. Good night." I felt the hands release Jenny Lind's bridle, and she moved forward up the trail. Invisible eyes were on me as I skirted the wagon pulled up in front of Fee's cabin — a grayish mass of undefined darkness in the surrounding black — and rode on to my own house, where I quickly unsaddled and stabled the horse. I pulled curtains over the windows before lighting a lamp.

Since Bill Lincoln had returned to Oberlin a few months before, I was alone with my thoughts. They occupied me till dawn.

Early the next morning, Reverend Fee came to my cabin. He indulged in no small talk. "Hacey, I regret that you happened along when you did last night. I suppose you have no doubts as to what was going on?"

"No, sir, no doubts at all."

"I may as well tell you that Berea has been a station for

over a year now. Deliveries are infrequent — once or twice a month at the most. Usually no more than three items in any shipment. Layovers are at my house only. No one in the village is involved at all. It is, of course, completely illegal and punishable by heavy jail sentences."

"Yes, sir."

"I've been particularly careful that you didn't get wind of it, because I know of your great admiration for Cassius Clay and his legalistic viewpoint. I wanted to spare you the pain of divided loyalties. But understand this" — he leaned forward and put his hand on my arm, squeezing it tightly — "I have no apologies to make for the work itself. It is God's work, and it will continue as long as I am in a position to carry it out."

"I can understand that, Reverend Fee, and sympathize with it, so long as it's a personal decision that affects only you. But it seems to me this affects the whole school. I wouldn't presume to question your actions as an individual, but your actions as the head of Berea — "

"Should be judged by exactly the same standard," he interrupted. "It is God's work, I said."

"But you know how many enemies we have already, Reverend. It's touch-and-go whether they'll let us open in the fall, right now. If anybody found out the Underground Railroad went through here, they'd burn us out in twenty-four hours. Five years of work would be wasted."

"Wasted? Do you believe the work would be wasted, Hacey? When a tree is struck by lightning, was its growing a waste? Was it a waste to the squirrels who ran through its branches, or the birds who raised their families among its leaves? Was it a waste to the tired traveler who rested a moment in its shade?"

"But we're just beginning to do some good here. The

mountain people are starting to come in, families are moving to Berea to live, so they can send their children to the school — why, Rogers thinks we'll have over a hundred students next term, if nothing goes wrong. How can you gamble the future of the college like this?"

"If the college's present doesn't mean anything, its future won't mean anything either; you can't make something out of nothing." He made a brushing gesture with his hand, as though clearing the air of a trivial nuisance. "But I'm not here to argue, Hacey. I just want to tell you, in all kindness, in all gratitude, that what you interrupted last night is as much the work of Berea as English and algebra. If you can't accept that knowledge, I can only thank you for your services and say goodbye."

I stared miserably at my shoes. "I don't know, Reverend Fee. I just don't know how I feel. I guess I'll have to think about it some. Can I let you know my decision in a day or two?"

"Of course, Brother Miller." He bobbed his large head at me, and his expression was gravely pious and his eyes serene. "We are all instruments in the hands of God." He rose and took his leave.

I lay on my bed and stared at the ceiling for two hours as I debated the right course of action. Should I stay, or should I leave? It was a tug-of-war, with one side seeming almost to win, then suddenly losing most of its hard-won ground to the other. Toward noon I got up and went looking for Ellie.

I found her dipping candles for the family with whom she lived. "Can you take a walk with me? It's important," I said. She immediately put her work aside and came with me up to the Ridge and toward The Glades oak. We walked in silence for five minutes or so. Then she said, "You going to say something, or you want me to guess? I could ask

'Twenty Questions' like we do with Mrs. Rogers. Only you got to tell me Animal, Vegetable or Mineral first."

Then I told her what I had seen the night before, and what it meant. "Whether it's right or wrong is one thing, Ellie. But the fact is, it's against the law. And if anybody in Lexington or Frankfort found out about it, why, they'd close Berea so fast it would make your head swim!"

She picked a stalk of high grass and began to chew it. She thought for a moment and then asked, "Hacey, do you think this Underground Railroad is a good thing?"

"Well, I think it's good and bad both. What it's doing is good — getting slaves away to freedom — but the way it's doing it is bad. Because it's against the law."

"What other way is there?"

"Well, right now there *isn't* any other way, short of a Negro being allowed to work for hire, so he can save up enough money to buy his freedom . . ."

". . . which don't happen so often as you would notice it, I reckon."

"No, and nowadays less than ever, since most states have laws against it. But that's not the point . . ."

"The point is, it's against the law," she interrupted.

"That's right — it's against the law, Goddamnit!"

"Whose law, Hacey? Nigger's law? Preacher's law? Your friend Wentworth's law?"

"*The* law, Ellie! Everybody's law — the law of the land. If people don't respect the law, they might as well be savages."

"I'm sure God wouldn't want you to do anything that would make you feel like a savage," she said primly.

We talked for another fifteen minutes, or rather I talked and she listened. Then she made me walk her back to the settlement. "I got to get back to my chores, Hacey. Don't fret yourself too much about all this. You do what comes natural, and it'll be as easy as picking ticks off an old hound dog."

But I did fret myself about it all the rest of the day, and when I went to bed that night my nerves were ragged. No doubt that explains the dream I had.

I was walking on a featureless plain with two companions whom I couldn't see, because they were just behind my field of vision unless I were to turn my head, and I knew I wasn't allowed to do that. All I could do was walk toward a horizon that looked and smelled like brass, and I knew it would never get any closer.

Suddenly there was something half concealed in the sand near my feet. I bent over and brushed the sand from it. There was a pounding either inside me or outside, no telling which — if it was inside, it was blood; if outside, drums. As the sand parted, I saw the thing was a baby, a Negro baby. I picked it up and held it in my hands. It was naked, very small, and had no eyes, only smooth skin over empty sockets. It opened its mouth and screamed, and out of its mouth crawled a small spotted snake. I tried to grab the snake and throw it away, but it avoided my grasp and wriggled swiftly into my sleeve. I could feel it as it worked its way up my arm and around my shoulder and down along my chest. Then I couldn't feel it anymore.

The scene changed, and I was walking along a dirt road, slowly climbing a hill. Again there were two other figures just behind my field of vision. I was in a hurry to get away from something, but I couldn't remember what; I had been running a long time and was too tired to run any longer. My feet kicked up little explosions of dust. I got to the top of the hill and started down. There was a large bush beside the road about a hundred yards away. Walking became easier, and my pace quickened. I knew I had eluded my pursuer. I broke into a trot and laughed aloud. I had almost reached the bush when I heard a dry, slithering sound, and saw something large and serpentine coiled among the branches. Then I remembered what had been after me.

The scene changed again, and I was walking up the front steps of White Hall. I was wearing black, so I knew there was death about. I went into the great drawing room, and saw an open coffin on a catafalque. Many people were in the room, and I recognized my brother Boone, Robards, the slave trader, Danford Ranew and Bryan Ledyard. Why were they at Cassius Clay's funeral, I wondered. I walked over to the coffin to look inside it. Clay was lying there, dressed in fine black broadcloth. But where his face should have been, there was a mirror. I looked into the mirror, but didn't recognize the face that looked back at me. It was a black face. Then I saw the reflection of two other faces behind me, and knew they belonged to the two followers who always stayed just outside my sight. I turned quickly to seize them, but they were gone, and in their place stood Robards and his "Choice Stock" girl, Cathy. Robards was cupping one of her breasts with one hand and rubbing his other hand down the curve of her belly. She looked at me with an expression of unutterable contempt and said, "Kill the white trash, Mr. Robards." Everybody in the room burst into laughter, and I dashed outside into the night.

Then came the oddest thing of all. I seemed to wake up from the dream, and to find myself in my bed with Ellie at my side. She was asleep, breathing lightly, a smile on her face, her chestnut hair spread on the pillow in a cloud. I put my hand on her warm shoulder to wake her so I could tell her about my dream. Just then I felt a weight on my legs, as if a large dog had silently jumped on the bed and lain down on the covers. I was surprised, but not apprehensive, for though I did not remember having a dog of my own, I had always gotten along well enough with them. I moved my hand gently on Ellie's shoulder. "Ellie," I whispered.

Then I felt *another* weight on my legs, higher up than the first, and at the same time a fetid odor assailed my nostrils. There was a dry, rustling sound I had heard somewhere before. Ellie's eyes opened wide, and her body stiffened. "Hacey, what is it?" she whispered.

"I don't know, honey," I answered. Then I felt a *third* weight. This time it was on my waist. The rustling was louder, and the stench was intolerable.

"Hacey," Ellie screamed, *"something's coiling around the bed!"*

Then, too late, I began to struggle against the great scaly body, as Ellie gasped and sobbed beside me in the remorseless coils. "Damballa!" I cried with my failing breath, "Damballa *loa!* Not yet, Dambella, not yet!"

I awoke lying on the floor beside my bed in a welter of bedclothes, alone, as I had been when I retired.

Next morning I told Reverend Fee that if there were an opportunity, I would like to assist him in the work of the Underground Railroad.

"Praise the Lord, Brother Miller," he said. "I'm delighted you reached that decision."

"Oh, I can't take all the credit for it," I said a trifle bitterly. "I doubt if anybody could hold out against a preacher, a mountain girl and a snake!"

XXI

———•———

THE RAILROAD

THE FACT that I had volunteered to help in the work of the Underground Railroad in no way indicated that I was reconciled to the dangers inherent in such action. Far from it: I was scared to death. Added to my fear for the fate of Berea in the event of discovery was a considerable nervousness about my own fate. All business was conducted at night, of course, and I was often on the road and in darkness at 2:00 A.M., the hour when the candle flame of courage flickers most erratically in the drafts of doubt and despair.

We received an average of one consignment a week. Generally the cargo was routed to us via Mr. Bird Cubbins of Rockcastle County, and he acted as conductor as far as Berea. Then Fee or I assumed the role, and after the freight had been warehoused through the day, resumed the journey the following night. Our leg of the Railroad went as far as Mr. Rawlings' farm outside Richmond, where we saw the cargo safely stored in his barn before we returned home. From Richmond the "tracks" contined to Maysville, where our branch line crossed the Ohio River.

The use of railroading terminology — "consignments,"

"cargoes," "timetables," "switching," "engineer" and the like — was almost a mania with us. Cubbins, our neighbor to the south, had a particular gift for communicating in cryptic railroad metaphor. I remember one note he sent us: "Dear Reverend Fee. As you requested, three copies of Calhoun's "Peculiar Institution," bound in black, are being expressed to you posthaste. Estimated date of arrival next Monday, at your siding."

But no amount of such foolishness could conceal the fact that we were playing for desperate stakes. I had not the slightest doubt that exposure would mean the immediate end of the college, and quite possibly the end of Fee or myself as well.

During the last week of April and the first two weeks of May, I handled three consignments. The business went uneventfully. Then came word of a fourth shipment, this one to include five articles. On the appointed night I sat up rereading *Walden* until 3:00 A.M., when I heard what was supposed to be the cry of a screech owl repeated three times outside my window. I quickly blew out the light and opened the door. My eyes were not accustomed to the darkness, and I could see nothing. "Who's there?" I called softly.

"A friend — with other friends," replied the voice of Bird Cubbins.

"You don't sound any more like a screech owl than I sound like Napoleon Bonaparte," I told him.

"You didn't like my tree frog, either, as I recollect. It may be your standards are a mite unrealistic. Come out here and help unload."

I followed him to the deep-bedded farm wagon standing in the road. There were five Negroes in the wagon, a family — father, mother and three children, one still a babe in arms.

We helped them down and into the cabin. When they and their bandanna full of possessions were safely inside, Cubbins and I locked the door and relit the lamp.

My visitors were a strangely assorted lot. Every time I saw Cubbins I remembered Shelley's "To a Skylark," for, his first name notwithstanding, I always thought, "Bird thou never wert." He looked like a tree stump, short, thick and with a skin as weather-beaten as bark. His shoulders bulged with muscle, his big hands were horny as a turtle's shell, but he had a literary bent that made his speech seem incongruous as it emerged from his lipless trap of a mouth. He picked up the book I had been reading and glanced at the title. "Ah," he drawled, "improving the shining hour with the Sage of Walden Pond? Or are you, like the mass of men, leading a life of quiet desperation?" He flipped through the pages looking for a favorite passage. He was very fond of Thoreau.

The Negroes stared at me with expressions ranging from uneasiness to fright. The father was stout, light-complexioned and about forty years old. His wife was younger and darker, and her eyeballs stood out apprehensively against her chocolate-brown cheeks. The three children seemed to be all eyes. The five of them ranged themselves on the floor with their backs against the wall and stared at Cubbins and me.

After a moment's perusal, Cubbins set the book aside. "You will no doubt be stimulated considerable to know that our consignment's routing arrangements are not entirely unsuspected by certain interested parties, friend Hacey," he said, with a lip-smacking enjoyment of his own polysyllables.

"Bird, what the hell are you trying to say?"

"Why, merely that there are Agents of Darkness sniffing

287

at our heels. Apparently our friends Jonah and Tibbie and their progeny" — he indicated the five seated blacks with a courteous nod — "had such a hold on the affections of their former master that he is loath to see them go. At any rate, he has employed two enterprising gentlemen of the genus Nigger-hunter to recapture them."

"How do you know, Bird?"

"Because they almost caught our friends crossing the Cumberland River and came close again near Somerset. The warning's been passed up from station to station."

I had a sinking sensation. "Did you see anything of them tonight?" I asked.

"Nary a trace. Which makes *your* chances of seeing them a good deal better, I suspect."

"What do you mean?"

"Well, the way I figure it, these two rascals will calculate that Jonah and Tibbie, en famille" (he pronounced it to rhyme with "steely") "will keep on going the way they was headed, which was northeast, to the nearest spot on the Ohio River, which is Maysville. And if you draw a line on the map from Somerset to Maysville, it just happens to go through one settlement which has achieved a fair amount of notoriety for antislavery agitation — one Berea, by name. Are you with me so far, Hacey?"

"Then you think these two slave-hunters will be watching the roads northeast out of Berea?"

"Either that or they'll wait on the Kentucky River near College Hill. That's where they'd expect anybody traveling from here to Maysville to cross."

If they waited outside Berea, they would be my problem; if they decided to watch the river crossing, they would be Rawlings' worry. "Which would you guess they'd do, Bird?"

"I'd say it was a mute point," he replied inaccurately. "But if I was you, I'd assume you'll run into them between here and Rawlings' farm."

"When was the last time these men were actually seen, and whereabouts?"

"I understand they were in Mount Vernon day before yesterday." Mount Vernon was less than twenty miles from Berea. "Which means they could be anywhere in the state by now, including underneath your bed. And on that happy note I'll take my leave, Brother Hacey." He turned to the five Negroes sitting against the wall, and shook hands ceremoniously with each. "Goodbye, Jonah — I trust your regurgitation from the belly of the whale is at hand. Goodbye, Tibbie, it's been a pleasure. Goodbye, Washburn. Goodbye, Crawford. And goodbye, Emmaline." The baby's hand disappeared into his great fist, and he pumped his arm up and down formally three times. The baby looked too startled to cry.

I blew out the lamp again and unlocked the door for him. "Be careful going home, Bird."

"Set your mind at ease about me, Hacey. You got other things to put it to." He widened his trap of a mouth in a smile, pantomimed a locomotive engineer pulling the cord of his whistle, said, "Toot, toot!" and disappeared into the darkness. A few moments later I heard the creak of his wagon as it began its homeward trip.

I bedded down my five visitors as best I could, and spent the remainder of the night wondering what to do with them. Reverend Fee was away from Berea, and I had no one to discuss the problem with. I decided I had four possible courses of action, and I argued the merits of each one with myself until daylight pushed under the heavy window curtain.

I could keep to the regular Railroad timetable, load my cargo that night, head for Rawlings' farm and take my chances. Or I could hold the cargo over for one or more nights, hoping that the watchers would assume they had missed us and give up their vigil. Or I could try to move the shipment by day, replacing the danger of the slave-hunters with the danger of an alert countryside. Or I could reroute the shipment and deliver it to another station entirely.

All four alternatives had grave drawbacks. Going out that night, as per schedule, was obviously a gamble; keeping Jonah's family in my cabin for an extended period presented all sorts of difficulties, and the risk of discovery would increase as time went on; trying to move them in the daytime would only substitute one threat for another; and as for rerouting, I knew of only two other stations besides Berea and Rawlings' farm — one was Bird Cubbins' place, and the other was a farm in Lincoln County, near Stanford — exactly the wrong direction for freedom-bound Negroes to travel.

It was a beggar's choice. I decided to keep the family in my cabin all day and all night and all the following day, in hopes that the twenty-four-hour delay might throw the pursuers off the scent. Then the next night I would deliver them to Rawlings' barn.

During the day I taught my classes, hunted up emergency rations of bread, cheese, side meat and beans, and, on the pretext of going into Richmond, rode over to see Mr. Rawlings. The leathery old man received my information coolly, and some of his quiet courage must have rubbed off on me, for as I rode up the trail to the Ridge through the gathering dusk, I began to feel almost confident.

That night I became acquainted with my guests. After I had served them their supper we talked until late in the evening, passing the time until we should be tired enough to sleep. Little Emmaline's eyes closed about nine o'clock, and her brothers followed her an hour later. Their mother dozed off before midnight, but it must have been two or two-thirty before Jonah and I finally retired.

He was a remarkable man, in his way. Tibbie was not his first wife, nor the three children his first children. He was half white, and had been raised as a house servant on a plantation just north of Memphis. He had been taught to read, write and cipher, and when he showed a gift for mathematics, was allowed to learn bookkeeping and simple accounting. By the time he reached manhood, he was capable of earning a fair income by hiring out as a bookkeeper around the neighborhood, and his master allowed him to do so a few weeks every year.

Jonah married an octoroon who was personal maid to the mistress of the plantation, and in time they had a child, with a complexion so light she could hardly be told from white. The master was indulgent; Jonah was allowed to save the money he earned as an accountant, toward the end of buying the freedom of himself and his family. The years went by happily as the little family's savings grew.

Unfortunately, as the slave's bank account increased, the master's diminished. By the time the latter died in a hunting accident, he had his house, land and slaves double-mortgaged. Everything went, including Jonah's bank account (which was not, of course, in his own name), his wife, his child and himself. The wife and child were bought by a Natchez slave-dealer; Jonah went to a tobacco farm near Murfreesboro, where he was expected to keep books two hours out of each work week and sweat in the fields for the remaining fifty-eight.

The helpless rage and bitterness he knew then almost

drove him to suicide. He felt he was the butt of a heartless trick, that God had allowed him to love, to marry, to father a child and work at his trade and save for the future, only to increase his agony when all of it was swept away. Day after day, his misery fed on him the way the tobacco borers fed on the plants around him, and when he fell into his bed each night he was no longer sane.

It was Tibbie who saved him. She was the daughter of a field hand, illiterate, the mother of two stillborn children before she was fifteen, married and widowed, already bent in the back and lined in the face when Jonah arrived to make his home in the wretched cabin next to hers. Ignoring his withdrawn sullenness and his wild rages, she proceeded to move into his life and into his bed. She calmed him with her patience, with her silences, with her cooking and with her body. In time she became pregnant again, and this time the child lived. Then she had a second, then a third.

Gradually Jonah began to believe in his own will again. He stopped railing at his fate and began to think about the future of his family. He resolved to escape to freedom with his wife and children. He concentrated on putting all his skill in accountancy to work for his master, with the result that in a few years he was given a share of responsibility in administering the farm. Through this work he met a number of influential white people in Murfreesboro — and one of them was a conductor on the Railroad.

I asked him if he wasn't afraid. He answered me musingly, "No, sir, I don't appear to be. It doesn't feel like I have any reason to be." He spoke with very little accent.

"How do you explain that? I'd be scared twenty-four hours a day if I were you."

"What have I got to be scared for? If they catch me, what

are they going to do to me? Take away my wife and children? What wife and children? Until I cross the Ohio, I don't have any wife and children. Sell me down the river? They sold me once, and I'm still here. Whip me? They've done that, too — but if they whip me too hard, I'm not much good to them afterward. Kill me? Yes, they could, but I don't reckon they will, and even if they do, there are worse things than dying."

We sat a moment in silence, as he rubbed a small scar on his neck with his finger. "No, sir, I don't have anything to be scared for now," he said quietly. "But just let me get across that Ohio River, and I'll be the scaredest-assed nigger you ever saw!" He looked at Tibbie and his three children, curled up together on a featherbed on the floor. "Just you let me get them up North, and I'll be standing with my back against the wall for the rest of my life. I won't even let my own shadow get behind me!"

The next day I tried to find out if anyone had seen the two slave-hunters in the neighborhood, but I could get no information. Fee was still absent from the college, and I had no one to talk to. I was tempted to take my worries to Ellie, but suppressed the urge. In the afternoon I walked out to The Glades oak and sat under it. I could look down the Ridge, past the clumsy new school buildings, to the settlement below. A heavy silence lay on the Bresh, and the slanting rays of the late afternoon sun created contrasts of light and shadow that lifted even distant objects into sharp dimensionality.

This is where it's all going to end, I thought despondently. *After the dream, the hope, the beginning, after the clearing of brush and the splitting of shingles, after the silent children who rode in on the bare backs of mules, with a couple of*

293

chickens tied feet-to-feet and draped over the bony back-
bones in front of them. Here's where it will end, wrecked by
two slave-hunters on the rock of the law.

With such gloomy forebodings occupying my thoughts, it
was after dark when I returned to my cabin. I found my
visitors ready to be on their way. I had kept my apprehensions to myself, and Tibbie and the children looked forward
to a continuation of their journey with pleasure. Jonah was
more sensitive to nuance, and his expression was grave.

A little after ten o'clock, I was outside my cabin with the
horse and wagon we used on such occasions. The moon was
in its last quarter, and was obscured by clouds more often
than not. The night was cool and damp. When I tapped on
the door, Jonah opened it quickly and shooed his wife and
children out ahead of him. I pulled up the heavy tail gate,
exposing the aperture under it that permitted entrance into
the foot-high space between the wagon's real and its false
bottom. The two boys crawled into the opening eagerly,
then Tibbie, with little Emmaline in her arms, wriggled in
after them. When they were safely inside, Jonah looked at
me somberly.

"What happens if those two nigger-hunters catch us, Mr.
Miller?"

"Well, first they'll have to find us, which I don't reckon
they'll do. Then they'll have to stop us, which could be a
considerable problem. Then they'd have to find the trapdoor, which they wouldn't even know to look for. And besides, I've got a pistol." For my pepperbox, unused for anything except target practice, was again in my pocket.

"Well, I don't have a pistol, but I've got a knife," he said
softly. "And I believe we're close enough to the Ohio River
for me to start feeling scared. Scared people know how to
use a knife the best."

"Just you concentrate on keeping those children of yours quiet, in case we get stopped," I told him. He crawled into the hiding space and I lowered the tail gate into place behind him. Then we began the trip to Rawlings' barn.

I had a strange feeling of powerlessness, and of inevitability, as I swayed on the wooden seat of that wagon, staring at the bony rump of the soot-colored horse in front of me. I felt that the fatal die was cast, and yet I experienced neither exhilaration nor fear; it was rather as though I were a swimmer carried on a wave, and for a brief interval of time that wave had become my universe. Above me the clouds scudded across the rind of the moon. The wheels creaked louder than the night sounds around me. I thought I heard a baby crying from underneath the false floorboards.

We were within a mile of Richmond, close to the turnoff to Rawlings' farm, when a light stabbed my eyes and a voice cried, "Stand where you are!" Instantly I snapped the reins, shouted "Yah," and grabbed for my whip. The old horse threw himself forward in the harness, and the wagon surged ahead. A rider materialized to my left, and I struck at him with my whipstock. "Halt or I'll fire," shouted a high-pitched voice. I remembered my own pistol and dropped the whip to dig for it in my pocket. I had it in my hand when another rider appeared out of the darkness ahead of me. He leaned to one side and seized my horse's bridle. I pointed the pistol at him and pulled the trigger. The gun misfired. I cocked it again, pulled the trigger again. It misfired again.

"God damn you, Cassius Clay!" I shouted furiously.

The rider on my left thrust his pistol in my face. It was a huge Colt revolver of Mexican War vintage. "You pull up now or I'll blow your head off," he yelled. His companion meanwhile had pulled my horse down to a walk, and a moment later we suddenly found ourselves at a dead stop. Except for the excited breathing of the horses, there was no sound around us.

Then the rider with the Colt said, "Now just you drop that little toy pistol on the ground and climb down from there, you hear? Real nice and polite." He spoke like Delta white trash. I climbed down from the wagon and stood beside it. "Just what the hell do you people think you're doing?" I asked angrily.

The light stabbed in my eyes again, and I saw that the lantern was held by a third man, who was on foot and standing to one side of the road. The man with the Colt swung down from his horse. "I reckon you got an idea what we're doing. Why, this wagon stinks of nigger a mile away!"

The voice of the second rider came from near the back of the wagon. "Ain't nothing back here 'cepting a couple burlap sacks and some loose straw, Jules," he said.

"I would have been surprised if there was," the man with the Colt replied. "Smelling nigger ain't necessarily the same as seeing nigger. Hey, you — Tuttle — bring that light around to the back of the wagon."

The light came toward us, and in its upward spill I recognized the fat face of Lafe Tuttle, a face I had first seen in The Glades Meetinghouse the day Reverend Fee preached his maiden sermon there. A moment later he recognized me as well, and said, "I seen him before. He comes from that nigger-stealing school."

"Well, what do you know about that? Hey, T.P.," Jules called to his companion, "Tuttle says this mean old gunfighter here comes from that nigger-stealing school."

"Well, we figgered that, Jules. I mean, hell, that's why we waited here, ain't it?"

"Yeah, but it kind of comforts a man to know he guessed right, damn if it don't."

"Now look here, you men," I said with as much righteous indignation as I could muster. "I don't know what you think you're doing, but if it's robbery you're after, you'll get slim pickings off me. I've got about two dollars in my purse." I started to put my hand into my coat pocket where I kept my money.

"You just keep your hands where they are, Mister," said Jules, pressing the Colt's muzzle into my belly. "It ain't money we're after. At least, not directly. Tuttle, shine that light into the back of the wagon, there. There's got to be a trick bottom. All we got to do now is find it. T.P., get up into the wagon bed and feel all them boards. Push on each one and try to wiggle it, you know?" He pressed the Colt tighter against me. "I wouldn't suppose you'd want to save us some time and tell us how to get into the false bottom, would you, nigger-stealer?"

"I told you I don't know what you're talking about."

"Well, it don't really make no nevermind. We'll find it directly anyway." The wagon boards gave off a hollow reverberation as T.P. stamped on them. "It surely does sound hollow, don't it? I expect them niggers are really shitting in their pants now." He chuckled softly. "Peee-yew! I bet it smells in there."

"How many times do I have to tell you —"

"No more times. You told me enough. Hey, T.P. — you find anything?"

"Not yet, Jules." The stamping continued.

"Well, take a look at that tail gate. Don't that look awful high for a ordinary wagon tail gate? Unhook it and drop it down." Lafe Tuttle moved in with his lantern, and T.P. pulled out the two pins that secured the heavy board in position. It dropped, revealing the black opening behind it.

"Well, I'll be dogged. Looky there," said Jules in a

pleased voice. "What you reckon we going to find in there? You like to make a guess, Mr. Nigger-stealer? Shine that light in there, Tuttle."

I watched, dry-mouthed, as the cruel light revealed Jonah crawling out from his hiding place. He emerged headfirst and dropped to the ground, then rose to his feet and stood between the light and the wagon. "All right, you got me," he said.

"Get outen the way, nigger," said Lafe Tuttle, pushing him to one side.

With the grace of a striking snake, Jonah brought his knife up and drove it into Tuttle's throat, just under the right ear. It happened so swiftly that Tuttle was unable to get out more than a single bleat before he died. He dropped the lantern and sprawled backwards on the ground.

Jules fired instantly at Jonah, and at the same moment another pistol roared from the darkness beside the road. Jules' bullet caught Jonah in the shoulder and threw him back against a wagon wheel. He clung to the rim with one hand and stayed on his feet. Jules gave a gasp, jackknifed with both arms pulled in tightly against his belly and suddenly sat down. T.P. stood frozen, his hands raised to shoulder height and his mouth hanging open. The lantern on the ground remained lighted, and the men at the back of the wagon cast monstrous shadows behind them.

"You there, wagon-driver," called a voice from the darkness. "No names, you hear? Now, pick up that pistol on the ground, there, and cover that man." I picked up Jules' Colt and pointed it at T.P. "Now get one of them burlap bags from the wagon and put it over his head!" I did as I was directed. When T.P. was hooded, Mr. Rawlings stepped out of the shadows. He held a revolver in his hand, and he jabbed T.P. in the side with it. "You touch that bag without

I tell you to, and I'll blow a bigger hole in your belly than I put in your friend's," he said.

"I ain't going to touch it, I promise," said the muffled voice under the burlap.

Jonah was still clinging to the wheel. Rawlings and I helped him into the wagon, and he lay down on the boards. I pressed another burlap sack against the bullet hole in his shoulder to reduce the loss of blood, and he gave a sigh and lost consciousness.

Rawlings knelt beside Jules and felt his pulse. "He's dead," he said calmly. "That's another one we don't have to worry about. The one in the bag — did he hear Tuttle say your name?"

"No, Tuttle didn't call me by name. I don't think he knew it."

"Well, that's all right, then." The old man stepped behind T.P., reversed his grip on his pistol, and struck the slave-catcher a powerful blow on the back of the head. The man dropped like a rock, and lay motionless in the dirt.

"Tuttle did say I was from Berea, so he knows that, at least."

"Well, I don't expect that'll do him any good, 'cause I don't imagine you'll be at Berea any time he's there looking for you." He hawked and spat. "You just skedaddle over to your pappy's house and hole up there for a while, and when all the hooraw's over, I'll send you word and you can come back."

We whispered a few words of reassurance to Tibbie and the children, who had huddled in the cramped darkness, silent and uncomprehending, through all the activity around them, and then, without bothering to refasten the tail gate, we drove the wagon to Rawlings' barn.

Rawlings elected to put as much distance as possible between the fugitive blacks and Berea, and so, after hastily bandaging Jonah and covering his unconscious body with a light blanket of straw, he began the next leg of the journey, while I rode for Hazelwood on a borrowed horse. I arrived by first light, having encountered no one on the way, and slept like a dead man for ten hours.

I stayed five days with my parents, until Mr. Rawlings sent word by a grandchild that T.P. had left the Bluegrass. My mother and father made no reference to the events near Richmond on the night I arrived, and neither did I. The *Lexington Observer* had a ten-line story on the discovery of the bodies of Lafe Tuttle and one Jules Catto, of Pass Christian, Mississippi, on the pike south of Richmond, but there was nothing about the Railroad in the story.

When I returned to Berea, I found that it had been searched from top to bottom by a sheriff's posse, acting with the advice of T.P. Rawlings' farm had also been searched, as had many other farms between Berea and Richmond. Nothing in any way incriminating was discovered.

The first time I saw Reverend Fee after my return to the college, he gave me a bland and gentle smile. "Ah, Brother Miller, I hope your family is in good health again?" he said.

"Yes, Reverend, everything is as snug and secure as could be expected," I replied. He gave me a pat on the arm and went about his business. Never after that did he refer to my absence from the school in any way. Of course, neither did I.

That was my last assignment as engineer on the Underground Railroad. I was never asked to handle another cargo.

XXII

Commencement

IT WAS A WARM, SUNNY DAY in late May, 1858, and nearly two hundred people were assembled in an oak grove about a mile and a half from Berea. Dinner was laid out on plank tables under the trees, and the air was heavy with the aroma of fresh bread and roast meat. There was music and singing and laughter, and the penetrating yells of children playing. Everybody had on his Sunday best, even though it was a weekday.

Berea College was celebrating the conclusion of its first term with class exercises. No one was graduating, but nevertheless I thought of it as our first Commencement.

Ellie and I sat in the grass near the road, watching the late arrivals. These included the dignitaries — judges, congressmen, state senators and the like. In between commenting on them, I was trying to persuade Ellie to marry me, and she was refusing. "I've told you and told you, Hacey, I won't marry up with you till I graduate. Now leave me be!"

"But that's so dumb."

"That's right. It's dumb, like I am, and like I'm going to keep on being until I graduate. So hush your fuss."

"Ellie, at least come over to Hazelwood for the summer and

let me court you right. There's no point in you staying here with the Waterfords just waiting for school to start again."

"Hacey, I ain't about to go meeting your ma and pa while I'm still too dang ignorant to spell 'slop' if I was sitting in it. There! You hear what I just said? Now, that was a downright vulgar remark, wasn't it? How'd you like it if I was to talk like that in front of your ma and all your fine friends?"

"I expect they've all heard worse. Gosh all hemlock, Ellie, do you think we're hothouse flowers or something? Why, they'll love you just the way you are — like I do. Except not so much — because nobody could love you as much as I do."

She looked at me gravely and put her small, cool hand on mine. "Let me do what I got to do. I reckon there's time. There's our whole life long."

I looked back into her big gray up-tilted eyes and knew I would never be able to refuse her in anything she asked.

Among the friends of Berea who were at the class exercises were Bird Cubbins and old Mr. Rawlings, each of whom came over to pay his respects. Cubbins appeared first. "Ah, Hacey, didn't anyone ever tell you it was downright antisocial to spirit away the most pulchritudinous filly in the herd and stable her secretly in the shrubbery, away from the eye of mortal man?"

"Howdy, Bird. How are things at Walden Pond?"

"Unquietly desperate. Well?" He waited to be introduced, his traplike mouth curled up at both sides in a smile of anticipation.

"Miss Padgett, may I present Mr. Cubbins? Mr. Cubbins, Miss Padgett — at least that's her name for the time being. But I have every hope of changing it shortly."

"Why, Hacey — how you go on!" exclaimed Ellie, dropping her eyes modestly, for all the world like a graduate of Madame Mentelle's Finishing School in Lexington.

"Your servant, ma'am," said Bird, bowing from the waist like a short, mean, ugly dancing master. "If I understand our friend correctly, I can only hope that you will be able to work the civilizing influence of which Hacey stands in so much need without sacrifice of your own loveliness, Miss Padgett." She bowed her head graciously, and I stared at the two of them as if they were two recently materialized Patagonians.

A few minutes after Bird took his leave, Mr. Rawlings strolled up. He shook hands with me and bobbed his head over Ellie's hand with a rough antique chivalry. "A real pleasure, Miss Padgett," he said, with a smile that showed his appreciation. Then he looked at me, and there was a glint in his eyes.

"Some amount of water's gone over the dam since we got together last, Hacey."

"Or you might say it's gone down the river."

"Yep. You might say that, if you had some reason for thinking about the river."

"Like as if you had some friends who were planning on crossing it?"

"Like as if."

"Didn't you have some friends who were figuring on crossing it a while back, Mr. Rawlings?"

"Yes, I did."

"I wonder if they made it."

"Last I heard, they was safe across and heading north like a Canadian goose with a tailing wind." His tobacco-colored face parted in a shy grin. "They sent back word thanking their friends for past favors."

"I'm real glad to hear that. Won't you sit down and join us, Mr. Rawlings?"

"Oh, I reckon not. I brought a passel of grandchildren here, and without me to keep them reined in, they'll devil folks worse than the Ten Plagues of Egypt." He made his adieux and sauntered off through the throng.

The singing had just began with a lusty "There were ninety and nine that safely lay/ In the shelter of the fold" when Ellie tugged at my sleeve and pointed. I looked where she directed and saw a tall, barrel-chested figure picking his way through the tag-playing children. It was Cassius M. Clay, dressed in black broadcloth and snowy white linen, hatless, brushing his shock of black hair impatiently from his eyes.

"Ain't that your Cash Clay?" asked Ellie.

"Why, yes," I cried excitedly. "Reverend Fee invited him, as a matter of course, but nobody thought he'd come. Mr. Clay — over here!"

He saw me as I was struggling to my feet — my left leg had gone to sleep. He smiled in recognition and altered his course toward us. "Hacey, it's a pleasure to see you again. You're looking fat and sassy — and I must say, you're in handsome company." He gave Ellie a warm smile as he shook my hand. "How did you manage to kidnap the prettiest girl in Madison County and keep her all to yourself?"

"I can thank a plausible tongue combined with a total lack of scruple. It's good to see you in Berea, Mr. Clay. We'd about given you up."

"Or vice versa, you might say. Well, Hacey, to tell you the truth, I got a little tired of sulking in my tent. There were too many alarms and excursions in the night around me. I was hearing so much about my college I decided I better come down and find out what was really happening."

"Have you seen Reverend Fee yet? He'll be tickled to death to see you, Mr. Clay."

"That's where I'm headed now. I think the time has come for a little fence-mending on both sides. Not that I'm prepared to accept any illegal activity, you understand."

"In my Father's House are many mansions," I quoted piously.

"My God, Hacey, you're getting as fast with Scripture as the Reverend himself. We've got to get you out of here." He struck me affectionately on the shoulder, causing me to stagger slightly. "Come and see me at White Hall sometime soon. Things are happening, and you've got some catching up to do."

"I surely will, Mr. Clay."

"Good." He bowed to Ellie. "Your devoted admirer, Miss Padgett." With a smile and a wave to me, he turned and started off through the crowd. Just then a high, piping voice called out, "Mr. Clay! Mr. Clay! Wait for me, sir," and a moment later the slight figure of John G. Fee appeared. His oversized head bobbed anxiously as he trotted through the groups of promenading visitors. Clay recognized the voice and turned back to greet his old friend. Fee stopped a few steps away and the two men looked at each other in silence for a moment. Then Fee said quietly, " 'Oh Lord, our Lord, how excellent is Thy Name in all the earth!' It is good to see you here, Mr. Clay. It is very good."

"It's good to see what you have done here, Reverend. I can't tell you how impressed I am."

"It's the Lord's accomplishment, not ours — but that doesn't lessen our satisfaction — or our gratitude to those who helped us begin it. Welcome to Berea College, Mr. Clay."

"Thank you, Reverend Fee." The two men shook hands

formally, then Clay impulsively wrapped a massive arm around Fee's narrow shoulders and drew him away for a few moments of private conversation.

Ellie and I held hands. Around us the other guests buzzed in pleasant anticipation. The students who were scheduled to address the audience with poetic readings and oratorical declamations squirmed nervously on their bench on the raised platform. The smell of roast meat hung over us like a benediction. Birds sang.

Then the voice of Reverend Fee rose to lead us, joined a moment later by the rough baritone of Cassius Clay:

> We are climbing Jacob's Ladder,
> We are climbing Jacob's Ladder,
> We are climbing Jacob's Ladder,
> Soldiers of the Cross.

We sang as if we wanted our voices to ring across every knob and hollow in the hazy blue Cumberlands that stretched out to the south.

> Every round goes higher, higher,
> Every round goes higher, higher,
> Every round goes higher, higher,
> Soldiers of the Cross.

In the trembling silence that followed the last note, Ellie whispered to me, "It's all going to be all right, I can feel it. Everything's going to be all right."